GIANT ON THE RAMPAGE!

Crossbows *thunked* up and down the line as men shot. Bolts sizzled through the air, aimed at the brute's eyes and mouth. But the bony ridges shielded the hidden eyes, and most of the quarrels bounced off like hailstones. Bolts fetching in the beast's mouth elicited no howl or groan of outrage. Even three bolts in the beast's trunk did little harm, though the monster's grasping fingers raked at them, snapping them off like twigs . . .

The line of men broke and ran. The battle chant died on their lips as they shoved at their fellows to get clear. Another man, falling, was snatched and crushed, then bitten in half.

SHADOW WORLD
THE BURNING GODDESS

IAN HAMMELL

ACE BOOKS, NEW YORK

This book is an Ace original edition,
and has never been previously published.

SHADOW WORLD: THE BURNING GODDESS

An Ace Book / published by arrangement with
Bill Fawcett & Associates

PRINTING HISTORY
Ace edition / August 1994

ISBN: 0-441-00086-X

ACE®
Ace Books are published by The Berkley Publishing Group,
200 Madison Avenue, New York, NY 10016.
ACE and the "A" design are trademarks
belonging to Charter Communications, Inc.

PRINTED IN THE UNITED STATES OF AMERICA

10 9 8 7 6 5 4 3 2 1

1
Ambushed
in
Hell

A STREAK LIKE LIGHTNING FLASHED BEFORE Zed's eyes, and the man beside him fell.

Zed couldn't see more than five paces in any direction through the fog and steam that enveloped them, but the spear had flown so close the shaft grazed his jaw. The man thrashed. The spear that pierced his chest was six feet long, made of some dense white wood, ash or oak. It was not straight, but crooked, with one long angled tine and a shorter side tine. It had been fashioned from a tree branch that had obviously been bent as it grew to form this odd fork, and resembled nothing so much as a bolt of lightning.

Zed had only a second to notice this, for a line attached to the shaft of the spear suddenly tightened and the spear was plucked out of the man's chest and pulled back into the fog.

The man at Zed's feet rolled and tossed. He clutched his bleeding chest, which oozed and bubbled, one or both lungs punctured. Wary of more spears, Zed scooched low. He slapped a hand over the wound in the man's chest, scrambled around him to grab his collar. But the man suddenly kicked and knocked the guide off his feet.

Zed landed on soggy turf amid roots and brambles. A sudden *chuff* made him lift his head. A lightning spear whistled above him, right through the space where he'd been standing.

Down the narrow, twisted jungle trail, Zed could hear men shriek, curse, shout, and die. They called to one another, "Where *are* they?" and "What *is* it?"

Zed shouted, "It's spears from above! Get to cover!" But his cry was just more noise.

There was always noise on this accursed island. Birds and monkeys and whatnot shrieked in the treetops. Sulphur pits blurped explosively. Hot springs bubbled and gurgled. Leaves rattled in the hot, uneasy wind and rain pattered or poured at least thrice daily. And always, unending as the pounding of storm surf, the three volcanoes that formed the north end of the island rumbled and guttered and grumbled.

If we survive the animals and the bugs and the heat and the spears, Zed thought, those damned volcanoes will finish us for sure.

Desperately, Zed clutched the fallen clansman's collar and rammed himself backward into the thickest patch of ferns he could see in the gray dimness. The ferns were taller than he, their pithy stems as thick as his wrists. He slammed through them like a bull, dragging the clansman behind him. The ferns bounced back to cover them. Zed, bent low as any snake, tried to tear loose a scrap of the clansman's tunic to patch the wound, but it had stopped bubbling. The man was dead. Zed cursed and slid over the body, back onto the trail.

He almost banged heads with Balka, the sergeant in charge of the scouting party. Balka was a typical Fulcrumian: loud, brash, rough, courageous, confident. In the tropical heat he wore only an undyed linen tunic and kilt strapped with tanned harness, a dripping cloth bound around his forehead, and tall stout boots. His face was tanned, lined, and bristly bearded. He was armed with a short heavy spear, a gladius that hung behind him, and a bullwhip coiled at his belt.

Behind Balka were half a dozen other clansmen, similarly dressed and armed, all drenched with sweat. Seasoned fighters, they hunkered along the edge of the trail, under the shelter of ferns or tree branches hung with moss, well spread out.

They watched above them and ignored the groaning, crying wounded. At least six men were down.

Balka thrust his hairy face close to Zed's and barked, "Jump us out of here!"

Still on his hands and knees, Zed shouted back, "I can't jump like that! You saw me! It takes hours to calculate—"

Balka grabbed Zed's collar and shook until his neck popped. "I don't want excuses! You guided us in here!"

"No one said anything about natives! There aren't supposed to be any!" He would have liked to slap the hand away, but restrained himself. Navigators were trained to guide and negotiate, not to fight. A frontiersman like Balka could break Zed in two with one hand.

"Then *talk* to them! You're good at that!"

"Balka!" a man cried. "On the ground!"

Like the white tongue of some giant snake, another crooked spear flew out of the forest and pinned that clansman to a tree, the long tine of the spear embedded in his throat. The hidden attacker jerked on its cord and the spear disappeared into the undergrowth. The man gargled blood and collapsed in the trail.

Zed knocked away Balka's hand. "Climb in here with me, through this fern bed! It'll turn spears! We can circle east where the forest is thinner—"

Balka suddenly lurched away from him. A spear from the other side of the trail had caught him low in the belly. He folded over the spear and fell on it. But even dying he fought. Clutching the shaft of the spear, Balka dragged out his gladius and severed the rope tied to the spear. The rope zipped back into the woods like a frog's tongue.

Their leader fallen, Balka's men panicked. Some spun about to run back the way they'd come, some dove to get to Zed's refuge. One man tripped over a body in the trail. Running half-crouched, two cannoned into each other. One went down with a lightning spear through his guts, then the other was lanced.

Whoever this invisible enemy is, Zed thought, they're quick to take advantage of a bad situation.

One clansman leapt for the branches of a tree, missed, and fell on his back, only to be pinned like a insect against the turf by a lightning spear.

Zed set himself to make a dive for Balka, to see if he could rescue him, at least, but something caught his eye and made him pull back. Zed was a navigator, a scientist, and a mechanic; his curiosity was not only a natural quirk but also an acquired trait. He paused now because he'd seen the enemy for the first time.

The man was of average height, with white hair and deep-tanned skin striped black like a tiger. He wore a short tunic of thin leather pinned together between his legs at midthigh. He held a hair rope like those attached to the spears. In his other hand he carried a short knobbed stick made of the same wood as the spears. He was barefoot and bareheaded. His arms were smooth and muscular as pythons—probably from throwing that spear all his life, Zed cursed. The native's foot, tough as boiled bullhide, stamped on Balka's head and then his hand. The dying sergeant let go of the spear, and the native—an Aranmorian, Zed decided—turned toward the navigator.

Zed went cold. His curiosity had held him too long. He scrambled backward like a crab and flipped over, but too late. The native slung the spear underhand. A streak of lightning chased Zed and ripped through his thigh.

Zed gasped and crashed to the turf. He tasted moldy leaves and damp soil. Pain shot through his body in ripping waves, threatening to blow out the top of his skull. He reached for his thigh and wished he hadn't, for his hands found the stout wood on either side of his outer thigh muscles. His hands slipped on the shaft, wet with his and Balka's blood. He was wracked with fresh spasms of pain. He bit on rich soil—as bright a taste and smell as an open grave—and tried to think. He couldn't run while hooked like a fish. He'd have to pull out the spear, but then it would bleed more freely. He'd probably black out. Either way they'd kill him ... his thoughts whirled.

A new pain ripped him, different but just as severe, and he sagged. The native had kicked him sideways and plucked out the spear. Through a red cloud and gray fog Zed saw him poised above, feet spread, the dripping spear ready to snuff out Zed's life ...

A bark, high-pitched, sounded on the trail. Zed sucked breath. It was the word "Stop!" though twisted by some barbarous accent. Even dazed with pain and the fear of impending death, Zed's curiosity rang a tiny bell in his fogged brain.

That was a woman's voice. The native above him grunted, then turned away.

Zed was alone and, as far as he could see, the only one of his party still alive. He rolled over—the pain felt like white lightning behind his eyes—and crawled deeper into cover. Maybe the natives would be too busy to come after him. Maybe he could get back to the army, warn them, get his maimed leg patched.

Maybe he'd bleed to death and scavengers would eat his corpse.

Using two hands and one leg, Zed pushed across the flattened center of the nest of ferns and into the next wall of stems. They snapped against his shoulders and gave off a dry, dusty smell. It was the first dry thing he'd encountered in the four days he'd been on this benighted island. Everything was wet and muggy, mildewed and rotting and soggy. Like the ground under him, wet with his blood.

Zed felt a chill and hoped it wasn't from loss of blood. He wished he'd drawn another assignment, but a journeyman navigator had to take what the guild ordered or else resign. Zed had studied too hard and persisted too long to quit the guild at his first big chance.

Still, it would be a shame to die on his first assignment, even as a full-fledged navigator.

He banged his head against a tree trunk, hard enough to hurt. He'd crawled out of the ferns and was elbow-deep in moss, on actual dry ground. But he hadn't noticed it. Was his vision going, or was the damned fog closing in again? Could—

A noise sounded off to his right. He stopped, slumped, tried to control his panting to listen. It was . . . a mewling. A . . . baby crying?

Zed twisted around and put his back to the tree trunk. It was a very rough trunk, some kind of palm scored by diagonal slashes. Even the trees were aggressive on this island. He caught his breath and looked down at his leg. That was a mistake. His trouser leg was soaked with blood from the knee to the ankle. His blood. Green crumbled moss peppered the wound.

Something toddled into his line of vision and put a chubby hand on his bloodied knee. A baby.

Zed gaped. It was an infant, barely walking, all round tummy, pudgy legs, and short fat fingers. It was naked and white-haired, like the natives out there, with big black eyes.

Its eyes and cheeks were red from crying. The baby put up his arms and ambled toward Zed.

Zed breathed a long sigh. He was going mad—no, there had to be an explanation. Maybe the natives were a nomadic tribe and took their children along when they raided. Maybe this infant had been stashed behind a tree, left momentarily by the woman (he had heard a woman's voice, hadn't he?) while she went to watch the ambush. In that case . . .

The baby toddled closer, about to fall. Zed instinctively put his arms up to catch him. Maybe if he held on to the infant, he could negotiate his freedom. Or maybe they'd lost the baby, and would be so grateful to get it back, they'd spare him. Zed caught the child and pulled it to his breast. He gasped as his leg throbbed. He hoped the infant's mother knew doctoring. "There, there . . ."

The infant grabbed Zed's ears and pushed its fat stomach against his face. He spluttered into the rolls of flesh. "Hey!" He tugged at the baby's arms, but couldn't get a grip. His hands were slippery, or the baby was. And it was astonishingly strong for a baby. He couldn't remember the last time he'd held one, except for his sister's . . .

Zed couldn't breathe. He shoved at the child and gasped for air. But he had a faceful of baby fat, clinging tighter all the time. Smothering him.

Zed's reason evaporated along with his air. Panic set in.

Wildly Zed slapped the baby on the back, ripped at its arms. His lungs began to burn, then hurt as if he'd been speared. He realized this was no baby. It was some enchanted thing, and it was killing him. He beat on the thing's back with his fists.

Zed thrashed and rolled, reared and spun around, banged himself and the baby into the tree. The rough bark gouged the monster, and it relaxed for an instant. Savagely, Zed ripped it off his face.

A searing burn like a monstrous mosquito bite shot through his leg. Another baby monster was latched to his knee, biting his wound. He could see its mouth was a maze of teeth pointed like a cat's. And red with his blood. He pounded on the monster's head and only drove the teeth deeper into his wound.

Then something bit his fingers and he found another baby on him. And another hooking toes into his belt to climb his chest. This was a baby girl, and it had a chubby fistful of moss. And an evil, hungry leer in her eyes. Zed lashed out a hand to fend the monster off, but the one at his thigh bit anew and Zed screamed. A fistful of moss was pressed into his mouth, along with the fist. Zed couldn't even bite down on the hand. He could only choke and watch the darkness close in around him . . .

The hand and the moss were jerked from his mouth. Screams like a slaughtered pig's rang in his ringing ears. Zed's mind climbed up out of darkness in time to see a woman warrior, a native, with one of the babies twisting on her forked lightning spear.

Not a baby any longer, but a dried-up thing with three fingers like claws and murderous teeth. An illusion-casting monster, he thought. What's more harmless than a naked baby?

Or I'm going mad. I was going to rescue the baby for the mother and she's spitted it. Zed reached for his forehead, missed, and fell sideways into the moss.

Zed was strangling. Some weight crushed his lungs, and he couldn't move his arms to push it away. The cannibal babies were back, he thought. Or one of the natives was standing on his chest, ready to spear him. He twisted in the air, turning to throw off the weight. His leg wound throbbed, and the new spasm of pain made him open his eyes.

He was hanging by his arms. Specifically, his forearms. From wrist to elbow he was lashed with hair rope to a stout stick that someone had hung in a tree branch. Ignoring the fresh jabs from his wounded leg, he got his feet under him and took the weight off his arms. He could breathe again. He gasped, hurting all over. He suddenly wished he were back on the home farm, boring as it was.

He craned his neck and noticed his leg was bound. Moss, the deadly stuff that had almost smothered him, was packed under a bandage of some light stretchy leather. From the many puckers and holes in it, and its grayish color, he guessed it was bird leather. Though where they could find a bird big enough—

A whapping of wings almost overhead startled him. A dark shape, giant, kite-square, soared over him, whapped some more, and disappeared into the murk.

It had been a featherless bird big as a horse.

Zed groaned and wanted to close his eyes, but forced himself to look around. He tried to find something that might keep him whole and healthy.

The navigator hung in a tree at the side of the trail. Eight white-haired, tiger-striped natives, five men and three women, worked nearby, ignoring him. All wore leather tunics and carried weapons. They stripped the bodies of the Fulcrumian clansmen. They took everything, including the men's loincloths, leaving the bodies naked and pathetic. One striped woman used a sword to chop off the metal tips of the Fulcrumian spears, which she saved. Some consolidated the clothing and gear into neat bundles, which they lashed to stout sticks they cut from the side of the trail. Others lashed the corpses by the forearms to sticks and dragged the bodies away down the trail. Within minutes there was nothing left on the trail except Zed. It was his turn.

A young woman was in charge of the party, it seemed, not that her people needed much instruction. She watched as the last body was hauled off and then approached Zed. He gritted his teeth and tried to look stern and haughty, as they had taught him in guild classes. But this slim woman, he remembered, led war parties and stabbed babies.

The woman didn't acknowledge his glare, or treat him as anything but booty. She reached up a brawny arm and tipped the stick he was lashed to. With a surprised grunt Zed fell to earth. The woman looped her weapons across her back, grabbed Zed's stick, and walked backward, dragging him along the trail. Zed felt his trouser legs and boots catching on the roots and rocks of the forest floor. He clenched his toes to keep his boots from being dragged off. That made his leg hurt.

As he was dragged along the trail, he found himself looking up at the leaves and branches above him, the ceiling of perpetual mist, and the woman's face.

Her face was by far the most interesting feature around, and he studied it. Her hair was barely shoulder length, as short as the men's, and white as cotton on the bush. Her skin was an even, appealing brown, although lined with faint scars in several places. The black tiger stripes were war paint. This woman had a stripe down her nose, two running diagonally across each cheek, one each on forehead, upper lip, and chin, and more painted on her ears and neck, down her arms and legs. Her eyes were yellow-brown. With or without the stripes, she looked startlingly like a tiger. It was clear she had no trouble towing Zed, who was not small. She had well-defined muscles across her neck and down her shoulders, and her arms and forearms were as thick as Zed's own. Her body was lithe and tawny. Her breasts were small, though they protruded because of the muscles behind them. Her nipples, noticeable under the damp leather, were pure female.

"What's your name?" he asked her.

She started and looked down at him. Her concentration had been on the trail and sky around them. She was alert for any threat, like a wildcat. More alert than Zed had been, he realized. He'd been attacked twice inside an hour and had seen neither attack coming.

"What?"

It took Zed a moment to grasp the word. It was barely recognizable, but it was in the common language of Jaiman. It sounded old-fashioned to Zed's ears, like the words of his great-grandfather.

Zed cleared his throat. If they could talk, they could negotiate. That was supposed to be his specialty. And any woman liked a man who asks questions about herself, he thought. Maybe she wouldn't kill him.

"What's—your—name?"

The woman grunted. A ghost of a smile creased the corner of her mouth. She seemed to ponder as she dragged him down the trail. Zed felt like a load of cordwood, and hoped they weren't going to burn him. Finally she said, "Tiger—Eye."

"Tiger—what?"

The woman let go of one side of the stick and Zed slumped to the trail, yet she still dragged him easily. She pointed to her face. "Eye. To see with." She caught up the stick again.

"Oh. Tiger Eye. Nice name. Pretty. I'm Zed. Zeddeth Toog Niarmon."

"Foolish name," the woman grunted. The ghost of a smile came and went.

Zed tried to guess if she were mocking him. If so, she was no naive jungle girl.

Zed decided to see how sophisticated she could be. It wouldn't do to insult her. "Why did you kill those men?"

The woman shrugged as she pulled. "Why not?"

"Why not kill someone?"

"Yes."

"They didn't mean you any harm."

Another shrug. "No. But the forest would kill them sooner or later. We can use their metal."

Zed digested that. He felt cold in the pit of his stomach. But he also realized she could speak as well as he, for all her old-fashioned accent. She had been mocking him. "What could kill them in the forest?"

She smiled now. "A hundred things. The Locharrion, the Children of the Moss, almost killed you. It's dangerous on the ground."

"But you live on the ground."

"We don't."

"Hunh?"

The woman smiled again, a sly smile. She spoke slowly, as if he were dim-witted. "No live on ground. Live up there."

Zed made a face—a navigator wasn't used to being teased—and she dropped him flat on his back.

They had come to a clearing. This one was larger than any other Zed had seen on the island—at least thirty paces across. The whole infested island was covered in oversize trees and thick underbrush. A clearing this large looked like a desert by comparison.

This benighted island, the land the Fulcrumians coveted, was a place of secrets and ancient treasures, men said. To Zed it was a doorway to hell. The air was dense and sulphurous, the land boggy and treacherous, shot through with hot springs and underground creeks, or sinkholes covered by dense mossy mats that gave way under a man's foot without warning. Elsewhere, it was brambles thicker than a rabbit could pass, or knife-edged palm fronds and elephant ears, or just roots piled on dead trees, on trash, on more roots, all entwined with vines. Zed had never seen, or even heard of, such a place, and navigators heard about a lot of treacherous places. When the twisted brush wasn't tangling a man's feet, the ground itself was unmanning him, shaking like a palsied horse fit to die. Even the sky was wracked, thick with gray clouds to a height of a hundred feet, and flames chased across the clouds from the three volcanoes. Zed would not have been surprised if the whole island suddenly split apart and sank into the sea. If ever an island on the planet of Kulthea suffered death throes, it was this hellhole, Aranmor, and Zed fervently hoped that whenever whatever happened to it happened, he would be somewhere else.

Right now he was tied like a suckling for market. His back

and rump were wet. He sat up—which made his leg throb—
and looked around. In the middle of the clearing, two of Tiger
Eye's warriors had propped up a dead Fulcrumian. The naked
corpse's head lolled obscenely to one side, but the warriors
were not reluctant to handle the body. They knew death and
did not fear it. Zed was repulsed, yet also curious. What was
the purpose of holding a corpse aloft—

One of the warriors, a woman with short-chopped hair and
wide hips, whistled, a short piercing sound. Silent as a cloud,
and almost as big, a gray monster dropped from the mists.

It was a bird, Zed realized, only some horrid one. It was big-
bodied as a horse, with wide, wide wings of featherless mem-
brane like a bat's. The thing was a sickly gray that perfectly
matched the sky, except for red eyes that seemed to glow. It
had claws bigger than Zed's hands and much, much stronger.

As the navigator watched, the monster bird swooped into
the clearing, wingtips almost brushing the boggy ground. The
fearsome claws opened and the bird grabbed. Deftly, gently
even, it caught the stick suspending the corpse. The bird
barely dipped as it connected, then the wings pounded air and
the bird was aloft, gone into the mist. Zed felt icy sweat pop
out on his forehead.

Zed watched as another body was propped up. This time a
man whistled, and another bird swooped down to grab its
load. Another four came and went the same way, then no
more. So, there were only six birds, Zed guessed, and they
carried their loads of dead men to their nests. The white-
haired warriors scanned the sky frequently as they waited, but
they watched the forest around them more. It was dangerous
on the ground, Tiger Eye had said.

Not as dangerous as these natives, Zed noticed. The warriors spaced themselves around the clearing, watching ...
watching. A woman clucked her tongue and pointed. Immediately three jagged spears came up. This time, the natives laid
the spears along the shorter knobbed sticks that rested along
their arms and shoulders. Quicker than Zed could follow, the
throwing sticks, the atlatls, snapped over, and the spears
whisked away into the bushes, trailing their light lines.

Ah, thought Zed, the throwing sticks acted as an extended
forearm. The spears went half again as fast as a man could
normally throw—so fast Zed could barely see them.

The spears pierced the bushes and something else, some-

thing that shrieked. Two warriors tugged their lines and
dragged forth a wild pig, fast dying from chest wounds. The
third warrior, who'd missed, was the butt of much ribbing and
low laughter. The dying pig was trussed to yet another cut
stick and added to the loads to be hoisted by the monster
birds. Zed continued to see the spears flash in his mind. The
Fulcrumians had had no more chance than that pig. Less, for
the pig was smaller and more adept at hiding in the brush.

A warrior looked up, whistled, and was answered by a
rasping caw. The man hoisted a pack over his head, stick up-
permost, and like something out of a dream, a featherless monster swooped out of the murk and snatched the load as a man
might pick an apple.

Once the corpses and packs and pig were gone, a warrior
held her crooked spear overhead, crosswise, and whistled.
These actions made Zed break out in sweat again. Sure
enough, a bird appeared and plucked her up like a dandelion.
She was gone in the fog, into the air.

Surely, Zed thought, they don't live in the clouds?

Someone prodded him in the back. It was Tiger Eye. That
half smile touched her lips again. Zed tried not to tremble, or
at least not to let her see him tremble. She prodded him,
forced him to limp toward the center of the clearing, then
pushed the stick strapped to his forearms in the air.

"Look, uh, Tiger Eye." Zed was babbling but he didn't
care. "I don't like heights. The highest I've ever been was up
the mast of a warship, and I didn't like it at all. I was terrified. I'll admit it. I've been in the mountains too, but that's
different. Everyone has a weakness. Mine is heights, understand? Maybe I could walk—"

Tiger Eye held the stick aloft, stepped back, and whistled.
She whistled very loudly for a woman, Zed noticed.

Then a huge bird swooped at him. The bird's straight,
razor-edged beak was open as if it would swallow him. The
red eyes burned as if they might explode into flame. Those
claws could rip his head off, he thought. He didn't want
to—

A grab, a tug. His feet left the ground and windmilled frantically. The ground was sinking away, then was gone.

With one long frantic scream, Zed the navigator was walking through clouds.

2
Above
the
Forest

WIND RUSHED PAST ZED'S EARS, SWIRLED IN-
side his mouth like cold water, slipped up
his trouser legs to chill his damp knees.
Above the noise of the wind and the beating of the bird's wings he heard a distant
howling and realized it was his own
screaming. He shut his jaw with a *clack*
and put an end to it. But he didn't feel better or in any kind of control.

Zed kicked his one good leg, hoping to
find solid ground under him. As best he
could, he wrapped his bound hands around
the staff above him. He couldn't tell how
high he was. There was only mist below
his feet, mist all around. Loremasters,
please don't let the bird hit a tree! he
prayed. Maybe he wasn't very high. How
high could a bird carry a full-grown man,
anyway? Not much above treetop level,
he was sure. Even if the beast dropped
him, he'd probably land safely—maybe
scratched, but alive—among the millions
of dense-packed trees all around. If the
bird could only get to the warrior's village

soon, just beyond the next stand of trees, say ... and land ...

Suddenly they broke free of the mist and Zed howled again.

They were higher than a ship's mast. They were higher than the volcanoes at the north of the island, for he could see all three, almost into the foremost's crater, where red flames licked the stony rim like the mouth of hell, and black smoke belched forth only to be whipped away by the perpetual winds. Zed could even see the peninsula of Fulcrumia to the south.

He didn't want to. He squeezed his eyes shut, but somehow not seeing was more frightening. He opened his eyes—which watered in the wind—and cast about for something familiar.

There! At the southern tip of the island he recognized Wistler's Island, considered the only safe part of Aranmor. For a fee (a very hefty fee, most of which went to the guild) he'd jumped the Fulcrumian army to that island. Crossing Mistroke Channel on rafts, they'd landed at the old ruined stone dock, and together had all climbed the Smoking Cliff for a bird's-eye look at the island. (Not as good as the one Zed had now.) Yet they couldn't see much for the constant mist and fog. They'd only been able to glimpse the beginning of that blue stripe below. The old Tradway Canal was choked with reeds and cattails and cypress trees. It split the island to the middle. To the west of the canal was the dismal Elder or Salt Swamp. Subterranean eruptions threw entire blocks of clotted salt into the sky as high as a man could shoot an arrow. To the east had been what the old map marked the "safe" route, but Zed could personally attest that was untrue. A dozen invaders had died in the first three days of setting foot on the island, either from the bites of poisonous mosquitoes or plunging into boiling mud pits. Some had just disappeared in the fog. Balka's scouting party—hand-picked hill men, at home in wilderness—had died under Tiger Eye's spears. In four days, the army had lost two dozen men, and had yet to penetrate ten miles into the interior. Welcome to Aranmor, he thought bitterly. We hope you enjoy your stay, which will be measured in hours.

Zed twisted in his bonds, his feet dangling. (His arms were falling asleep. Would they slip out of the bonds if they went numb?) He tried to see to the head of the blue stripe that was the canal. According to the one water-stained map known to exist, at the head of that fetid canal, on a hilly island encircled by the canal, was the army's goal—the Lost City of Tarek Nev. Zed could see nothing but the tips of brush, forest, and tall trees. No sign of a city. A lot of men were going to die before the army got there, if it ever did, and there might be nothing at all in the spot.

Zed craned around to see more. On top of all his other troubles, he was flying backward and couldn't see their destination. There wasn't much more to the island, for it wasn't more than thirty leagues long. Half the north of the island was laid waste, singed to ash and black crazed glass by the belching volcanoes, like erupting pustules spitting death. The big one was Mount Kadaena, named for a bloodthirsty and headstrong god, the middle-sized one Mount Orso, and the little one, almost pushed into the sea by its brothers, was Mount—Something Horrible. Zed didn't care. He wasn't going near any volcanoes.

Was he? *Were* they flying north?

All around the island boiled the Sea of Fire, named not only for the torrential storms that wracked this part of the world, but also because whole acres of the sea actually were hot, if not boiling, from underwater volcanic activity. Zed had heard fishermen and merchant masters brag of sailing into the boiling waters to kill the sea worms and barnacles along their wooden hulls.

Zed flinched as the bird banked its wings idly. It had stopped beating its wings and glided over the salt marsh to catch a warm updraft. Now Zed lost his stomach—he would have lost his lunch, but he hadn't eaten today—as the animal swooped east toward the one place Zed would have said was truly impenetrable—the forest of giant trees, which grew to three hundred or more feet tall.

They were, a clansman had guessed, some sort of freak stag oaks. The mysterious Wyr Forest, where no man had ever set foot, even in the dim reaches of time when men and gods had lived side by side on the island of Aranmor. The forest was a world apart. Fed by nutrients washed from the bottom of the sea by geysers and driven ashore by storm tides, warmed by underground springs, enriched by potash and lime from the volcanoes, the trees were more like mountains than living things. As the bird swept closer, Zed could see the trees were indeed oaks with dark creviced bark and widespread twisted limbs. The trunks stood well apart from one another, thick as large hills, so thick a team of men could never cut them down. The branches reached sideways and up, so that, hundreds of feet above the mist-shrouded ground, they created almost a separate forest risen on stilts. All this Zed glimpsed in an instant, then the bird banked sickeningly, dipped, and shot among the monster branches. As leaves began to tick against his heels and shoulders like hailstones, Zed closed his eyes and prayed to every god he could think of.

The bird banked suddenly, stalled in midair (Oh, gods, please don't let it crash!) and Zed's boots touched solid ground. Zed sucked in a breath he didn't know he needed and almost cried with relief. He opened his eyes—

And two warriors grabbed his shoulders, tripped him backward, and slammed him against the very solid ground. Oh, yes. He wasn't dead, but he was a prisoner of steel-eyed savages.

On his back, a woman's foot planted on his chest, Zed could only lie with his arms bound and numb and look around. What he saw was leaves, mostly. Oak leaves, lobed and pointed. Black oak leaves, or something similar. He could see the leaves clearly, see everything clearly for the first time in days, for they were far above the island mists. The air was cooler too, and refreshingly full of winesap, not the boggy fog of layers of decay. Zed wanted to imagine he could see the sun, but this part of the world had been overcast for years. Fulcrumian highlanders his own age had never seen their shadow.

To his left he could see a towering trunk, its top lost among a million—no, billion—leaves. The bark was stained black in long stripes where channels of water had run down, but wide patches were white as a ship's sail. There was another giant trunk far to his right. He turned his head to see and the woman above him—her leg was more muscular than Zed's, though not as hairy—stomped harder. She didn't like strangers in her tree, evidently.

Someone appeared over him, in stripes he recognized. Tiger Eye caught him by the shoulder and jerked him to his feet. "I'll take him," she told the two warriors. Zed was spun around and pushed down the wooden causeway.

As he was shoved along, Zed found more to look at than he could grasp.

The natives—these "lost" Aranmorians—lived in these trees. There was a whole community nestled among the branches. This immediate area was a nexus where a dozen branches came together. Over years, maybe centuries, the natives had worked the trees as a man might mine a quarry. At the juncture of many branches, where natural cracks in the bark were as wide as caves, people had built houses with wide doored fronts and roofs fashioned of shed bark layered in shingles. In some places the houses were three or four stories tall. In front of the houses and along the wider branches, the wood had been worn and polished by generations of bare feet, forming walkways as wide as cart paths. Bridges abounded, spanning branch to branch and hanging over an unimaginable drop, though nowhere did Zed see handrails or guide ropes. He couldn't have used them anyway, for his bound hands were numb and swollen. Off-balance, Zed balked when Tiger Eye pushed him onto one bridge, for it wobbled underfoot, but another shove put him across. Struggling would only tumble him into the depths, but he shivered uncontrollably. His wounded leg threatened to collapse under him at any moment, but oddly it didn't hurt very much.

Passing around one huge trunk, on a path partially notched into the bark, partly shored with more wood, Zed found an even bigger community of some two dozen houses. This one centered around a pool some thirty feet across, formed in a natural pocket at the base of a branch. It was fed by a waterfall that tumbled down a trunk from the heights, and excess water spilled out a channel in the far side to break into spray far below.

Tiger Eye spoke to him for the first time since their arrival. "Do you thirst?"

Zed tried to answer and could only croak. "Y-yes."

Without any warning, Tiger Eye shoved him to his knees at the edge of the pool. Zed's trussed arms were thoroughly dead, so he couldn't stop himself from plunging headfirst into the water. He spluttered until Tiger Eye hauled his head out, laughing. Zed was furious at this shabby treatment, and by the laughter of the crowd that had gathered to see him suffer. But he was thirsty, and he managed to slurp up enough water to slake his thirst. The water was sweetened with sap, refreshing.

As he shook his head to clear the water out of his eyes, Tiger Eye jerked him upright and hauled him along more paths.

Over his initial fright, Zed's anger was building. "Where are you taking me? What are you going to do with me?"

The voice came from behind, slightly mocking. "We'll ask you questions. About the invaders you've brought to our island."

"It wasn't my idea for them to come here. I only guided them. I'm a navigator."

"A what?"

Zed stumbled in his surprise. "You don't know navigators?"

He could hear her laugh. They were moving toward more populated territory. At a juncture of many giant branches was an area entirely floored with planks, a common kitchen or marketplace. None of these people wore tiger stripes. Children laughed at play, women and men gossiped as they stirred pots and cut meat and vegetables at tables. The smell of cooking made Zed's stomach squeak. Tiger Eye teased, "Should I know of navigators?"

"We're the most important guild on this planet! Nothing important happens that we don't partake in! We can jump *anywhere*!"

"Oho." Her mocking tone nearly drove Zed berserk. "Then we can't be very important people, because we never heard of you. How high can you 'jump'?"

"No! *Jump*, damn it! *Teleport* from one part of the earth to another, riding the Essence!"

"Oho," she said again, while Zed raged. "Handy, I'm sure. What gives you this power, that you can 'jump'?"

They'd reached a crevice in a tree trunk. It had a woven latticework ceiling and a latticework gate. Zed spun to face her, almost falling because of his leaden arms. "It comes from long hard hours—*years*—of study! And from our—" Involuntarily he half looked down at the fine black leather pouch fastened to his wide belt. He looked away too quickly.

Tiger Eye smiled, the smile odd and whimsical, surrounded as it was by stripes. She snapped out a foot and hooked it behind Zed's heel. As he fell, she unhooked his belt and took it, pouch and all.

Zed tumbled onto his rump and landed in the crevice. Tiger Eye caught his stick in one hand and unwound his bonds, taking her time with the knots to preserve the valuable rope. Zed's arms flushed with pins and needles so sharp he groaned. He cursed at the tingling and at the loss of his belt. "I want that pouch back!" He tried to point and couldn't. His hands were dead as sausages.

For the first time he noticed that the crevice was boxed tight. The sides of the crevice were polished and scarred, as if by clumsy tools. Angry, in pain, he gasped, "What is this place?"

"This is the pen where we hold pigs and monkeys for slaughter."

"You're not—not—going to eat me, are you?"

She gave an ambiguous toss of her shaggy white head. "Not until we've asked you some questions."

She smiled again, flipped the belt and pouch over her shoulder, and sauntered away.

Zed sat and waited and stewed. At least he was on solid ground again, or a solid surface. He noticed he could feel the trembling of the distant volcanoes even through this massive tree. Why didn't the whole island shake apart?

The children had lost their initial fear and came to gawk through the latticework. They were all sizes and mostly naked, but even the littlest carried a spear. The children's spears were all straight, whereas the adults carried crooked spears. Zed wondered what that meant. For that matter, he wondered long and hard about these Aranmorians, for he was the only man in the world who knew they existed. (Another bad omen. Either no one else had poked into this corner of the world, or some explorers had and never returned.) After a while the bolder children took to poking at him through the latticework with their spears, but Zed just snatched their spears away and kept them. When a child went crying to its mother, a woman arrived and shooed the children away. The woman even returned with food, meat and flat bread and fruit, on a platter. Zed had to return the children's spears to get it.

He wolfed his food, surprised at this kindness. But maybe they were just fattening him up. The woman watched him eat. She was old and wrinkled, old as Zed's mother, sagging with fat around her middle and bottom, but her legs were still knotted with muscle. Even she looked strong enough to thrash Zed.

Later a man came and unlocked the door, and changed the rude bandage and dressing on Zed's leg. The spear point had passed through only the outermost muscle. The medicine man pronounced it not serious. He rubbed a salve from a leaf into the wound, and the pain eased.

As darkness fell, Tiger Eye returned. She didn't have his belt and pouch. She brought him more food and waited while he ate it. Then, spear in hand, she unlocked the gate and told him to follow her. "And don't try to run off. We'd only catch you. And you might fall," she added with a chuckle.

"Where are you taking me?"

"To the elders. They'll ask you questions."

"May I spruce up first?"

"Spruce up?"

"Clean myself. Relieve myself."

Tiger Eye pouted prettily and nodded. She led him around a tree trunk and pointed to a short shelf. Oak handles were fixed at various heights above the shelf. She told him what to do and then walked back around the tree. Clutching an oak handle with a death grip, Zed pissed over the edge, the stream falling far, far down toward the forest floor. He wondered what he was pissing on, and how the denizens down there liked it. Well, at least sanitary arrangements were adequate.

Next Tiger Eye led him to a pipe of water that also ran off into space, and Zed washed himself. He took his time: He was in no hurry to explain himself to any elders.

Tiger Eye asked suddenly, "Why do you wear so much clothing?"

Zed looked down as his disheveled garb and wondered the same thing. The largest damage he'd done to his uniform was sweating into it in this infernal heat. A navigator of the Guild of Vurn-kye wore black or dark gray trousers and hooded tunic, with a small skullcap and usually gloves. His clothing was all fine, soft, durable wool. An icon of his compass was embroidered in gold and silver thread on each shoulder. Zed was tanned and handsome as any other outdoorsman and sported a neat black beard, though he suspected it was currently full of moss and twigs. The bandage and bloodstains on his leg didn't help, either. He scrubbed at them ineffectually. "A navigator's uniform is his badge of authority. Same as your tiger stripes, I imagine." She only laughed in reply.

Finally Zed could put it off no more and announced he was

ready to "pay his respects to the elders." Surprisingly, the pain in his leg was mostly gone. Whatever had been smeared in the wound was strong medicine, the most potent he'd ever heard of. But his leg was stiff and he limped. Tiger Eye gave him her atlatl to lean on. Together they made off across the branches and bridges of "Treetown" or whatever these people called it. Zed set the pace, slowly.

"What do you call yourselves?" he asked.

Tiger Eye looked at him sideways. "We are the Nureti. We are an ancient race descended from the gods."

"Which gods?"

Tiger Eye frowned. Her eyes warned him not to mock her, but Zed remained bland. "The gods of this island. We are the scions of Argamanthol, and him from Solus the Entrapped. Argamanthol wielded the Lightning Lance, and we bear these in his honor." She waggled her crooked white spear in the air. Zed congratulated himself: They were meant to resemble lightning bolts.

Tiger Eye studied his face. "You are educated, yet you do not know of these gods?"

Zed thought of all he did know, but decided to withhold it for now. "Why are you the leader of the war party? Where I come from men lead."

Tiger Eye tossed her head with a snort. "Women always lead. Women are more levelheaded, less apt to go berserk. They do not endanger themselves to prove a point. They do what is sensible and right and best for the people."

"It doesn't seem right a woman should be fighting at all."

Tiger Eye stopped short and faced him. They were on a branch that dipped in the middle, the path as wide as a man's reach. She took away the atlatl and handed him her spear. "Try and kill me."

Zed took the unfamiliar lance gingerly. It was slim and cool on his palms. "I don't want to—"

Tiger Eye spread her hands wide. She was not three feet away. "Try. Here." She pointed to her belly.

Zed demurred, but when she refused to move, he made a tentative jab at her middle, nowhere near touching her. Yet, faster than he could follow, she leapt back like a cat, brushed the spear aside, then was chest-to-chest with him, her fingers rigid and resting below his Adam's apple. Then she hopped back lightly. "Again."

Zed set his feet (none too steady up in this tree) and lunged with the spear. This time she hooked past the end of the spear. She flashed along the tree trunk. Zed would have sworn she scrambled sideways along the edge of the branch like a squirrel. Then she was behind him, with her fingers on each side of his head, her fingertips poised over his unprotected eyes.

Her voice was mocking. "I am gentle with you because your leg is hurt. Do you need another demonstration?"

"No, no." He handed back her spear.

Her eyes glinted. "Are women fit to fight? To lead?"

Zed tried to rub his nose and couldn't. The inconvenience irritated him. He was growing tired of being pushed around. Very casually, he replied, "Some are."

She frowned and pointed along the branch. "Walk." He walked. Limped.

Zed was marched for miles, it seemed, across bridges and branches, up slopes and down. Gradually, they went higher, until he could see their destination in the distance. It was a monstrous tree, twice as thick as any he'd seen, a mountain of wood. And as they drew closer, Zed sensed something familiar. First he noticed a high whine, a singing in his ears like mosquitoes all around. Then there came the smell of ozone, burned air as one found in alchemists' shops. Then a tingling along his skin. In fact, the tingling increased until the hairs on the back of his hands rose of their own accord. Zed looked at Tiger Eye for some recognition, but she showed no signs of encountering anything strange. "Do you feel it?"

The woman glanced over. "Feel what?"

"The charge? The aura? This tree is crackling with Essence! It's pure magic, more than I've ever felt in one place!"

Tiger Eye shrugged. "It is Calagrog, the Most Ancient Tree. The elders live here, and meet here for council. It is a special place."

Zed shook his head. "I'll say."

The warrior led the navigator across a broad planked expanse to a cavernous opening in the side of the tree. Inside, torches lined a huge chamber, a room almost as wide as the tree itself. Zed wondered how the tree could be so hollowed and yet live, but perhaps the Essence sustained it. Certainly it contributed something, for Essence sparkled on the walls like fox fire.

The chamber was an amphitheater, with descending steps

or seats, all carved or worn into the wood, dropping to a dais in the center. On this dais sat three elders, two women and a man. They had elaborate chairs carved of some ancient stained wood. There were animal skins and robes under them, and padded stools for their feet, but their clothing was only the simple tunics everyone else wore. The three had turned their chairs to address one another. Two of them smoked clay pipes from charcoals in a stone brazier on a small three-legged stand. Three natives stood in attendance behind each chair, their arms folded across their chests.

Zed began to relax. These simple tree people couldn't help but be impressed by the knowledge a navigator had at his fingertips. He could promise them no end of trade goods too. Primitives would barter gold nuggets for mirrors and knives, he knew. These isolated folk would be no different.

Tiger Eye and Zed sat and waited until the elders finished their mumbled conversation. Then at a word, their seats were turned, and the two came to stand before them. Without preamble, the oldest woman said, "Tiger Eye, tell us why you have let this man live. He should be dead on the forest floor."

Zed's stomach dropped into his feet.

Tiger Eye's tone was cool but respectful. "Elder Water Rat, we attacked the party and wiped them out to the man. No one escaped to bring word back to the army. But this man"—she pointed to Zed as if he were some animal specimen—"looked different from the others. His clothing is different, and he carried no weapons. Only that jeweled tool in a belt pouch."

An elder man reached into the robes of his chair and produced Zed's belt and black pouch.

Tiger Eye went on. "I thought this man might be a man of science, of books and natural history. An alchemist, perhaps, or a seer. I thought he might be able to tell us why the Three Masters smoke so, and the ground trembles—"

"Child," interrupted an elder woman, "we have stalked these trails many times. The masters rumble and speak, and that is good. As long as they vent their spleen, they cannot explode. A shrieking cat cannot bite. Now go on. Your other reasons."

Tiger Eye licked her lips. She didn't speak, and Zed felt his stomach sink even lower and drain out his feet, leaving him hollow and unsupported. Tiger Eye had only one reason for keeping him alive, and they'd just thrown it out the window like a pot of piss. What now?

The eldest woman nodded. She'd silenced Tiger Eye and taught her a lesson. She asked the other elders, "Is there more?"

The man holding the pouch nodded and took up the questioning. He opened the pouch and extracted Zed's compass. It sparkled in the torchlight and seemed to glow even more than usual in the presence of all this Essence. The glister was of gold, for the compass was plated. It resembled a mariner's sextant, a telescope mounted on a triangular frame, yet more elaborate. It had filigree and curlicues for ornamentation, but had also a number of slides, internal pendulums, clockwork timers, set stones and lenses, and jeweled cambers and pivots. Zed had built the instrument himself as part of his training. He prayed the old man with the palsied hands didn't drop it.

The elder cradled it gently enough and asked, "You speak our language?"

"Yes—sir. Master." Zed felt as if he were back in college.

"What is this? What is it for?"

Zed wet his lips, unconsciously imitating Tiger Eye. "It is a compass, sir. It allows me to find my way along the Essence flows, to guide others the same way. I am a navigator."

"And what is that?"

Zed's eyes bugged. This was impossible. Everyone on Kulthea knew—but obviously not. Not these lost people of the trees. Monkey people. "Sir. Navigators travel Essence flows. We can open doors in space and cross the planet in minutes. We guide people who want to travel. We perform good works. We're uncovering much of the ancient knowledge lost when the Loremasters disappeared . . ." Zed talked about the guild at length, warming to the subject, as the elders listened—or seemed to listen. He finished, "I'm here to lead the army to the Lost City of Tarek Nev. I was hired by Aroth Cutthroat's army to help them decipher the maps, jump to this island, find the easiest path into the interior."

It was silent awhile. Then the old man shook his head. Zed hoped he couldn't read his mind. There was more to Zed's mission, of course, that he mustn't talk about. Guiding the Fulcrumian army to the interior was only half of Zed's job. Once the army had entered the city, his second task began. Using his compass, he was to find a suitable and safe place to set up a locater focus, a black disk currently in his pack in the army camp. Using the disk as a placeholder, his guild, the Guides of Vurn-kye, would send a team of engineers to fix a black obelisk that couldn't be disturbed. From then on, navigators could jump to this city with ease, and specially trained scavenger teams would move in to search the city thoroughly. Zed wasn't about to tell these tree people that the navigators planned to pilfer their ancient treasures. But then, the guild hadn't known these natives existed. No one had . . .

It was unnerving the way the elder stared Zed in the face, as if peeling back his soul. "Young one, do you think yourself educated and us ignorant?"

"Umm . . ."

The elder interrupted, "So you know a great deal?"

Zed was puzzled by the question. "Yes, sir. I think so."

The elder was shaking his head. "What of yourself?"

"Myself, sir? Umm . . . I was born on a farm, but I didn't like farm work. It was boring. I had a good head for figures, so my father apprenticed me to the Navigator's Guild. I passed their tests and studied hard, eight years, and became a navigator. I hope to become a master someday . . ."

The elder raised his bony head on his scrawny neck. He put his fist over his breastbone in a dramatic pose. "I am Bluebird. My father was Milkweed. His father was White Leaf. His father was Broken Tooth. His father was Long Journey. His father was Boiled Oil. His father was Cinnamon Bear. His father was Feather. His father was Sharp Edge. His father was Hair Rope. His father was Glass Rock. That is the history of my family for ten generations. I can tell you the lives of each of them. Can you do that?"

"Umm, no, sir. I can only remember my great-grandfather. But umm . . . I don't recall his name."

The elder persisted. "Had I your strength, I could tell stories of our people for five days running and never repeat one. Any of us elders can sing three hundred songs. *This* is knowledge. You know only things and figures. You know this bauble." He weighed the compass in his hand. "Yet you know not yourself. So your knowledge is worthless. Who is ignorant here?"

Zed felt he had to say something in his defense. "Sir. I studied for *years*. I know—"

The elder wasn't listening. He shook his head. "He has

nothing to tell us. Toss him, is my vote." He lobbed Zed's compass to Tiger Eye. "Toss him, and his toy after him."

Tiger Eye nodded solemnly. Zed didn't like her nod. He raised his eyebrows in a question, and she hooked a thumb sideways and down. Off a branch? Zed's knees turned to water. So they didn't take prisoners or keep them for long. No wonder they were an unknown people.

But the third elder, the woman who hadn't spoken thus far, took her pipe out of her mouth and pointed it at the navigator. "I would hear a little more of this army on the ground. But first we need to teach him humility, so he speaks true and does not waste our council. Hold him down."

Tiger Eye grabbed Zed by the neckline. The three attendant warriors came down off the dais and grabbed him also. Zed, on one good leg, was powerless in the grip of four doughty fighters. His struggles only made them lock iron hands deeper into his flesh. Tiger Eye herself stripped his tunic off over his head, then his chemise. He was laid barechested on the wooden floor of the amphitheater. A warrior held down each leg.

The interested elder, the woman with the pipe, got up, creaking, picked up the stone brazier full of glowing charcoal, and stepped arthritically off the dais.

Zed clenched his teeth.

The elder dumped the hot charcoal onto his chest.

3
Tossed

ZED'S CHEST WAS AFIRE. THE BOWLFUL OF ashes and hot chunks of charcoal scorched his skin and gave off a nauseating burnt stink. He could hear his flesh sizzling.

The pain—three or four burning holes on his breast like knives—made him buck so hard the warriors holding his wrists and ankles could barely restrain him. He screamed, swore, shouted, panted, and yelped like a whipped dog, feeling more like a craven animal than a man. The burning and sharp stabbing pain went on and on, and he swore it would pierce his heart and stop it, if not burn a cavity in his chest and bleed him to death. He kicked some more, but the straining had exhausted him. He fell limp, pain eating into him everywhere, sweat flushing him all over, and prayed he wouldn't die. Or if he did, that it was over quickly.

Through a haze, Zed saw the elder woman gesture. A woman upended a pail of water over Zed. The ashes and charcoal extinguished—Zed actually heard them

hiss out. More water was sluiced over him, then the medicine
man was there. He mopped Zed's chest lightly with a green
leaf, then applied the salve used on his leg wound. The navigator lay back, panting as if he'd run five leagues, and felt
the cool balm seep into him. He cursed these people in his
mind. He'd been speared, burned, terrified, and humiliated,
and he'd done nothing against them. He'd find some way to
get revenge before this was over, even if they did kill him.

Then he realized the pain was fading. Only the aftermath of
it, the horror of it, lingered in his mind. The warriors let him
loose, and he was allowed to sit up. His chest was plastered
white over puckered skin. He looked at Tiger Eye for her reaction, but her face was stony.

The elder woman took her pipe from her mouth. "In teach-
ing a child or a flete, you must first get their attention. Now
that we have your attention, perhaps you would please explain
yourself, your companions in the forest below us, and your
purpose here in our land. Why have you come to Aranmor?"

Zed shifted himself to his knees. He moved very slowly so
as not to create any spasms in his charred chest. He felt
twinges, short stabs, but their painkilling medicine had
worked marvelously. He hated these people, wanted to kill
some or all of them, but—he admitted it—he was afraid of
them. He didn't want to be burned again. So he sat back
down, took a deep breath, and talked. The elders sat and
smoked, the attendants resumed their positions behind the
council chairs, and Tiger Eye crouched on her haunches on
the first seat of the amphitheater. All listened.

He started by describing the army and its leader. Aroth,
called Cutthroat, was a clan leader from the peninsula of
Fulcrumia, to the south. (Here Bluebird interrupted him. The
Nureti knew of this peninsula. Their island had once been part
of it, eons past, before the Lords of Essence fought their Wars
of Dominion and ravaged most of the world, splitting whole
continents asunder.) Cutthroat had lately been visited by
dreams. Visions of churning, smoking seas, mountains of emeralds, jets of scalding water, and bubbling volcanoes plagued
him for many nights, then starting impinging on his days, until he didn't know if he were awake or asleep, and almost lost
his reason. Centermost in the dreams were pictures of the
Lost City of Tarek Nev, and whisperings and callings in the

night, a siren's song. Beneath the city, the dreams promised, was wealth to stagger a man's mind. (An elder sniffed.)

Cutthroat commanded the largest of the many clans that dotted the hills of Fulcrumia, with three hundred families under his troth. He bound five hundred stalwart fighting men to his quest, and put in motion the gigantic machine that was his army. Yet Cutthroat knew the legends of the lost city that died in blood, and knew even so large an army might not breach its magicked walls.

Then came Darroc the Sailor with the key to the city. Darroc was wizened and gnarled as a winter apple, battered and salt-streaked as a Fulcrumian coaster, gray-haired and pointed-eared, so that no one could tell if he was a man, a dwarf, a black elf, or some bastard mixture. Darroc had heard of the pending quest, and came to Cutthroat with a ring and a story. The ring was green, marked with some strange sigil. He called it a "Pax" ring, and swore it protected him from dying at sea, whether from serpent, wind, or drowning. Darroc also claimed to have actually been to the gates of Tarek Nev. (The elders exchanged glances. Zed had finally surprised them.) Furthermore, he claimed to know the secret word that would open the gate. He would open the gates for a share of the treasure. So Darroc was signed on, and the army prepared to depart.

But to get anywhere on Kulthea, Cutthroat's army needed a navigator, and that was where Zed came in. Zed tried to explain what he thought everyone knew. Essence, the magic stuff of life itself, the power of the Loremasters and the Lords of Orhan, flowed to and fro across the planet's surface, thick in some places, thin in others, especially strong in "foci" like this tree. The navigator guilds had learned how to tap into this Essence, bend it here, shift it there, and use it (almost) as they wished so men might journey safely from point to point. Even these isolated tree people understood that the seas of Kulthea—and Kulthea was as much sea as a frog pond was water—were too dangerous to be traversed by ship, and the skies too turbulent for skyships, except in rare instances. Even birds hesitated to fly from island to island. Thus, two islands on Kulthea only ten leagues apart might as well be on separate moons. Except for the navigators.

Here Zed's voice began to glow with pride, and Tiger Eye shot him a warning look. Zed tried to remain humble: his blood fluids leaking down his stomach and pooling in his navel helped remind him. There were many navigator guilds: the Navigators, the Daruni Olkanin, the women of Cypharia, the Pathmasters of Hulgan, and (the best for last) the Guides of Vurn-kye, which was Zed's guild. With secret knowledge gathered over centuries and passed orally from master to apprentice, the Guides could traverse any spot on the globe, and take whoever could pay with them.

Cutthroat had laid his hand on a black obelisk in Jaiman's port city, Blackwater, and intoned "I require a navigator." An assessor navigator had negotiated the terms, and Zed had been assigned the task. He'd met Cutthroat's army at the tip of Fulcrumia. Over many days, he'd consulted his compass, the skies, the heavenly tracks, auguries in the wind, and—at the propitious moment had jumped the entire army across the shortest gap possible, to Wistler's Island off Aranmor.

(What Zed didn't tell was that much of his calculating was dross, that navigators always took as much time as they could, and that Zed—a journeyman-in-training—had been sent because the task was simple. The mystique of the guild required a "lot of sweat and mumbo-jumbo" to justify their outrageous fees. Still, it had taken him hours to calculate a jump across even that short path.

That left little to tell. Cutthroat's army was here, however many leagues from this forest, ten miles into the interior, and losing men right and left as they penetrated deeper. Zed was in a tree full of hostile savages.

The elders had their chairs turned together again, and they consulted in quiet tones while the younger people waited. Zed jumped when a voice whispered in his ear, "Are you a man of science? True science?"

Zed turned his head. His whole body was sore from wracking and twisting himself under the coal torture. He felt limp as a galley slave. But Tiger Eye's were burning a question into his. Maybe he could turn her eagerness to his advantage. Maybe stay alive. He whispered, "I know some science. My teachers know more. I can summon any number of learned men to help you. What is it you want?"

But then the attendants cleared their throats as they turned the elders' chairs again. The old woman, the one who had spared Zed's life, spoke. "Much of what you say makes sense, man not of the Nureti, but much does not. Why would men work so hard to journey when they have what they need at home? It is not right or just. We need not fear the army. There are five hundred of them—or less—and only some four hundred of us, but we need not lift a hand. The forest will finish them. It is dangerous on the ground. Since you accompany them, you shall share their fate. You are to be tossed."

Tiger Eye stood up abruptly. "Elder Tree Sap, I'll do it." The elder nodded. She accepted Zed's belt and pouch from an attendant and gave them to the warrior woman. "Toss this after him. Then go and watch the army and see they all die. That is all." Together the elders rose to leave the dais.

Zed was in a daze. Toss me? he thought. From these trees? How long would I fall? He tried to think of something, anything in his defense. A lie, even. "Wait! Wait! My guild will pay to get me back! They'll pay handsomely! Whatever you want! But if you kill me, they'll come for you! Their vengeance will be terrible! Retribution—"

He stopped as a noose of hair rope dropped over his neck, then wrapped around his wrists. It was pointless anyway. The last was all a lie and no one was listening. The elders shuffled out, aided by the attendants. Zed was jerked to his feet and dragged stumbling out of the council room. Tiger Eye led him like a pig to slaughter.

Outside, there were few people in sight. Even the elders were gone, perhaps taken to apartments higher in the tree. A covey of naked children with spears came trotting toward Tiger Eye and her prisoner, but she shooed them away. She jerked the rope taut and led Zed off away past the council house, off the giant enchanted tree Calagrog, toward some remote section where Zed hadn't been before. The children trailed behind, curious.

"Where are you taking me?" Zed's voice was a croak, but not from the noose.

Tiger Eye didn't look at him. "Out a ways, where the stink of your corpse won't waft up to us."

Zed shivered and stumbled. It was hard walking with his hands tied behind him and limping besides. Tiger Eye led him farther out along smaller and smaller branches, until they were walking a branch no wider than a ship's plank. Leaves were thicker and closer around them, and they lost sight of the community behind. For a moment Zed considered throwing himself off the branch and pulling Tiger Eye after him, but he didn't have the heart for it. The leaf wind was chill on his sweaty back.

Eventually they reached an actual clearing, where the giant oaks had left a "hole" in the sky, hundreds of feet across. The branches across the hole showed no sign of foot wear. This was past any part of the forest community. The sky above the clearing was a roiling gray of clouds and smoke shot with red: reflections of the tortured hell amid the volcanoes. Zed could smell soot on the wind. Looking into the gulf made him dizzy.

Tiger Eye stopped and turned to face him. Zed took a breath. This was his last chance.

He ducked his head and butted Tiger Eye in the breast. She let out a surprised bleat, but leapt back a spear length and landed lightly on her feet. Zed scrabbled with his feet for purchase, ready to ram her again. But she was gone, then tripping his feet. He crashed onto his scorched chest—which wracked him with pain, medicine or not. His head was hanging on the far side of the branch, facing down. The tree trunks around him descended in his vision, growing smaller and smaller till they were thin as sticks, then disappearing into the fog. Layer upon layer of leaves shrunk from sight. Billions of them. He wondered if they'd brake his fall in any way.

"That was foolish," she muttered. Tiger Eye rolled him over. Besides her spear and throwing stick, she still carried his belt and pouch, and his chemise and tunic. She balanced them on the branch carefully, as if she'd need them later.

He grunted, "I had to try something. Give me credit for that. You don't have to kill me, you know. You could disobey them."

"Anyone who stands against the tribe is no longer part of it and must leave." To Zed's raised eyebrows, she replied, "Tossed."

"What about your questions? For the man of science?"

She ignored him, slipped the noose from over his neck, and stepped past his head. The yawning gulf behind her was just at the edge of her heels, but she showed no fear of it. Zed would be in that gulf in a moment. She caught his wrists and dragged them over his head, lashing his forearms to her atlatl.

He tried, "We could go away. I could show you the world. Haven't you ever wanted to travel?"

Out of sight above him, Tiger Eye chuckled. "You heard the elders. Why would anyone want to leave home?"

"There are wonders out there. Things you can't imagine—"

"Hush," she told him. Almost gently. She put a strong gentle hand against his chin. Her yellow-brown eyes were deep and sparkling as gemstones. Her lips were full and pouty and kissable. The smell of her clean body was warm and womanly. Zed suddenly realized she was beautiful.

She said gently, "I'm sorry."

She shoved his head sharply.

Zed's butt left the branch, his boots ticked against the edge. Then he was falling.

Zed fell and fell and tumbled as he fell. Wind hissed in his mouth and made his eyes tear. Leaves whapped at him with tiny rippling sounds until he was dappled with leaf slime and sap. He smelled of the forest, and soon he'd be feeding it. He had vowed not to scream, but could not tell if he was or not. A branch popped against his wounded leg and he shed more leaves. As he revolved, his vision was a blur of leaves, tree trunks, the angry gray sky, more leaves. Then he was falling in the open. It was hard to breathe, and he wondered if he'd black out before he hit whatever was below. Surely he'd never feel it. Damn those people, and damn himself for—

He heard a sharp whistle far above.

Something wide and gray, with burning red eyes, swooped toward him, like a wayward storm cloud. A hand or claw tugged the stick binding his arms. He struck a branch and leaves exploded. The tug was gone. He fell, parallel to a tree trunk now, as if he'd fallen down a wooden mountain. The air was thickening—either he was entering mist, or he was losing consciousness.

Then the red-shot storm cloud was upon him again, and he reached for it, stretched out his tight-bound arms.

He gasped as the stick was snagged by craggy claws. The skin on his forearms was chaffed by the drag of the rope, his wrists and elbows and shoulders almost dislocated. The giant featherless bird clung to the stick holding him and flapped its wings furiously. Zed couldn't see well, for the mist was all around them. They were still falling as the bird struggled to gain altitude. Swooping and picking up a man in a straight flight was one thing, snatching a plummeting one and then reversing direction was another. Zed watched a knot on a nearby tree trunk. It neither went up nor down, but wobbled from side to side. The noise of the bird's wings was tremendous, like the rumble after thunder. Then, slowly, the bird rose, and Zed went with it. Within a minute it had regained its graceful soar, and the two were sailing upward.

Their destination turned out to be a crotch in a tree below the Nureti community. It was too steep a crotch to use comfortably, but someone—perhaps Tiger Eye, for she waited there—had bridged the space and built a platform big enough for the bird to land. Far above them, some hundred feet or more Zed could see the underside of planks that made the community proper. The giant bird flapped clumsily into the crotch, its wingspan restricted, and crashed to a halt with Zed underneath. He got a faceful of dusty, leathery gray skin before the bird could release the stick and climb off him. Both the bird and Zed rested, panting, for some while. Tiger Eye sat and watched the two of them get their breath. Next to her were his clothes and more besides: a bowl of food and medicine, a varnished leather bottle of water, more rope. She also had his belt and pouch strapped around her waist.

"I thought—" Zed gulped. "I thought to disobey the elders was death."

"It is," she said calmly.

Zed stared at her bug-eyed. He'd met a lot of women, had a lot of women, but they had always been giggly, soft, painted city girls. He'd never met a woman like this one, a scarred spear-throwing savage who talked about killing and dying as casually as other women talked about attending a dance. And who threw men into the void without a qualm.

The warrior went on, "This disobedience is for the good of my people. If I am right, I will be vindicated."

"Right—in—what?"

Tiger Eye put her legs out, feet together, back against a bole. She laid her weapons across her lap, as if ready to tell a long story. She spoke quietly, so her voice wouldn't carry. "I think the elders are wrong. I don't think the Three Masters venting steam and smoke is good. I think they're going to explode and kill us all. Yet I don't think it's a natural occurrence. I think something in the city is stirring them up."

"In the—lost—city?" Zed tried to sit up, but gave up. It was wonderful just to lie still and be alive. He hoped they could lie here and talk for—weeks, maybe. But his dratted curiosity wouldn't let him rest long. He croaked, "Why?"

She shook her head. "I don't know. I know the volcanoes haven't behaved like this for twenty generations or more. Our history would say so if they had. And the tremors in the ground, they are also new."

"I thought the ground always shook here." Everything else was treacherous, why not the earth itself?

"No, they've never been this common. And I find your account of—Cutthroat's?—Cutthroat's dreams interesting. Something calls him from the city. And if something long dead has power to call a man in his dreams, can it not also stir up volcanoes?"

Zed nodded. It made sense. Two never-before things suddenly occurring were probably linked.

Behind them the giant bird had recuperated. It stuck its scaly tail out over the edge of the platform and shook it vigorously. It opened its beak to caw, but Tiger Eye flicked out her spear and rapped it on the beak. The bird gurgled instead.

"That bird does everything you command?"

Tiger Eye scratched her knee idly. "Not a bird. A flete. A product of the ancient gods' magic. It does most of what I want. It does not belong to me, though. It belongs to the tribe, for use by our war parties."

"Which you lead." Zed almost had his breath back. "I've always thought women should lead war parties." He grinned like a gargoyle in joyous relief, and Tiger Eye smiled back.

Then his grin faded. Zed remembered his predicament. She'd obviously saved him for a reason. If he couldn't supply the reason, she'd no doubt toss him again, for real this time. "So. To business. Why did you save me?"

"You're a man of science and magic. If we got inside the city, you could find the source of the volcanoes' muttering, couldn't you? Perhaps stop it?"

Zed licked his lips. "Perhaps . . . So the city is real. You've been there?"

Tiger Eye shook her head. "Better to show you than waste time talking. You rest here. I'll summon my warriors and we'll go look at the city." As Zed began to protest, she added, "They're all pledged to me and will follow my orders."

She stood up, inches from the hideous drop alongside the

platform, and nudged the bowl across to him. "Wait here." She added a grin. "Don't go away."

She whistled to her flete and pointed. The bird hopped across Zed to the edge of the platform and hopped into space. Its wings beat mightily as it soared out and circled back. Tiger Eye turned to go.

"Wait," Zed croaked. "Why did you have to toss me?"

"The children were watching."

"Oh. How did you know the bird could catch me?"

Tiger Eye shrugged her solid tanned shoulders. "I took a chance."

She whistled again, turned to the edge of the platform, and held her weapons over her head. As the bird swooped up from below the platform, she tilted outward, stiff as a plank. Just as she toppled toward the far-distant forest floor, the flete snagged her weapons and hoisted her into the air.

Zed leaned back against a tree trunk and wrapped his fingers around the edge of the thickest plank in the platform.

Zed rested, wiped leaves and sap off himself, washed his face, slathered more salve on his increasing number of wounds, dressed. He ate the food, rested some more. He was exhausted. He couldn't count the number of times he'd almost died today. It he thought about it, he could have gotten very angry. But for now . . .

A shapely foot nudged him awake. Tiger Eye's. Zed was surprised to find it was morning. The air had a morning dew smell and freshness. Birdsong rang all around him. He'd slept like the dead, without moving, on a wooden platform hundreds of feet in the air.

Tiger Eye handed him food and drink and waited until he'd finished. After that, she wasted no time. "Come."

"Wait a minute. I need my compass back."

"No." She slapped a strong brown hand over the black pouch.

Zed wanted to curse, but didn't. "It's my tool, my livelihood. It's no use to you."

Her hand stayed in place over the pouch.

"May I check if it's damaged?"

"No. You'd 'jump' away, wouldn't you?"

Zed cursed to himself. That had been his idea, though any

jump was never a quick activity. He finally sighed and followed her.

There was another short flight by flete, him going first. He was grabbed on a lower branch by a dozen tiger-striped warriors. The flete disappeared and returned with their leader. Without a word, with Tiger Eye in the lead and Zed in the middle, the party set off through the forest.

The journey was one that Zed would not have repeated if he were voted Guildmaster for it. The words "monkey people" rang in his brain more than once as Tiger Eye's male and female warriors leapt incredible distances and drops, hung on to one of six fletes to span gulfs, backed down bark chimneys, swung on vines. They went for mile after mile, twisting, turning, dipping, climbing, always descending, down down down, until they were not fifty feet above the mist, which resembled a placid sea as seen from a masthead.

Zed leaned against a tree trunk. He gasped, "Are we near the ground yet?"

A woman chuckled. "Oh, no. That's another hundred feet below."

Zed groaned. He was a strong man, used to walking miles, climbing, rowing, and running when need be, but this quest used muscles he'd never suspected he had. His leg was stiff too. The warriors rested often, but not often enough and never for long. They were eager to press on. Zed grew physically tired from the constant climbing, and mentally tired from being helped up and down, over and around, like some crippled child. But there was nothing for it but to grit his teeth. The day was hideously long. He wasn't any less afraid of heights at the end of the day than the beginning, but he'd begun to care less if he fell and were killed. He was tired of being frightened. Bored with it, almost.

At rests and where the going was not strenuous, he passed time by feeding his curiosity.

He asked about the tiger stripes. Were they the mark of a warrior? A woman told him yes, it's to help hide them near the ground. But also to keep off the mosquitoes, for they mix the juice of a forest floor plant into the dye. People don't need it higher, for the bugs don't reach there.

And who were these gods that once lived in the city? Were any of them still alive?

There was some disagreement among the warriors on this,

for even their oral history reached only so far, and the time of the gods had been chaos and upheaval.

They could agree on the main of the story. The ancient people of the city had been the Nureti, and the tree people were their offspring. They were a wise and happy race that dwelt side by side with the gods of the city. (Zed thought they were more likely descendants of some aboriginal people, or else shipwrecked sailors or colonists, but he kept quiet.) As thinking beings eventually will, the gods fought among themselves for control of the city and its treasures (no one knew what they were, except they were fabulous). One goddess was Orgiana, Mistress of the Underworld, the Place of the Dead. She was a revered god of the city, for death is part of life, and even the dead need gods. She took a lover, either god or man, from somewhere off the island (or perhaps it was still part of Jaiman and the peninsula of Fulcrumia then). He was Tilak, a champion, but for his cruelty he became known as Tilak the Defiler. He defeated—some say in a fair fight, some by cheating—Solus, a beautiful and popular god, and imprisoned Solus in the sword Soulcrusher. He also wore the all-powerful Helm of Kadaena, which some said Orgiana had fetched for him from the nethermost regions of the Underworld.

As the power of Tilak and Orgiana grew, the other gods put forward their champion, god of the sky and storms, Argamanthol (the Nureti's direct ancestor). They met in a fierce battle over the city, some say growing to the height of the trees of the Wyr Forest, battling like two thunderclouds itself. Argamanthol caught the very lightning from the clouds and hurled it headlong. Tilak was slain, and Argamanthol wounded. With her schemes and lover destroyed, Orgiana, the fire goddess, burned white-hot, hotter than a dwarf's furnace, hotter than Mount Kadaena, and set fire to the city. Many people and demigods and full gods were killed. Some escaped and were scattered to the four winds. (Maybe they fled to Jaiman.) One god who survived was Belkor the Immortal, the Tiger King, a shapeshifter, for he had feathered his own nest throughout all this scheming and betrayed everyone, as shapeshifters will. In punishment, he was bound with a silver collar and forced from the city with whips, driven into the forest. No one knew the fate of Argamanthol, or the other gods. Somehow the fires of the city were snuffed out, but no one was left alive within the walls. The people who survived took to the trees—for it was dangerous on the ground without their gods to protect them—and built a life there. The tree people, the Nureti, scions of Argamanthol, even today carried the crooked spears in his honor.

After the end of the story, there was quiet everywhere. Zed asked no more questions. He had a picture of them, though. A hard people, descended from cruel gods in a savage land that could kill in an instant in any of a hundred ways. Yet they climbed above the forest and prospered, even retained a sense of humor. But Zed didn't fool himself—they'd kill him if he proved useless. As he trudged along, he juggled escape plans in his head until it ached.

At the end of the day they came to the end of the forest.

They were still very high, sixty or seventy feet, but Zed found the air muggier, heavier. The mist was almost at the soles of their feet, but less thick here, for the winds of the Sea of Fire could tear at it. At their right, to the north, the Three Masters smoldered and whispered of death to come. Flames and lava would occasionally spout forth to scorch the low clouds. They could feel the earth tremble through the soles of their feet, the tremors shaking even this mighty tree whose branch they occupied. A wasteland of cracked, burnt earth and ash stretched from the feet of the volcanoes down to the sea beyond, and somewhere to the edge of the northern forest. Down and to the southwest was the dismal Salt Swamp, though most of it was hidden by sea fog or salt mist. Along the edge of the swamp, out of sight below a lower screen of trees, ran the choked Tradeway Canal. They could see to the head of the canal, maybe a half mile distant, for the swamp had undercut the forest there.

In a bog formed by the head of the canal, raised on a high hill, was the Lost City of Tarek Nev.

The city no longer resembled the tiny scrawled picture on the only map Zed had seen. The hill was lapped by swamp and bog water, encircled by thick yellow reeds and cattails. The reeds gave way to salt grass and then vines, then low brush and finally scraggly trees. The trees were level with the outer walls of the city, which were strangely intact. They were tall as five men, Zed guessed, of stone that looked white at this distance, cut into blocks and tightly fitted. Within the city, the hill continued to rise, so that ruined crumbling tiers could be seen, rising in rings, the houses increasing in size, till at the peak was a round palace or temple crowned by a great dome. The whole city was huge, perhaps five miles across. It was obvious the Nureti had once been a prosperous and popular people, though there was no trace of them now except for these simple tree people who wore skins and carried wooden spears.

It was so quiet, Tiger Eye's voice startled Zed. "This is the back side of the city. A road used to run along this side of the canal, then bridge just below the city, so one might enter by the gate on the west. It's a giant's face, leering, but his mouth is closed and none of my people have ever discovered how to open it."

Zed thought of the boasts of Darroc the Sailor and his secret word. He asked, "Can no one climb the walls? They're not that high."

Tiger Eye pointed. "Someone tries, one of our foolish men, about once a generation. The Raven Guardians see to them. Notice how no tree is higher than the wall?"

"Yes . . ." Zed could see the walls were surmounted by some thirty black statues like squared-off hunched gargoyles. Now that he knew their name, he could make out their sharp beaks and clawed feet.

Tiger Eye said, "They—but wait. I'll show you."

The warriors sat down on the branch with their feet dangling over open space. Zed sat too, but with his back to the trunk and his feet tucked under him. He was glad to sit, for the muscles in his legs trembled. Tiger Eye walked, then slid to the end of a branch and cut a long stick crowned with leaves. With a steel knife (Zed thought it likely looted from Balka's scout party), she cut the long stick and started to thread leaves. Zed watched, curious. Before long, she had fashioned a glider in the shape of a bird. Tiger Eye stepped along the branch and drew back her arm. She smiled at his stare. "It's a skill learned as a child. See if I can catch an updraft." With that, she leaned far back and shot the glider into the air.

The twig and leaf construction soared out, graceful as a flete, looped and banked, then caught an updraft above the hot swamp and wafted toward the city. Tiger Eye called, "Watch the ravens!"

Sure enough, they moved, as if stirring to life, yet stiffly, awkwardly. Machines, Zed thought. A half dozen of the raven statues swiveled in place. Four heads came up. As the glider neared the walls, suddenly three beams of red light fired from the ravens' eyes. The glider was instantly crisped to ashes that blew away on the wind.

Tiger Eye stood with her hands on her hips. "Now you see why the trees are level with the walls. Each spring when they send out new shoots, the ravens cut them back. Even the birds of the marshes have learned to avoid flying over the city. It's a cursed place. A place for the dead. And there's no way in."

Zed stroked his chin, thinking, plans and contingencies again jumbling his mind.

Finally he said, "I can get us in. If you let me go."

4
Cutthroat's Army

THE WARRIOR'S YELLOW-BROWN EYES SNAPPED. She tightened her grip on her spear and swung the point to touch Zed's chest. "Why should I let you go?"

"So I can rejoin the army and guide them to the city. The old sailor can open the gate with his secret word."

"Why that? Why can't you 'jump' inside, if what you said is true?"

"If I could jump into the city, I would have taken the army straight in, wouldn't I, instead of just bringing them to the coast. If those ancient engineers went to so much trouble to protect the walls from physical assault, they no doubt placed guards to prevent jumping too." This was half truth. Zed had never encountered a barrier to jumping, though navigation theory didn't discount their existence. "The solution is to let me rejoin the army. Once the sailor opens the gate, I can see it stays open. You and your warriors can slip inside the city and do your own searching."

"You'd betray the men who hired you."

"I'm betraying nothing! I got them onto the island, and I'll lead them to the city. That fulfills our contract. They don't need to know about you. Stay out of sight. You'll have a friend on the inside. We can meet in secret and look for your magic source."

"Why would you be friends with us, when we have tortured you?"

"I'm trying to forget that!" Zed snapped. He pushed the point of her spear away from his chest. "And would you stop poking spears at me? Look. Let's remember our missions. You want to get inside the city and find out what's causing the tremors. I have to get inside the city and set up a locater focus, a black disk. If I fail my assignment, I won't be a navigator anymore. And if you don't get inside the city, you won't have an island anymore. And I'm no good to you here," he added.

"You'll tell them about us, the Nureti."

Zed put a hand up, palm out. "I swear I won't. I'll say the party was ambushed by those wretched pygmies, the Children of the Green."

"Moss."

"Whatever. I'll just tell them to stay out of the forest. That's not news. Logic, negotiation, is the thing we navigators excel at. I'm a great talker." Tiger Eye smiled at that. He went on, "Considering you live in trees and hang from giant birds, I don't think they'd believe me anyway."

The woman said, "They'll torture you if they don't believe you."

"I don't think so. I've been tortured enough lately."

Tiger Eye's face showed her confusion. "My task is to watch the army die. The ground will kill them all before they reach the city."

Zed shook his head. "Not this lot, it won't. Cutthroat became head clansman because he's good with his fists *and* his brain. And those clansmen are tough as these oak trees. They're probably your distant cousins, as hard and stubborn as you folk. They'll get to the city on a corduroy road of bodies if need be. Do it the easy way. Let them cut a path to the city and coax the door open while you sit back and watch."

Tiger Eye tapped the butt of her spear on the branch they stood on. Through this discussion, her dozen warriors had listened without commenting. Zed thought that a sign of good discipline, or else their faith in Tiger Eye, that they didn't interrupt. Finally she said, "I see no other way into the city, and I need to enter. I've already defied the elders, and so am already marked for death. Defying them further risks nothing."

Zed wanted to groan with relief. But suddenly the spear whistled back at him, to stop just below his chin. He could feel the longer point nestling in his short beard. She added, "But you have much to lose if you betray *me*! Remember *that*!"

Zed said without moving, "I'll remember."

Having made her decision, Tiger Eye relaxed. She was a woman of action, and having a plan calmed her. "We'll take you to within walking distance of the army. Tell them nothing of us. Say the Children attacked and you climbed a tree to get away. Say you burned yourself attempting a fire."

Zed rubbed his chest absently. "Very well. May I have my compass back?"

Tiger Eye set her hand on the pouch at her hip. Zed liked the jaunty angle at which it rode on her hip, and would have liked to place his own hand there. She said, "No. I'll keep it as a hostage. We will watch the army always. We'll contact you if need be, try to safeguard you where possible. If you need us, just walk into the bushes as for a nature call. And remember these things. Wrap your head tightly before you go to sleep, leaving only your mouth exposed. And sleep as close to the fire as possible."

"Why those things?"

"As you penetrate deeper into the forest, the dangers multiply. The insects grow bigger where the water is warmer. Other things will come from the depths of the forest to hunt when they discover the army."

"What things?"

"Just heed my words. It's dangerous on the ground."

"So you keep telling me." He scratched his raw chest. "It's dangerous up in the trees too."

At that all the warriors smiled or chuckled. Tiger Eye turned and pointed. "Go."

They walked south for a time, though their trail twisted with the tree branches, and finally camped for the night. Four of the warriors hooked to flete and dropped to the forest floor. They returned at dusk with a brace of raccoonlike animals and a small pig that they cooked over a tiny fire built in the crotch of a tree. Zed pulled his arms under his tunic, wedged himself where he hoped he wouldn't fall, and nodded off. Tomorrow night he could sleep on the ground, he told himself. That would be heavenly. Except the tough, brave people who lived here considered the ground too dangerous a place to set foot for long . . .

By late afternoon of the next day they smelled smoke. Then they heard the army. Sergeants shouted, axes and swords chopped. The men were not much farther than when Zed had left them, maybe fifteen miles into the interior. They'd have to go twice as far again to reach the city. The warriors picked along branches, silent and slow as ghosts, and after a while Tiger Eye urged him forward. The mist was less thick here. Eventually he could see the army. Men slashed a trail through scrub brush and burned reeds along the water's edge. An ancient road ran along this side of the Tradeway Canal, but it was so overgrown and awash as to be useless except as a guideline. The army was crawling where the forest met the swamp and suffering the disadvantages of both.

Tiger Eye admonished Zed to make no noise, nor talk, and pointed him to descend a vine. A long downward climb later, his arms aching, Zed touched solid earth after what seemed like weeks, but had actually been two days. The woman followed.

Zed stamped his feet. The forest floor was a thick, steaming, quivering mat of dead leaves and large and small branches, but it seemed like home. He turned to Tiger Eye. "It's been—not a pleasant experience, but a pleasure to meet you, mostly. You're quite a woman."

Tiger Eye cocked an eyebrow. "We'll see one another again soon. I have your friend here." She patted the compass on her hip.

"I remember. Take good care of it. I built it."

He turned to go, but something tangled his feet—her spear butt—and he fell down. Tiger Eye knelt her weight full on his back. She was solid muscle and not light. She told him, "You need to look more mussed if you've survived the forest." So saying, she rooted under the leaves, grabbed a handful of loam, and ground it into his hair, face, and beard. When he squawked, she shoved some dirt in his mouth. She shoved more leaves under his tunic and down his pants, then let him up. By the time he arose, spluttering and scratching and cursing, she was twenty feet up in a tree and still ascending. She called merrily, "Watch yourself. It's—"

"Oh, shut up!" Zed marched off toward the army.

Zed waved his arms and shouted to alert the guards along the periphery of the forest that he was coming. These men carried heavy crossbows and were known to be jumpy, seeing as how so many had been killed on duty by unknown somethings. Before long, he was past the guard and before a sergeant with sword and whip on his belt. Zed was reflecting on how glad he was to see these brash men, among whom he felt safe, until he caught sight of the sergeant's face.

Like the ill-fated Balka, the sergeant, along with most of his men, wore a thin linen shirt and kilt, with his weapons strapped on. All of them wore stout leather kneeboots with hobnails. This man was tall and red-haired, with a fierce red beard and more red curly hair standing above his shirt collar. He grabbed Zed by the shoulder and gave a squeeze, not in greeting but to see if the navigator were real. He snarled, "Where the hell have you been? And where the hell are Balka and the rest?"

Zed's euphoria evaporated. He shook his head, suddenly exhausted. "They're all dead. I'm the only survivor."

The man shook Zed's shoulder until his head rattled. "*What?* A piece of worthless rye bread puke like *you* lives through an attack where real *fighting men* are killed? I don't *believe* it! What got them?"

Zed gave their formal name before realizing it. "Children of the Moss. These horrible little—cannibal buggers that look like children but aren't."

"Unlife! You don't say! And why are *you* alive?" Other clansmen had gathered around to hear Zed's story.

"I, uh, ran away. I got into a tree and stayed there. They fought and were chopped to pieces. Eaten, actually, after being smothered."

The clansmen exchanged glances. The sergeant let go of Zed's shoulder and put a hand to his whip. "So a rabbit lives where a wolf was pulled down. Maybe. Cutthroat will get the truth." He turned and barked at two clansmen. "Rupert! Danno! Drag him to Cutty and be quick about it!"

More hands were laid on Zed, and he was marched down the slashed, burned trail.

The trail was rough, and the navigator stumbled over slash, roots, hanks of tall grass and reeds, stumps. The smell of burnt brush and salt was heavy, and their feet stirred up gray ash that settled on his clothes. The trail was more like a tunnel, for little of the boiling gray sky showed: Fern fronds and tea trees overhung the trail on one side and odd tall purplish flowers like swords overhung the other. Cedar roots tripped him. Zed and his escort dodged and sidestepped swinging axes and swords. A third of the clansmen were employed in clearing the trail so the army could pass. Another third spent the day packing the tents, food, tools, and other equipment along the trail and pitching camp in a spot cleared the day before. The final third guarded the perimeter of the camp and trail, and guarded the men who fetched water for boiling or hunted for fresh food. Zed knew that Cutthroat had planned to make ten miles a day in this fashion, to arrive at the city after four or five days, but the island had stymied him. They actually made something like three miles a day, and were losing speed steadily as more men went missing or were wounded by animals or bugs or disease or their own comrades.

Zed personally thought the men were the greatest danger to themselves. These highland clansmen were independent men, used to braving the frontier alone, relying on their strength and wits to protect their families. They didn't like taking orders. Cutthroat sometimes quashed men himself or let them kill each other to settle a dispute. There was nothing they couldn't turn into a bet or a fight, and they engaged constantly in one-up. No sooner was an exhausting day's work done than the Fulcrumians spent half the night wrestling, fighting, singing, even out-eating one another. Everything was a contest.

Some two miles down the trail, they came to a clearing. The camp couldn't extend into the marsh, so it stretched out against the trees, many of which had been hewn down to fall among their brothers. The trees here at the edge of the forest were not giants, but were still some hundred feet high, and Zed wondered what Tiger Eye and her companions thought of their being cut down. The camp was some hundred and a quarter tents, pale yellow like ships' sails. Since the camps were only for a night, they were not arranged neatly. Fulcrumians didn't take to neatness anyway. There was just room enough to move between tents, and dust and ash filled the spaces between them. Litter and garbage and beef bones and shit were everywhere, along with clouds of flies. Fires burned unattended. Water buckets were upset and fouled. The only sop to order was that a wide central area was always kept clear before Cutthroat's large tent. In any other army this would have been a parade ground where soldiers learned to drill together and follow orders. Here it served as an arena where two men sought to one-up each other to death.

Their latest sport was fighting with whips, a trick learned from an army of mercenaries in northern Jaiman called Brownboots. Two men tied a rope to their ankles and whipped each other until one collapsed. A fight was well along, and Zed's guards stopped to watch.

Tied together, in boots and kilts, were a tall, dark-haired man without a beard and a shorter, bald man with old galley-slave scars on his back. Both breathed heavily. The bald man had welts across the top of his head and shoulders. The tall man had welts wrapped around his arms, waist, and back. As Zed watched, the tall man made a play. He hopped backward suddenly, snubbing to the end of the rope, at the same time snapping his long black whip over his shoulder and forward at the smaller man's face. He hoped to tag the man in the face as he fell forward. But the stouter man used his weight to keep his feet planted and upright, and was only jerked forward a hair. The whip popped harmlessly a foot from his chest. He was quick, though. He caught the end of it—bright red with his own blood—in a callused palm. He couldn't hold it long, for its owner tugged it loose easily, but the bald man had time to lash with his own weapon. The whip ripped skin from the tall man just by the right armpit, his whip hand. The tall man gasped. Men in the crowd—for a couple hundred had gathered to watch and wager—hooted or groaned.

The tall man instinctively grabbed at his torn flesh. With that much irritation, he'd find it difficult to drop his arm, and the arm, leaking blood, would tire quickly. The bald man laughed through the streaks of blood on his face and seemed to dance in the air. Actually he hopped up, spun on the foot anchored by the rope, completed the circle, and whirled his whip again. The crowd jumped back as the circle of death whizzed by them, then the whip smacked into the tall man's unprotected neck on the left side—for his hand was still in his armpit. Blood welled there darkly and the man looked stunned. He reached for the new wound—

—and the bald man jerked his feet backward. The tall man's feet shot out from under him and he landed heavily on his back in the dust. The bald man laughed with glee and slapped his whip high, brought it down flat on the man's stomach. He snapped it aloft again and struck the man in the groin. The audience laughed as the tall man shrieked. He grabbed himself, half-stunned. The bald man flogged him as the man shouted and the crowd roared. The tall man fell still and someone called for the bald man to quit. Immediately a voice went up. "Ten crowns says he's dead!" Another retorted, "Ten he's dead by morning!"

Zed groaned to himself. He wished again he'd been given another assignment on some other island. Any other island. In a moment he'd have to face Cutthroat. That worthy would use every trick he could think of to get the truth out of Zed, stopping only at violence. (Like most, Cutthroat believed there was danger assaulting a navigator. The danger was mostly rumor fabricated by the guilds.) Still, Zed knew if he kept his wits, he could talk rings around Cutthroat and confuse him enough to get off unscathed. He'd keep his word to Tiger Eye and show her up besides.

Cutthroat's tent stood open in front, the long flaps held up and away by fresh-cut slanting poles. In the tent a number of lesser chiefs pored over the ancient map laid on a rude table. Bowls of food and jugs of ale pinned the map at the corners. At the far end of the tent was a portable throne that packed flat, and upon it sat Cutthroat. Beside him was Darroc the Sailor. Zed was marched to the opening and men turned to look. Cutthroat blinked, then waved a hand, beckoning. Zed was dragged inside. He tried to walk in a dignified manner, but the guards had him by the biceps.

The tent was lit by dim yellow light filtering through the canvas, and it smelled of mildew. Cutthroat sat on his throne and frowned at the navigator. The head clansman was larger than most, with shaggy corn-yellow hair and beard. He was big in the body, but his hands were huge, gnarled, and knotty as an old fisherman's. Aroth of Fulcrumia had earned his nickname not for his bloodthirsty habits, though he was fierce in battle and always in front, but rather for the long slash square across his throat. He'd had his throat split by a polearm in his youth, but he'd held the ends of the wound together and had a friend stitch his neck shut there on the battlefield. He'd lived and gained fame, but he spoke like a box of rocks grinding together. It was painful to hear, and probably painful to produce. The man's clothing was plain and unadorned as any other's, mostly because Fulcrumians didn't like to see their leaders dress any better than themselves. A long sword rested in its scabbard beside the throne.

"How," rasped the gravelly voice, "have you survived, Navigator? Where are Balka and the rest?"

"Dead, Lord Aroth." (Navigators applied titles whenever possible. They cost nothing and yielded much.) "The party was ambushed by little babylike monsters—they have some witching shapeshifting power—who cut the men down, biting and smothering them."

"Biting? And smothering?" The words ground like a ship on the rocks. "How can anything small take down grown men with swords in their hands?"

Having suffered at their hands himself, Zed had no trouble spinning out a tale of how the Children of the Moss had surprised the party in deep brush, pulling them down, biting deep into limbs to drain blood and weaken the men. Zed added lots of graphic description, so the listeners would fix on details and miss the big picture—in this case, that it was all a lie. He went on about hiding in a tree, attempting a fire, finding his way back.

Beside the throne, Darroc the Sailor listened. Man, or elf, or dwarf, he was squatty, white-haired, and pointy-eared. He smoked a pipe. The hand that held the pipe sported the round green Pax ring with its odd sigil. His clothing was old, worn white at the creases, with a rope belt and ragged pants, and battered boots shot with holes. Darroc listened without nodding or shaking his head.

When Zed was finished, Cutthroat stared long into his face. "Is that all there is to your story?"

Zed raised his nose. "All."

Cutthroat shook his head. He gargled, "I don't believe you. A man soft as you couldn't live in that forest where I've lost near twenty men. Not with forest creatures like that after you. And a man two days or more in the woods would be starved by now, yet you haven't looked once at the food on the table behind you."

Zed blinked and spun around. He was thirsty, but he'd eaten with Tiger Eye's people at noon. He turned back, and

Cutthroat was again shaking his head. Cutthroat dismissed the lesser chiefs and ordered the tent flaps closed. The dim room was suddenly stifling to Zed. Cutthroat stepped down from his throne and motioned the guards to put Zed on it. Darroc stepped behind Zed and clamped his hands around Zed's arms. The sailor's craggy hands were strong as iron. Cutthroat, who was not an old man, though he walked slow as one, like a great bear, trudged to a green rope-bound traveling chest against one wall of the tent.

Throughout, Zed kept a stony and dignified silence. But as Cutthroat rummaged, he told the chief, "I hope, for your sake, you don't plan assaulting a navigator, Lord Aroth. No man's done that and lived to brag of it. We navigators can reach anywhere and find anyone, and have in the past."

Cutthroat pulled a purple velvet bag from the chest and walked toward the throne. His huge fingers delicately undid the gold knot that shut it. "I am assaulting no one, nor even laying hand to you. Darroc is doing that, and he's a peasant."

Zed forced a laugh. "Hairsplitting will avail you naught when a team of navigators stands by your bedside some lone-some night."

The clansman shook out the contents of a sack. It was a necklace of soft silver or platinum links. A pendant cut with a single staring eye hung from it. Cutthroat laid the necklace over Zed's head gently as a maid might a necklace of daisies. The necklace was cool on Zed's shoulders even through his tunic. Cutthroat turned the necklace slightly so the pendant hung over Zed's left breast. "I'd be willing to talk to some master navigators. I could tell them a thing or two. For instance, that I paid them a thousand pounds of gold, almost, to jump a distance I could see. That they then gave me a upstart guide who goes out with my scouting party and returns alone with a mouthful of lies. Why, if I believed the word of this navigator—and we all know the old expression 'Nobody lies like a navigator'—I might lose a dozen or two dozen or three dozen more men in my ignorance. But now, with that necklace around your neck and near your heart, I'll learn a few things, and the damned navigators be doubly damned. Tell me, who killed my brothers?"

The gentle words in the gravelly tone sounded strange, but not as strange as Zed's own words when he blurted, "Tree people."

"Ah." Cutthroat almost smiled. "And what do they look like?"

"Us. Tanned. White-haired."

Zed was shocked at himself. So much for his word of honor, his promise to Tiger Eye. He looked down at the pendant. Damn! The eye made sense to him now. This was a Necklace of Truth-Telling!

"What weapons did they carry?"

Zed tried clenching his jaw. He couldn't stop the words. "Crooked spears, like lightning bolts."

"They throw lightning bolts?"

Zed groaned, but answered. "No, they're just shaped like lightning." Damn, damn, damn! He couldn't resist answering any question hurled at him. He could keep the answers short, but whatever sprang to his mind first popped out of his mouth.

Behind Zed's back, Darroc sucked on his gurgling pipe and chuckled. Cutthroat began to pace back and forth in front of the throne, studying the ground, thinking. His questions had to be very specific to get the answers he wanted.

"These people live in trees?"

Zed bucked in place, but the hands held him fast. His tongue betrayed him again. "Yes."

"A whole village of them? How many?"

"Yes. Some four hundred." Zed shook his head violently. The necklace rattled softly, but still he talked.

Cutthroat started at the beginning, and Zed blabbed for two hours or more, about everything: the Nureti's wiping out Balka's squad, the shapeshifting Children of the Moss, his rescue by the tree people, the giant fletes, the tree community, the history of the people and their claim to be dispersed descendants of the city folk, the journey overlooking the lost city, the gate, the raven guardian statues. Cutthroat asked hundreds of questions, calmly, thinking the while. He might have gained the position of head clansman with his fists and sword, but he kept it with his wisdom.

After a long while Cutthroat ran out of questions. He paced back and forth across his tent and muttered to himself. ". . . seek to oppose me, do they? Not when I'm so close! Not by the Lord of Orhan's teeth, not by the gods! I'll show them . . ."

The other chiefs watched their leader uneasily. Everyone in the tent knew how solidly Cutthroat's dreams gripped his mind.

Darroc took a moment to hiss a question in Zed's ear.

"These tree folk, did they mention the King Under the Forest? Old Man Malosho?"

Zed shook his head. "No."

The sailor clamped hard on Zed's arms. "You can't lie! They must have mentioned him! They had to!"

But Zed just closed his eyes. He was exhausted, as if he'd been stretched on a rack, or his brain had. He despaired. He'd betrayed Tiger Eye thoroughly. Well, he told himself, not so thoroughly. Cutthroat couldn't ask questions he couldn't imagine, and he hadn't asked if any of the warriors were women: fighting females were beyond his ken. He thought Tiger Eye was a man. Cutthroat had been sharp enough to ask the whereabouts of Zed's compass, and was interested to hear it was "held hostage." He muttered, "A curious phrase. They expect to see you again, then?" When he'd asked why they'd let him go, Zed had replied Tiger Eye had no use for Zed, but simply wanted something in the city, the source of the tremors. Cutthroat stopped asking questions there rather than reveal details of his own dreams.

Early evening flies entered the tent and Cutthroat waved at them unconsciously. Out on the parade ground, the loser of the whip fight had lain in his own blood until someone hauled him off by the heels. A cook brought food for Cutthroat and he munched salt pork absently.

Maybe, Zed consoled himself, it wasn't so bad. Tiger Eye's warriors would no longer attack the Fulcrumians, though they'd gladly watch them die from forest dangers. Cutthroat's route pointed toward the lost city, nowhere near Wyr Forest, and the tree folk were three hundred feet up anyway. There was no reason for the Nureti and Fulcrumians to clash.

Maybe Tiger Eye wouldn't learn Zed had exposed the secret of the Nureti, and wouldn't kill him for it.

Cutthroat paused in his pacing, about to say something, when a muffled shout came to them from outside the tent. "Elephants! Elephant attack!"

Darroc loosed his grip on Zed's arms. He grunted, "There ain't no elephants on this island."

Cutthroat moved to the flap and drew it aside. All three men could see the lumbering beasts bearing down on the camp.

They weren't elephants.

5

At War
with the
Forest

THE BEASTS THAT LUMBERED FROM THE FOR-
est toward the camp looked like elephants.
They towered into the air, twenty or more
feet high, had thick, gray, baggy skin, legs
like tree trunks, and massive flat heads.
But they had small ears, and their long
trunks that swung like restless pythons
ended in a cluster of gray fingerlike grasp-
ers. Their eyes were buried deep under
bony ridges, and they slavered as they
walked in a curious sidelong swing. Zed,
who had seen real elephants on the grass-
lands and steppes of southern islands,
didn't like the curious intensity of these
beasts as they approached. They walked
too quickly, eagerly, as if hungry.

The guards from the perimeter of the camp
had backed at the first sign of the giants, and
now they turned and ran. The gathered Fulcrumians laughed as the monsters ambled
from the woods like oversize pigs, and
laughed at the fleeing guards. The lead
beast, the largest, must have been a bull.
Behind him, from the depths and dimness

of the forest, came a handful of others, six or more of various sizes, including a tiny one not much higher than a man. It became apparent the monsters were going to plow right into camp.

Some men formed a line and shouted and waved their arms to frighten the beasts off. Others ran to the weapons racks by their tents for crossbows or spears. A couple shoved torches into cooking fires to whip up flames. Yet more grabbed their weapons and haversacks from their tents lest they be stepped on. Inside the tent, Darroc let go of Zed's arms and moved to the tent flaps. Cutthroat stood there with his hands on his hips, evidently wondering how to tackle this latest menace.

Men with crossbows and torches joined the shouters. Having left the forest, the beasts fanned out behind the bull, until they were a wall five monsters wide bearing on the camp. The Fulcrumians shouted, just noise at first, then broke into an age-old battle chant:

> "We will de-*feat* you!
> Burn your hou-ses!
> Slaugh-ter your men-folk!
> We of Ful-*cru*-mi-a!"

The chant buzzed in Zed's skull, set his blood racing, and prickled the hairs on his arms. He shook his head and tugged off the Necklace of Truth-Telling, laid it on the throne. Outside, in the early evening dusk, the chant rose, timed with the beating plod of the animals' feet. The plodding shook the earth as did the volcanoes, but regularly, as if Zed stood on some giant's drumhead. The elephant beings didn't waver, and neither did the men of Fulcrumia, and Zed had to admire their courage. Though he did wonder which line would break.

It broke in a way no one could have predicted.

Faced with tons of oncoming gray flesh, the men had to fall back. The line split that the lead bull might pass. But suddenly its trunk flicked out, quick as a frog's tongue, and the grasping fingers at the end seized a man. Before he could even shout, the trunk whisked him to the bull's mouth. Then the Fulcrumians could see the monster had not the round flat teeth of a grass-eater, but a mixture of flat and sharp teeth, like a man's.

The captured clansman was stuffed into the beast's maw to

his waist, and the monster bit down. Blood exploded from its gray lips and spurted along the trunk, danced over the ground. Another shove of the obscene fingers and the man was swallowed whole. Only one of his boots, with a splintered foot still inside, escaped to plop onto the dusty soil.

Pandemonium.

Crossbows *thunked* up and down the line as men shot. Bolts sizzled through the air, aimed at the brute's eyes and mouth. But the bony ridges shielded the hidden eyes, and most of the quarrels bounced off like hailstones. Bolts fetching in the beast's mouth elicited no howl or groan of outrage. Even three bolts in the beast's trunk did little harm, though the monster's grasping fingers raked at them, snapping them off like twigs. Several men with torches tossed them under the monster's feet, or tried to set fire to tufts of grass, but the stubborn weed took a long time to ignite. A man too absorbed in firing grass was snagged around the legs and whipped into the gaping maw. The man shrieked, jammed his hands against both sides of the monster's mouth, but the immensely strong trunk simply broke his back and stuffed him in sideways.

The line of men broke and ran. The battle chant died on their lips as they shoved at their fellows to get clear. Another man, falling, was snatched and crushed, then bitten in half.

Farther down the line, a tall man with an ax, shouting a berserker chant, dashed past a large cow to the smallest beast, the calf no higher than a man. He lashed out with his fighting ax and struck the youngster full in the knee. The beast squealed, a trumpet like a walrus's. Black blood spurted from the calf's leg and it went down to its knees from the pain. But its mother turned and reared on the berserker, and, swinging with her trunk, knocked the man down and pinned him. He beat with insane fury at the trunk, then a gray foot as thick as a hogshead barrel descended on his chest. His face turned red as a beet as his vitals were crushed to pulp. The calf continued to trumpet, a shrill sound that grated on Zed's soul.

Elsewhere the nightmare elephants thundered into camp, crushing tents, supplies, and weapons underfoot. They scattered fires in a cloud of ashes and ignited tents and men's clothing drying on makeshift lines. At every hand the trunks grabbed for fleeing men, some who got away, some who didn't and were ripped, crushed, or bitten to death.

Free, alone with only Cutthroat, Zed poised in the mouth of

the tent and choked in the dust. He wondered which way he should run. The swamp behind them was dangerous, but so was the forest from whence these monsters came. He suddenly wished he were back in the treetops with Tiger Eye's people.

Behind him, Cutthroat had run to a chest and thrown back the lid. He lifted out a wooden rack of bottles packed in straw. They were filled with yellow fluid, tightly corked and waxed shut. Cutthroat gave the navigator two bottles and kept the rest of the rack—four more—for himself. He barked, "Come! We'll see if my gold bought good magic!" More wary of Cutthroat than any monsters, Zed followed.

The beasts were all over the camp, except for the wounded calf and its protective mother. Five great beasts stood on and amid the ruins of the camp, trumpeting, chasing and seizing men, crushing the army and the expedition under their feet. Only Cutthroat, leader and organizer of the expedition, ran to the attack. With Zed following.

"Don't let the bottles break!" the head clansman called over his shoulder. "And you must hit the beasts! Don't miss!"

Zed stumbled on roots and potholes and wreckage while holding the bottles far apart so they wouldn't strike together. As usually happened in a crisis, his curiosity surfaced to slow him down. What was in these bottles?

Cutthroat ran directly toward the lead bull. The beast was red with its own blood that leaked from a dozen crossbow bolt wounds, but redder with the blood of Cutthroat's men. Zed gasped as the leader stopped no more than twenty feet from the monster. It was flailing its trunk wildly, clutching here and there, and now it paused and snaked its trunk toward Cutthroat.

But the leader had his own attack ready. He pried a bottle from the rack, bent a powerful arm, took aim as if along that long deadly trunk, and snapped the bottle over to crash directly into the nightmare's forehead.

Zed watched the yellow fluid trickle down the animal's face. Momentarily confused, it probed with its trunk at the oil, or whatever it was. Then it ignored it and returned to the attack. Cutthroat had backstepped quickly, very quick for such a large man, and almost slammed into Zed, who barely got his two bottles out of the way.

Cutthroat cursed long and hard. The beast stepped toward

them, marching like a wall of muscle. The leader blasphemed the name of Kuriac Su, presumably the alchemist or magician who'd fashioned the bottles. Cutthroat ranted, "We must run! My expedition is lost!"

But Zed interrupted. "No! Look!"

The monster had stopped, confused again. A wisp of smoke curled from the patch of oil on its forehead. As the two men watched, flame suddenly blossomed and banished the smoke. The oil had ignited. The fire spread quickly, licking up the oil on the top of the beast's head, down its trunk, and around its mouth. Spots of splattered oil on the ground near its feet also ignited quickly, feeding on the air itself, the fire rose in pitch and intensity. Zed, some thirty feet away, could actually feel the heat on his face.

The beast could feel it too. It roared with pain and shock. Rearing on its back feet, the creature pawed with its front feet, mopped frantically with the trunk that was also afire. A waft of scorched flesh, sickeningly sweet, wafted toward Zed and he gagged. The beast broke and ran.

Thundering, hooting, burning until its flesh bubbled, the monster charged straight across the camp, smashing and sundering poles, sticks, tents, and pile of supplies as if they were anthills. Then it left the camp and burst among the reeds. Its feet pitched into black stinking mud and reeds and snarled on hidden roots. But the momentum of its charge carried it forward, and its rump flew over its own feet so the beast splashed into the water with a sound like a thunderclap. Sheets of dirty water geysered into the air. The fire hissed and bubbled, the oil trickling across the water and igniting reeds at either side. The beast kicked its trapped legs, twitched all over, and, its face underwater, slurped water into its lungs and drowned.

Juggling his rack of bottles in one hand, Cutthroat turned to Zed and slapped him on the shoulder hard enough to stagger him. He spun Zed around and pointed him toward one end of the camp where a beast ravaged men. "Go get him!" he crowed. Zed jogged off. He marveled that, in all this confusion, Cutthroat had reverted to the clear-eyed and cogent leader he'd been originally, as if action banished the dream-fog that clouded his brain. Zed wondered, not for the first time, if the man were wholly sane.

Zed ran, ducking and weaving between wreckage and flee-

ing men. A large cow had cornered some men who had gi-
sarmes, long polearms with wicked spearheads. She had them
trapped on a tiny spit reaching to the fetid water of the canal.
They prodded the female to keep her trunk at bay. Zed saw no
need to attack her head on. He ran alongside her and planted
his feet to take aim.

The cow noticed him, turned from the prodding spears, and
swung to face him. Zed goggled as the deadly trunk snaked
out, then aimed and pitched the bottle. The thin-walled flask
crashed against her underside. Zed stood, waiting, for the
smoke to rise, wishing it to ignite.

But the cow had no clue she was in danger. She was hungry and Zed was unarmed. The beast lumbered in a half circle, took three great steps, and reached for Zed.

Zed turned and bolted.

Clutching his remaining bottle so hard he feared it would
break, he jogged and then pelted across the smashed camp
with the thundering steps of the beast behind him. The men
with the longarms sent up a cheer, though whether they
cheered for Zed or the beast he didn't want to know.

Then a roar sounded behind him, and he heard flames
crackle. He risked a glance over his shoulder and saw the cow
had stopped. She whapped at flames along her side and belly,
setting her trunk afire. Zed stopped, panting, well out of
range, and scanned the camp for some target for the second
bottle. The men with longarms rushed alongside him with
thanks and congratulations, then snagged his arm and pulled
him along running. One shouted, "Come on! Here's two
more!"

Cursing his own foolhardiness, Zed trotted after the clutch
of men, blowing. They ringed the cow protecting the
wounded calf. A brawny highlander nudged Zed forward.
"Pitch it! It's your kill!"

The navigator hooked his arm and lobbed the bottle. It
dashed against the side of the cow and her calf, and the two
caught fire. Zed tried to block his ears to the calf's squealing.
The highlanders fell back, and everyone cast about.

Flames spouted all over the sundered camp. The bull in the
swamp was dead. The first cow Zed had burned had fallen on
her side, dying. Another by the woods was on its knees and
afire. The air was thick with stench.

By and by the men returned to camp from the woods or

trails. Some who'd blundered into the canal howled when they discovered leeches large as sparrows attached to their legs. Everyone avoided the mountainous corpses and picked through the ruins of their supplies. Under the shouts of Cutthroat and captains and sergeants, they cleared spaces and assembled their tents in a tight cluster near the parade ground. As dusk settled, men had food propped over cooking fires. Someone cut a hunk out of a beast and found it good enough to eat, if a man weren't fussy.

Zed sighed and wondered where his personal baggage had gotten to. Probably it was lost, and he'd sleep in his clothes. As he cast about dully, a hand clamped on his shoulder.

It was Cutthroat. The man's bearded grin was wide. "Good work, Navigator! You did well, for a man who can't fight! I guess we'll keep you after all, and put you to further work. We'll make a man of you yet!"

He laughed uproariously and Zed smiled, but he resented the words. He was tired of being pushed around and used, whether by this man or a girl from the trees. Idly he wondered what would happen if Cutthroat and Tiger Eye were to fall into battle, and who would win. But right now he was too tired to care. He'd be glad to get some sleep, on the ground or in a tree if he must.

The corpses of the dead Fulcrumians were stacked along the fetid canal. In the morning, as had many others, they would be pushed into the water to "find their way home."

To his surprise, Zed was suddenly a hero. Rough men invited him to share a tent and a fire. They recounted acts of bravery, inflating their own and Zed's achievements. He ate basic rations but no roast beast, and wrapped in a borrowed blanket early.

When the men tied the tent flaps back to escape the heat, Zed remembered to sleep close to the fire and to wrap his head. Between the hard ground, the stench of camp and the scorched beasts, the grumbling sky and the quaking ground, he thought he'd have trouble sleeping. But he dropped off as soon as his head hit the blanket.

He dreamed of burning elephants that pursued him over trembling ground. Tiger Eye rode behind the beast's head and prodded it with her spear. She wanted it to eat Zed.

He was awakened by screams.

* * *

Screams sounded all over the camp.

The dawn was obscured by mists thick as broth. Zed had jerked upright at the screams, unsure if he were still dreaming. He wondered if the elephant beasts had returned. The ground shook under him, but it always did that. He struggled to unwrap the blanket from around his head.

The Fulcrumian next to him, who'd invited him to share the tent last night, was awake too, though his head was canted at an odd angle. Zed reached to shake him and recoiled at some slithery, leathery fabric wrapped around the man's head. Zed peered closer, straining his grainy eyes in the dimness, then recoiled bodily.

The man was still stretched full out. The leathery thing on his head was some sort of bird or giant mosquito. It had pale naked skin, like Tiger Eye's flete, and bulging yellow eyes. Its scaly claws were dug fast into the clansman's face. The thing's mouth was not a beak, but rather a belled trumpet, and this trumpet was fastened over the man's ear. The creature's narrow chest pulsed in and out, like a mosquito sucking.

Tangling in his blankets, Zed scrambled backward from yet another deadly forest denizen. But he thought of the clansman's kindness and was suddenly enraged. Furious, he snatched up his boot and swatted sideways at the bird or bug or whatever it was. He fetched it a solid shot, but the creature clung tight to its prey. One grubby claw was hooked into the man's unfeeling eye. Zed swung with both hands and bashed the creature free. Its mouth came free with a grotesque sucking noise, and blood and brain matter—a putrid gray— slopped around the inside of the tent. The bird-thing flopped on the ground, one webbed wing bent. Its gory tongue, they could see, was round like a rasp, like a lamprey's tongue. Another soldier in the tent, toward the back, whipped up his heavy leather boot and pulped the thing. He picked it up by two fingers and threw it out of the tent.

Zed bent over the afflicted man, but he was dead. The whole side of his head was bored open, directly down his ear canal, and blood and brains swirled in the depths. The other clansman grunted, "It ate his brains . . ."

Zed crawled out of the tent and retched into the dirt.

When he'd settled his stomach and racing heart, he realized this beast was why Tiger Eye had told him to keep the blankets wrapped around his head. Like the carnivorous elephants, the brain-sucking things had come out of the forest after the army. If not for her advice, that could be him in there. He almost retched again.

Other screams came and went as more men discovered their comrades dead or dying, their brains gulped by more of Aranmor's horrors. Yet that was not all of it. Many men who'd slept near the water had to be dragged on their blankets to the parade ground. These men had been victims of mosquitoes, only giant ones, and in many places they'd lost not only blood but muscle. Men had shallow pits under their skin where the meat was missing, sucked away. The wounds looked like old arrow scars. And these men were debilitated, either by loss of blood or injection of disease. They couldn't lift their heads; they could barely beg for water.

And that's why, Zed thought, Tiger Eye told me to sleep close to the fire. The insects were getting bigger with every mile. And more numerous.

Drenched in sweat before the morning had even started, he peeled off his shirt to wash in a bucket of water. He discovered a rash in his armpits and crotch. Scratching made it burn like fury. He turned his clothing inside out, figuring to smoke the insects out, and found not only sand fleas, but tiny red spiders that chased the fleas. As he stepped near the fire, a foot-long centipede dashed from amid the firewood, spooking him. And all around, ordinary mosquitoes came and went in clouds, yet they were no more than a nuisance at this stage.

"Loremaster's Luck," he said to no one in particular. "What a hellhole!"

Breakfast was very quiet. There was none of the joking and chaffing there had been in previous days. Zed found that worrisome. A silent army was a resentful army.

Cutthroat and the other clan chiefs had no trouble urging the men to break camp. Everyone was eager to get away from the stinking corpses of beast and man. Short prayers were offered to various gods, and the dead men committed to the canal. The current would wash them to sea shortly, for even with all this suffering, the army was not far into the interior. And they had twice as far to go yet, everyone knew.

Once work was ready to commence, Cutthroat decided to try something different than cutting trail. At the head of the trail, at a solid spot along the water's edge, he ordered men to cut softwood trees to build rafts. Broad daylight put the men in a better mood, and they worked with a will to get away from this cursed spot. There were plenty of trees, plenty of muscle, and plenty of rope, and by midafternoon a dozen long rafts hugged the water's edge. They were some thirty feet long but only ten feet wide, so as to allow many men to pole against the lazy current. Zed had helped lay the logs straight and tie knots. Cutthroat asked among his chiefs for volunteers, and one loudmouthed chief announced he and his cousins would go first, pole upriver, and find someplace to camp the next day. So with hale cheers and good-natured jeers, he and twenty others boarded the foremost raft, shoved their poles outboard, and poled into the canal.

The Tradeway Canal had once been perhaps a mile wide and perfectly straight. Zed didn't know the method once used to dig it: magic or slaves or beasts or something else. But over centuries silt had drained from the hillsides and heavy ash had rained from the volcanoes, until the canal had grown so choked and reedy there was only a trickle a few dozen feet wide in the center, and that track was jammed with white-flowered lily pads. If there had ever been a dike separating the Elder Swamp from the canal, there was no trace of it now, and the canal water spilled into furrows in the swamp in a thousand places. Healthy reeds petered out in the distance, where they died in the hot salt bogs. Still, the men would have no trouble following the main channel.

The army, watching from the shore, gave a cheer when the chief and his men made the center of the canal. With broad sweeps of their brawny arms, and a chant to mark the rhythm, they plunged their poles deep and pushed mightily. Water lilies bobbed and piled up before the bows. The raft shot forward and men cheered again. At this rate, they could be out of sight in minutes, and the army could be in the city in a day or two.

Then something roiled behind the raft, something long and black and sleek, like a seal, and a man who'd climbed a tree for a better view shouted, "Look out! Behind you! Look—"

With a roar and a splash, to the screams of startled men, the long black shape opened jaws like a shark's and clamped onto the back of the raft. Men howled, lost their balance, grabbed for a hold on the slippery logs. The monster evidently couldn't sink the raft, for it let go, and the nose slapped down in the water with a crash. But it came back, and another water monster attacked the front, and—to the groans of the watchers ashore—dragged one side of the raft under in their mighty jaws. With the stress and added weight, the ropes around the logs sawed against one another and parted, and the raft broke into a jumble of logs. Every man was spilled into the water.

Zed couldn't see over the reeds along the bank. The lookout in the tree shouted the men were being bitten and dragged under by the giant serpents, or eels, or whatever they were. Other men were caught between the logs and crushed, or stunned so they slipped under the surface. Cutthroat ordered another raft out to rescue them, but no one hurried to obey. Finally the clan leader himself jumped onto the next raft and called men by name to join him, damning them as cowards if they didn't. Reluctantly, some of Cutthroat's kinsmen jumped aboard. The men on the raft shoved one empty raft ahead of them, pushing it with another, and got to midstream easily, for the doomed raft had pressed the reeds and lily pads out of the way. Cutthroat hopped from one raft to another, whapped at something with his pole, shouted and swore, hauled men dripping from the water with one hand as if they were children.

Cutthroat only managed to rescue a handful of men. These survivors were black and lumpy with leeches, and men had to pin them to rip the filthy things off. They bled from a hundred punctures. Gasping, they cried or moaned or begged to return home. None of them could identify what had attacked them. All they could say was that there were as many serpents as there were leeches.

The rafts were left to rot as men returned to cutting trail.

Without his compass, Zed could only rely on his instincts and training to mark the straightest yet easiest path the trail should take. He put in a long weary day squinting at the jungle and swinging a short sword. The crossbow-toting guards beside him were too nervous to be company.

That evening he again wandered the camp hunting his bedroll and pack. Inside it was a locater focus, a flat disk like a black dinner plate. This disk would eventually cap an obelisk brought in by navigator engineers. He was to place it in the center of the lost city—if he ever reached it. He asked around, but men were sullen and uncommunicative: Zed's hero status for setting elephant beasts afire had evaporated with the onset of new horrors. He never did find his pack, lost in the panic, and he tried not to take the loss as an omen. There were blankets and kits aplenty: dead men's. By firelight he sewed rents in his once-proud uniform.

He was cutting trail the next morning when he had to hit the bushes, and he stumbled behind a small birch copse on the forest side of the trail. He was urinating against a tree when a female giggle startled him. Zed jumped and wet himself.

When Zed had put his trousers aright, he glared up into the tree, which was another fifty feet into the forest. In the crotch of a shaggy oak, thirty feet up, sat Tiger Eye. She carried her spear and atlatl and rope, and still wore his black belt and compass pouch. She tossed him the end of a looped rope and he put his foot in the loop. By leaning back and tugging on some elaborate knot that worked like a block and tackle, the young woman easily drew him into the tree. He sat beside her sulkily, covering the wet spots on his trousers with his hands.

"You might allow a man some privacy," he scowled. "I doubt a woman would want to be interrupted so."

Tiger Eye smiled. Her face was tanned and clean and healthy-looking, fresh as a sun-washed flower, especially after Zed had been staring at grimy, haggard men. The tiger stripes only made her more enticing, for he wondered how she looked without them. She fluffed up her white hair and lay back against the trunk. Zed wondered if she were teasing him with her charms. Or testing him.

She told him, "If you choose to inhabit our forest, you must get used to being watched. There isn't anything we don't see from our perches here. We've the eyes of eagles, and wings to match."

Zed found anger burning in his stomach. "You knew then, of the elephants that stomp men like ants and then eat them."

The woman nodded. "Dawn Reapers. They're rare, though. They live in the scrublands east of the forest. I'm surprised they came this far to feast on your army, but they must have heard all the noise. You lot are louder than the volcanoes."

"A lot of men died under their feet and into their maws."

Tiger Eye shrugged. "It won't happen again. That's the only herd, and you killed five of them. Those are the last of the Dawn Reapers, the last of the city's herd, if that's where they were fashioned."

"Why are they called Dawn Reapers if they attack at dusk?"

"I don't know. I didn't name them."

Zed shifted his butt against the rough bark of the oak tree. His feet dangled over the side of the trunk. After spending a couple of days hundreds of feet in the air, a height of thirty feet didn't move his stomach a jot. It just looked like a big step. "You also didn't tell me about the—brain suckers."

"The arvi. I warned you to wrap your head. You still have your brains. What little you started with," she added.

Zed ignored that. "And the giant mosquitoes? And the leeches?"

Tiger Eye sat up. She picked up her spear and touched the point to Zed's chest. "*I* told you it's—"

Zed pushed the spear point away. "I know, I know. It's dangerous on the ground."

She said nothing, just pouted. Was he supposed to kiss her? If he tried, she'd probably shove him out of the tree or spear him. It was growing more difficult to resist her charms every time he saw her. She was so damned healthy, vibrant, alive. Womanly. But she was also stronger, braver, and tougher than he was, and probably despised him as a weakling, as her elders had despised him as a know-nothing.

Abruptly she asked, "How's your chest? And your leg?"

Zed rubbed both absently. He'd almost forgotten about the earlier wounds. Compared to bug bites, they were negligible. "They itch. Like everything else. That salve they rubbed in really is a miracle cure. If you could get me a steady supply, I could get it to my cousin and he could market it."

Tiger Eye laughed. "Money." She tsked and shook her head.

Zed shot his own barb. "What do you care about my wounds anyway?"

Tiger Eye dropped her eyes. Was she blushing under her tan? "I don't," she mumbled.

Zed changed the subject, whatever it was. "You know, the army's moving slower than before because I don't have my compass to fix directions. May I have it back now?"

She put a strong brown hand on the pouch. "No. Later, maybe. I want to see you 'jump' sometime."

Zed crossed his arms and scowled. "If you want to see a performance, go to the marketplace and watch jugglers and acrobats. Navigators are scientists."

Tiger Eye squinted, mocking him. "Dedicated to a life of poverty and sacrifice, ferreting out truth, no doubt."

The word "truth" made Zed jump. To cover his nervousness, he reached out a thumb and touched the end of her spear, testing the point. It was sharp enough to draw blood. A good trick for plain wood, he thought. He was struck with a pang of guilt, reminded of his inquisition under the Necklace of Truth-Telling, how he'd betrayed Tiger Eye's secret. He pondered whether to tell her, then decided not to. The less talking he did, the better. He had a mission to fulfill, and he might need her help. And she still had his damned compass.

To say something, he asked, "Where are your warriors?"

She nodded vaguely. "Around. Watching. You can't scratch your armpit but we know it. Why were you so long inside the tent with the clan leader, the one with the scar on his throat?"

Zed ahemed. "He wanted to know if I could jump into the city in case the sailor's charm didn't open the gate. I told him no. He didn't like it, but there's nothing he can do about it."

Tiger Eye studied him curiously, weighing his words. Zed didn't look at her. He stood up in the tree. For one dizzy moment he thought he could make the one long step to the ground and almost fell. Tiger Eye snagged his tunic tail and arrested him. She laughed. Zed gasped and sat down again, but he was glad the subject had been dropped.

They talked awhile longer, him trying to learn of more dangers ahead, she making a game of not telling him. Finally he stood up and asked for the rope. "I have to get back or I'll be missed."

Tiger Eye nodded. She held the rope for him to step into, steadied his shoulder with more contact than was really necessary. "Good-bye," she said. "Keep your head covered."

She dropped him down the tree trunk. He said, "I will. I need my brains."

A chuckle.

The navigator reached the ground and headed for the trail. But he stopped suddenly when a flash of white flitted ahead of him in the dimness. White hair, a short, squat form, hunched over.

Zed damned himself. Darroc the Sailor must have been listening, had heard every word he and Tiger Eye had said. Was there anything he hadn't known before? What might he do with his information? Blackmail Zed? To gain what? Tell Cutthroat? Keep it a secret? Zed rubbed his temples. All this intrigue made his head spin. But then he huffed. There was no way to undo the damage, so he might as well get going. He marched out to the trail to rejoin the army.

He found the path strangely still. Nowhere were men working. Instead, the entire army was crowded in a circle around what was becoming the day's parade ground. In front of Cutthroat's newly erected tent, the clan leader faced three lesser chiefs who stared back with their arms folded across their chests.

Zed stood at the back and craned to see. He asked anyone, "What's happening?"

A clansman half turned. "It's three of the high chiefs. They're demanding to call off the expedition and go home."

"Go home?"

The navigator stopped, stunned, his thoughts a jumble at more news. If the army turned back, Zed would have to accompany them to jump them to Fulcrumia. Without the army, and Darroc's secret word, he'd never get inside Tarek Nev. He couldn't fulfill his mission. He'd be thrown out of the Navigator's Guild. And he'd never see Tiger Eye again.

He was surprised to find that bothered him most of all . . .

6

Madness
and
Betrayal

THREE MEN FACED AROTH CUTTHROAT. THE high chief's brow was cloudy, and Zed saw death in his eyes.

The three chiefs were Bashol Bullneck; Fiala Mac Finn; and Durl Churk, called the Prince for his handsome face and lofty airs. All had sworn loyalty to Aroth Cutthroat, but that was only a political necessity. In their hearts the men were as free as wild geese. There wasn't a man in this loose collection who couldn't bring a grievance to his chief, nor a chief to his high chief. Men of the highlands valued their independence above all else.

The Prince spoke now. Though he was not ten feet from his leader, he shouted so the assemblage could hear. "Cutthroat! We've lost more than three score men to this accursed isle! That's more than one in ten, too many for having never seen an enemy! We agreed to accompany you to find glory for Fulcrumia, to extend our lands, and to make safe our borders! We came with you because you *dreamed* of riches!

But your dreams will not sustain *us* any longer! Every man here wants to turn back, for we gain nothing and lose all! I speak for these two chiefs and for all the men! Will you turn back?"

Zed, the only one in this army besides Darroc the Sailor who was not a Fulcrumian highlander, listened to the mutterings of the men around him. He wondered if the Prince did speak for all the men, or if the men even knew what they wanted. Too much independence, Zed thought, could split this army like an anthill and leave it just as exposed. A rising wind rustled the scrub and tall trees at their backs, and Zed wondered if this was an omen.

Cutthroat stood with his back to his open tent. A handful of his attendants and many lesser chiefs stood before it, lending their support by their presence. Cutthroat raised a broad hand, so large it was almost deformed, and pointed into the distance at the rumbling Mount Kadaena. His voice was loud as the gutterings of the volcano. "Men of Fulcrumia! I speak not for myself, but I speak for the mountain, for this very island, for the spirit of the god that is Kadaena! He speaks to me, through my dreams when the night is blackest, and tells me— tells *us*—to seek out the Lost City, Tarek Nev, and bring forth to the light the lost spirit of that city and its people! There are untold riches deep in that anguished city, and artifacts that can make me—make *us*—rulers, conquerors of whatever we wish—the continent of Jaiman itself! Men, with me at your head . . ."

Around Zed, men muttered loudly. This was new talk, talk of conquering. They had thought they were on a looting expedition, after gold and jewels and magic artifacts, all the while investigating a mysterious neighbor to the north. What was Cutthroat going on about? And he was going on, interminably, his voice rising, ranting. Zed, who knew much about magic, speculated. If the source of Cutthroat's dreams was the spirit of Kadaena, then that spirit would gain more power over the man the closer he came to the source. In other words, under Kadaena's spell, Cutthroat would become more singleminded, more fanatical with every mile. And if he were springing surprises on this astonished army now—talk of conquering continents—what more would he espouse when they reached the city itself? How crazed was Cutthroat, and how much more crazed could he get?

While Zed pondered, Cutthroat ranted, the men muttered, and the three chiefs waited sullenly. Finally Bullneck waved his arms to get his leader's attention. "Cutthroat, enough! We've had our say and you yours. The men who want can stay with you, and die, making for the city. My menfolk are moving south! You know this is the law, that a clan can refuse battle, and so we do! What say you?"

Cutthroat, red in the face, stopped suddenly with both arms in the air. He stared blackly at Bullneck, as if trying to kill him with a basilisk gaze. Cutthroat turned to an attendant, gave a quick order. Presently the aide came out of the tent. He placed the butts of two long blacksnake whips in either of Cutthroat's massive hands.

The high chief said, "Choose whatever weapons you wish! I'll fight you all three at once, and cast your corpses into the canal for the leeches! Then *my army* will move on, toward the city!"

Bullneck looked startled at the other two chiefs. They shook their heads sadly. The Prince hitched up his kilt and called for his own weapons.

Within minutes they were all outfitted. The Prince had a short sword in his right hand and a long dirk in his left. Bullneck had a whip of his own and a studded club. Fiala Mac Finn carried a sword and a targe, a small round shield with a long point for its boss. The three men fanned out to form a semicircle. There were no more speeches, no rules of conduct read aloud. The three chiefs would try to kill Cutthroat any way they could.

The men around Zed whispered in shocked tones, jostled each other for a better view, or stood on stumps or stacks of supplies. They placed bets on which chief would deliver Cutthroat's death blow, but quietly so as to show respect.

Then a man shouted Bullneck's name, and another Cutthroat's, and then everyone was shouting, calling, jeering, insulting. The din was awful. The only quiet ones were the four chiefs and Zed. He couldn't imagine how Cutthroat could survive this fight. So the expedition was as good as over. And so was Zed's career . . .

These chiefs knew how to fight almost as well as Cutthroat, with weapons and wits. They crouched and shuffled forward to keep their balance, watched their enemy for any fault or sign of weakness, planned their strategy even as they closed within striking range. Cutthroat alternately flipped the whips before him into the dust of the parade ground, then back behind him, getting their feel and a comfortable stance. Zed wondered whom he'd attack first: Cutthroat was famous for doing the unexpected.

Quick as a snake, Cutthroat raised his whips and skipped in short sure hops toward Bullneck. That chief snaked out his own whip while readying his club. Without looking back, Cutthroat whipped. A long razor-sharp end licked out and sliced the Prince along the sword arm. That man hissed and dropped his sword and arm by his side.

As men watched, fascinated, the first blood well along the cut and drip into the dust, Cutthroat popped the twin whips again. One snapped at Fiala's crotch and made him jump. The other shot for Bullneck's face. The big man shoved his club aloft for protection as he hooked his own whip, but too late. Cutthroat's whip slapped around the club. The tip gained speed as the lash wound around the wood and it sliced Bullneck across his forehead and brow. Bullneck barked in surprise, then cursed as the gash ran blood into his left eye and blinded him on that side. He had to turn sideways to see Cutthroat clearly.

But the highland chief moved faster now, faster than Zed could follow. For an instant the navigator wondered if Kadaena was not empowering his champion. The bloodied whip snapped backward in a wide arc that made Fiala jump again. As Fiala sliced at the whip with his sword, Cutthroat spun. Completing a circle, the second whip slid under Fiala's arm and tore his thigh half to the bone. That man hissed also.

Three cuts, thought Zed, three men crippled.

Cutthroat spun in a full circle to gain speed and to disentangle his whips. The Prince rushed his back. His sword arm was almost powerless, but he held it upward with the sword still in place. He drove straight with the short dirk. Men gasped as Cutthroat threw himself against both blades.

His bulky body crashed full into the Prince. The dirk arm went wide, and Cutthroat caught it under his arm, trapping it momentarily. He blocked the limp sword arm with his own forearm, then brought an elbow up under the Prince's chin with a crack painful to hear. He smashed another blow to the man's throat and the Prince went down, gagging.

Bullneck and Fiala had rushed in too. Bullneck raised his

club to smash onto Cutthroat's head. Fiala led with his sword, with his pointed targe in reserve. Cutthroat spoiled both their charges by skipping backward behind the Prince. The Prince struggled to rise, and the other two chiefs paused to dash around him. Cutthroat struck.

He actually threw the whips backward through his hands so the long black braids hissed against his palms. He clamped his hands shut near the long black handles, which were weighted with lead for balance. Now he held two short flexible clubs. One sang through the air, hooked over Fiala's shield, and struck him on the head. The other hissed in front of Bullneck's nose. With one eye damaged, the man hesitated to endanger the other, and he hung back.

Cutthroat skipped behind the stunned Fiala, dropped one whip, slipped a hand under his armpit and behind his head, and bent his neck almost double. Bullneck didn't hesitate, though Cutthroat was shielded by Fiala. He slung his arm full length and pitched his war club.

The studded end missed Cutthroat's face but smashed into his shoulder. The high chief lost his headlock on Fiala. But he wasn't through. He dropped his other whip, snaked a hand along Fiala's side, clamped his hand over Fiala's sword hand, and crooked it backward savagely. The short blade jabbed into Fiala's neck and he rasped, a broken bloody sound. Bright red blood spurted onto his front and sprayed on Bullneck.

Cutthroat shoved the dying man toward Bullneck, who stumbled when Fiala struck his legs. Cutthroat leapt like a tiger with both giant hands outthrust. He snatched Bullneck's throat and mashed the man to the ground.

On his back, crushed by Cutthroat's weight, Bullneck grabbed at his leader's brawny arms, but they were locked tight in his throat. Clumsily, Bullneck turned his whip around and tried to hammer at Cutthroat's head with the weighted end, but his opponent ducked his head away from the feeble blows. Bullneck's face turned purple and his eyes bulged.

The Prince lurched against Cutthroat and slid a dirk into his side.

Cutthroat let go of Bullneck and jumped to one side, pulling his body off the blade. He rolled and rolled in the dirt as the Prince struggled to keep his feet and get after him. The Prince had been clacked under the jaw and elbowed in the

throat, and he wheezed painfully. His right arm hung uselessly, dripping blood along the whip wound. But the dirk in
his left hand was red with Cutthroat's blood.

Cutthroat rolled once more, then got to his feet. He had no
weapons at all, and the Prince still had the dirk. The two
men's tussle had brought them to the edge of the crowd,
which shuffled back awkwardly. The pressure even carried to
Zed at the back.

The Prince, hacking like a man with a bad cold, closed to
finish the fight while he still had his strength. Blood ran down
Cutthroat's side and leg all the way to the ground. But he
wasn't finished, nor had he even slowed down.

Cutthroat crouched far forward, almost on all fours, as if
ready to topple over. But he snatched a double handful of
earth and flung it in the Prince's face, blinding him. The gagging man swung wildly. Cutthroat grabbed the Prince's dirk
hand and punched the man in the throat once again. As the
Prince fell, Cutthroat held on to him and kicked him savagely,
then stamped on his throat as he hit the turf. Prying the dirk
from the weakened grip, he bent over his fallen foe.

The Prince was not handsome now. His face was white and
tear-streaked where there wasn't dirt and brown blood. He
couldn't even raise his hands to defend himself. Cutthroat
raised the dirk high and drove it into the man's throat so hard
it punched clean through his neck and grated on his backbone.
Men nearby groaned to hear it. Blood fountained over the
Prince, turning him into a red fallen statue.

Some men cheered, but most were silent. Even these hard
men were stunned by such savagery. Cutthroat stepped over
the dead man and moved toward Bullneck.

The big man had gotten his wind back, and he could see
Cutthroat coming. He scooted backward on his haunches,
croaking something unintelligible. Cutthroat ignored his en-
treaties. He stopped only to pick up the fallen war club. Raising it high, he smashed it on Bullneck's head as calmly as a
farmer killing a chicken. He struck the man so hard the club
cracked along the shaft. The man's head was a pulp of blood,
dust, hair, and brains. Cutthroat threw the broken weapon
away and walked toward Fiala.

Fiala's throat had been torn open by his own blade turned
against him. He lay unmoving, probably dead. Yet Cutthroat
picked up the targe with its wicked needlepoint boss. He

kicked Fiala in the ribs to turn him over, kicked his arms aside, then set the point over the man's heart and leaned on the shield. The point pierced his breast, but the man neither shuddered nor thrashed.

Cutthroat still wasn't through, and Zed wondered if he'd carve the men to pieces and eat their livers for all to see. The high chief grabbed Fiala's long twisted hair in both hands and dragged him. He hauled him across the parade ground, past his tent, beyond the edges of camp to the canal. When Cutthroat was knee-deep in the slimy water, he tossed the body farther out to splash amid the smaller reeds of deep water. Fiala's body sank, though Zed knew it would rise later when the gases inside built up—if something hadn't eaten it by then.

Still bleeding freely, Cutthroat hauled the two other losers to the water and cast them in. Only then did he pay attention to the wound in his side. He clamped a broad hand over it and faced the army. He was covered with dust streaked in long rivulets by sweat and his enemies' blood. His hair stood out all over like a lion's mane. His tanned face was pale from lost blood. But his voice was strong as ever. He bawled, "There! I have bested three traitors and fed them to the leeches, as I swore I would do! Is there anyone else who needs the same?" No one answered. "Then I am leader, now and forever, and will hear no one oppose me! We—I and the spirit of Kadaena—*will* go forward to the city and claim my birthright, and *you* will follow or die! We have two hours yet until the sun sets, and that trail *will* advance another mile! Or *I'll* feed the leeches until they sink under the weight of *your* blood! GO!"

Silently, men turned toward the trail and went. They picked up their cutting and digging tools on the way. Zed went with them.

The rising wind had been an omen, but only of shifting weather. Raindrops big enough to fill a canteen began to pelt them. The drops gathered into sheets that drenched everyone to the skin. Where a day before the men's tongues had hung out from heat, now men clenched their jaws to keep their teeth from chattering. The ground underfoot turned to sucking mud. Leeches left the canal and slithered from puddle to puddle, slipping up men's boots and fastening to their legs. The wind could not banish the mosquitoes now, and men wrapped spare clothing around their arms and necks to keep their blood under their skin.

For four more days the men struggled onward. The rising canal made the marsh more boggy and dangerous than ever, and men walking across solid ground would suddenly disappear with a yelp into a sinkhole. These men were usually hauled out by whip, gasping but alive. But as they pressed on, they discovered hot spots below the turf and grass tussocks. These marked hot springs, and the first man to fall into one of those was fished out dead. His skin was red, split in a hundred places, but there was no blood. He had been boiled alive. Men lashed long poles across the soles of their boots like snowshoes, but that slowed them down and made their legs ache.

The highlanders were sulkier and grouchier than ever, but kept their complaints quiet. Two men had tried to slip away at night, bound for the south, but were caught. Cutthroat assembled the army and pronounced sentence. Any man found going south, he bellowed, would receive this. And two attendants stepped forward to slice the bound men to death with metal-tipped whips.

As the army and the men deteriorated, only Cutthroat seemed to thrive. His knife wound had healed almost at once. It was, men muttered, as if this spirit of Kadaena had reached his divine hand down to seal it. The high chief looked taller, stronger, and grander every day, holding his head high and even laughing at the difficulties the army encountered. Men swore by Cutthroat's name now. No one cared about treasures, artifacts, or borders. They cared only about staying alive.

This was harder than ever. One night a horde of men ran screaming from the camp. They babbled that women with red skins, or no skins, had crawled from a boiling spring stinking of salt and made off with the night guard. Four men stood guard together now, costing everyone sleep, and the days and nights became a grind of pain and fatigue.

But trail was cut and the army moved forward. Men guessed it was only three leagues to the lost city. They cursed its name, but would be glad enough to reach it. Perhaps that would satisfy Cutthroat, and then they could go home. Though he had no particular home to go to, Zed shared their sentiments.

When he stepped in the bushes these days, he was especially careful to look about him. The forest was more dangerous than ever, and he didn't like being surprised by Tiger Eye, though she could seemingly materialize out of a berry bush. She'd visited him only twice since he'd rejoined the army, and had had little to report.

He admitted now he looked forward to seeing Tiger Eye. She even haunted his dreams. Zed had never had much time for women. During his apprenticeship, he'd been too busy to chase girls except on rare days off. And then it had not been difficult to catch them. Many women were attracted to the handsome mysterious navigators in their dark uniforms—it was one of the unspoken advantages of the trade. In the city, Zed often had his pick of women. But he found himself thinking of Tiger Eye in different ways, as just being with her and talking to her. It was almost as if she'd bewitched him . . .

He'd finished his business when a voice above him called, "Zzzzzed . . ."

Zed blinked at the trees overhead, pushed through more wet brush to stand under the dripping trees. There she was. Up in a tree. The dim, damp light slanted along her brown legs. Zed blinked rain from his eyelashes. He was glad to see her, but she looked at him . . . strangely.

Tiger Eye lounged on a tree branch not eight feet up. Her long legs dangled down along the trunk. Her arms were over her head, playing with her short hair. Her leather tunic was plastered to her body. Her nipples poked up round and high. She smiled and licked her lips.

Tiger Eye hopped from the branch and landed in front of him lightly, more like a tiger than a woman. Rain on her cheeks made her face shine. She smiled again without opening her mouth. Her lips were red as blood. She had a garland of white flowers around her neck, the first decoration he'd ever seen her wear. The green stems were tightly woven, so it looked more a choker collar than a necklace. Had she donned it just for him? Also for the first time, she was without weapons. This was a special occasion, he thought. And an odd one.

Tiger Eye paced forward, smiled up at him, put a hand on his shoulder. Her voice was a purr. "I'm glad you've come. I've missed you."

Zed smiled back. "Have you? I've been thinking about you too."

Tiger Eye put her other hand on his shoulder and drew her face closer. She still smiled that tight feline smile, and she purred like a house cat. Her eyes were bright under the dim trees. She sniffed. Zed wondered if she'd caught cold. The pressure of her hands was increasing until his shoulders ached. He wanted her to let go, but would have felt stupid telling a woman she was too strong. Instead he ran his hand up her shoulder, reached for the garland of flowers that encircled her neck. But she jerked her neck away from his hand. "No!"

Zed found his heart beating faster, and not from lust. Why was Tiger Eye suddenly hungry for him? Was this some savage ritual? He realized how little he really knew about the tree folk. Had she been joking when she hinted they might eat him?

Tiger Eye's view shifted over his shoulder and then back behind her. She dragged him toward the deeper forest. "Come. We'll be alone."

Zed was towed—there was no breaking her grip—farther under the trees, where it was really dark. He'd never been this deep into the forest along the ground. Huge roots like stone walls tripped him. His foot sank into a pool of water and leaf mold and almost sucked his boot off. He stumbled, but he continued to yank his shoulder. He felt like a fish on a hook. "Wait. Shouldn't you have your spear? It's dangerous in here."

"No, it's not. Come. Hurry."

It's not dangerous on the ground? he thought. That was the one thing she'd drummed into him all along. Something was wrong. He planted his feet.

The tugging fingers at his shoulder sank in like claws. Zed slapped the hand away. He looked about for a weapon: a stick, a rock, anything. There was nothing on the ground but muck and roots big as felled trees. Zed backed away from the woman—or whatever she was. Once he got back to solid ground, he'd run.

The woman padded after him in the dark. Her eyes and fingernails shone like a cat's. Her shoulders were hunched, ready to strike. Zed hopped backward, rapped a root with his heels, scrambled over it backward. Tiger Eye pounced atop the root, crouched.

We'll keep an eye on you, the warrior had said. He prayed that was true. He put his head back and hollered with all his might, *"Tiger Eye!"*

Zed turned to run, but the cat-woman leapt upon him, knocked him sprawling in the muck. She bounded onto his chest, driving the air out of his lungs. Her hand clamped down on his mouth. Her other hand thunked on to his throat. Zed felt fingernails dig for his windpipe.

He raised a fist and clobbered the woman hard as he could alongside the ear, half rolled and punched her in the other side of the head. Neither blow disturbed her cruel cat's smile. He kicked his feet but couldn't connect with her. He slammed her head with both fists, but it was like rapping a tree. Air squeaked in his nostrils, his last. He was blacking out.

Helpless, Zed watched as she opened her mouth to bite his throat. Her teeth were round and pointed like a cat's. Like the cannibal children's . . .

Something flashed in the dim light. A crooked spear pierced the cat-woman's back through the lower ribs. The wicked point stopped inches from Zed's own ribs.

He watched, stunned, as the cat-woman grunted in pain. Then she straightened up and hopped off him. Zed tried to sit up and gulp air and watch the cat-woman die from the spear thrust.

But she merely snarled, twisted her back in an impossible way, caught the shaft of the spear with one hand, and jerked it out of her back. It came out bloody. She tossed it away and turned back to Zed. Her fingernails had grown to inches long.

With a snarl she snapped out a hand for his throat. Zed put his arm up and was raked half to the bone. He heard cloth tear. The wound burned. He let the blow tumble him over another giant root. He hit the loam and rolled, scrambled up, and tried to guess which way to run.

With a cat's scream the cat-woman leapt for him.

Another spear came from the sky, this time from a different direction, and took her in the thigh. The stroke knocked her sideways and she tumbled alongside Zed. He kicked out and caught her under the chin. The blow hurt his foot. What *was* this thing?

Another spear sailed at the cat-woman and pierced her

hand. She shrugged that one off, ripped loose the spear in her thigh, and vaulted to the top of the root. Zed saw another spear miss her. At this rate, he thought, the forest will be littered with spears like jackstraws.

With a final baleful yellow-eye glare over her shoulder, the cat-woman bounded away into the darkness. He watched as the woman breasted another root, but it was a woman no longer. It was a white tiger with a shiny silver collar. Then it was gone, leaving a white hole in the forest and his mind.

Zed trembled so hard he had to sit down. His knees rattled and his teeth chattered. Suddenly he wished he were mucking out cows on his family's farm.

Tiger Eye stepped alongside him and he jumped. But this woman was tanned and smelt of sweat and the forest, a healthy, clean smell. She wore no flowers or collar and was decently garbed once more, if still wet. She picked up a spear and examined the tip.

Without looking at him, she said, "I'm sorry. I should have warned you. That was Belkor the Cursed."

Zed sucked air and wiped sweat from his face. He managed to stand again, with one hand on the giant root. "The— shapeshifter?"

"Aye. The Tiger King is another of his names. He wanders the forest as a tiger, or whatever form he takes."

"He took yours."

Tiger Eye smiled slyly at him, and for a second Zed wondered if this wasn't another cat-woman. "Yes. I wonder why?"

Zed thought of himself being sexually attracted to the— god—and said nothing. Tiger Eye stropped her spear on oak bark. Three more of her warriors dropped from the trees, two women and a man, and retrieved their spears. A woman teased, "You missed, Blackbird."

The man returned without heat, "On the run and the drop, Falling Leaf. That's not much of a miss. We can throw at leaves later if you like."

The woman giggled. They mounted the tree trunk, climbing with their toes and fingers, and disappeared upward. The other woman climbed another tree.

Tiger Eye and Zed were alone. The woman hopped to the root and hung with one hand to the bark. "Remember what I told you. It's dangerous on the ground. *Everything* is dangerous. So watch yourself."

Without warning, a whip snapped out and snagged her ankle. A Fulcrumian popped up from around the tree. With one mighty jerk, he plucked Tiger Eye from the tree trunk. She sprawled on the root.

Another man knocked Zed aside and leapt to pin Tiger Eye. Zed spun as a voice crackled, "You should watch out yourself, tree woman! You're our prisoner!"

Zed blinked. Grizzled Darroc the Sailor and a dozen Fulcrumians pounded across the twisted forest floor at them. The men had whips and spears.

A grunt sounded and the man who'd leapt for Tiger Eye sailed into Zed. Tiger Eye's gaze blazed at the navigator.

She hissed, "You *betrayed* us!"

7

The King under the Forest

In the dim forest twilight, dusty highlanders surged around Zed like a herd of stampeding cattle while white-haired tree people fell like leaves.

The man whom Tiger Eye had kicked into Zed lost his balance and both men went down. Falling Leaf, the warrior who'd teased Blackbird, dropped onto the Fulcrumian's shoulders from above. They tussled in the darkness, the man cursing. Blackbird himself swung from a rope and thumped Darroc in the chest with both feet. He spun the rope around the sailor's neck and pulled it tight. A clansman stabbed his spear at Blackbird, but the tree man hoisted the sailor in the air as a shield. There were shouts, screams, and angry curses at every hand.

Tiger Eye battled the man who'd ensnared her ankle with his whip. She tried to jump up and away, but the man jerked again and she landed painfully on her back across the root. The man leapt to grab her other ankle and she kicked him in the face.

His nose broke with a pop and blood spurted down his face. Tiger Eye rolled from sight behind the root, wrenching at the leather around her foot.

Zed and the man on top of him pawed one another trying to get to their feet. Zed was hampered by one bleeding forearm the Tiger King had slashed. The navigator rose just in time to duck a spear's backswing. A highlander lifted his spear to stab Blackbird, still strangling Darroc, and Zed grabbed the shaft long enough to spoil the man's thrust. Blackbird leapt out of the way. The Fulcrumian whirled and rapped Zed alongside the head with the haft. "Whose side are you on?"

It was a good question, the navigator thought blearily. His vision winked on and off from the blow. He didn't want to see any tree folk killed, but neither did he want any Fulcrumians hurt. He was always in the middle of something. He shouted, "Wait! Stop fighting! Stop it!"

Tiger Eye must have had the same idea, for she leapt atop the root again and shrilled, "Nureti! Flee! We have no fight with these men!"

But there were more than a dozen clansmen in these woods under Darroc's command, and only five tree people. Where are the others? Zed wondered. She had a dozen warriors before. Three clansmen closed on Tiger Eye, recognizing her as the leader. The first lunged at her with his spear, whether to kill her or scare her Zed didn't know. He didn't find out. Tiger Eye snapped her atlatl over her shoulder and whipped it at the man's head. The smooth stick with its solid knob hit him plumb in the forehead and toppled him backward. Tiger Eye followed up the soldier's surprise by dancing into the spot the man had occupied.

In seconds she was with Blackbird, who still spun a purple-faced Darroc in a circle as a shield. Tiger Eye fended off another spear thrust with her own spear. A man stroked his whip at her, but she caught the leather—the rough leather couldn't cut her callused palms—and kicked the man in the stomach.

Tiger Eye grabbed the rope around Darroc's neck, jerking the sailor away from Blackbird. She shouted, "Blackbird! Go! Up!" When he hesitated, she shouted, "GO!"

Blackbird didn't entirely obey. He hopped behind Tiger Eye and slashed at Fulcrumians with his spear. They fell back. Swift and canny as jungle animals, Tiger Eye and

Blackbird had slipped through the ring of clansmen to the open. They could have fled then, up into the trees. Two other Nureti warriors were on the far side of the ring. They dodged blows and jabbed their spears at the enemy, but refused to engage and risk being trapped.

Yet Falling Leaf was still stuck in the middle of the soldiers, along with Zed. She had backed into Zed, using him as a wall, knowing he wouldn't attack or help the soldiers. She was smaller than Tiger Eye, lithe and brown, and the navigator could feel the supple flow of her muscles against his side. A knot of three highlanders tried to snag her with whips. Zed raised his hands again, shouting to stop the battle, trying to establish a truce, but he was stung on a hand with a whip hard enough to draw blood.

Suddenly Falling Leaf whirled, ducked under Zed's bleeding hand. She batted a highlander aside with her spear and charged for Tiger Eye's protection. Zed breathed a sigh of relief. Once this last tree dweller was free of the ring of clansmen, they'd have a standoff and could talk sense. He called to Tiger Eye to ease off strangling Darroc.

But the hope for peace shattered when a whip snapped out and caught Falling Leaf's wrist. She thudded to the ground. A clansman above her raised his steel-tipped spear.

Blackbird hurled his spear and pierced the man's throat. He rocked onto his heels, gargling blood.

With that death, the scene exploded. Fulcrumians leveled their arms and hurled their spears, Darroc be damned. Tiger Eye deflected a spear that would have killed both her and her captive. Falling Leaf, scrambling up, grunted as a spear glanced off her hip. The man who threw it received one in kind through his shoulder. Men howled. Tiger Eye shouted but no one listened. Zed wondered what to do. Everything happened so fast in a battle!

Two highlanders were down. Ten were up and poised to spear or whip anything they could get a shot at. Falling Leaf was wounded, down behind Tiger Eye. The Nureti, scarce as they were, held the ring of clansmen at bay. The fighting lapsed for a second.

"Fulcrumians, stay put!" Tiger Eye shouted. "We'll disengage—"

She lost the words as Darroc smashed his elbow into her midriff. The sailor whirled, jerking at the rope with one hand.

The other fist he slammed into Tiger Eye's face, a blow hardened by years of wresting ships through storms and around rocks. The warrior was knocked flat on her back. She curled into a ball and tried to roll away, but was too stunned.

A crooked spear flashed toward Darroc through the dimness, but caught in the tail of his leather shirt. He was roping Tiger Eye now, and lying low to use her as a shield. A clansman stamped on Falling Leaf to keep her on the ground. The tree people dashed toward them as more Fulcrumian spears came up to the ready.

Zed took charge before there was a bloodbath. "Nureti! Go! Get away! I'll protect her! Go now, before you're caught too!"

The tree warriors glanced at each other and the snarl of highlanders swarming over Falling Leaf and Tiger Eye. Then they flickered, like candle flames in the wind. Zed caught sight of Blackbird scaling a trunk like a squirrel, then they were gone.

Darroc rose from the tangle of taller Fulcrumians. In his strong hands was Tiger Eye, trussed with rope as securely as a netted fish. Only her head was visible, and Zed saw that one side of her face was swollen large and bright pink. Falling Leaf, the gash on her hip bleeding heavily, was smothered by men who fought to tie her. Zed staggered toward them all, clutching his slippery sliced left forearm in his right hand. He didn't know what to say, or even where he stood. He called Darroc's name.

The sailor turned, spotted Zed, and snarled, "Him too!"

Zed protested, "What?" But someone rammed him from behind and knocked him to the turf. He tasted dirt and leaf mold and blood from a cut lip. Then rough hands yanked his arms behind his back and trussed him.

Birds of a feather die together, he thought grimly.

A short while later Zed, Tiger Eye, and Falling Leaf were on the camp's parade ground trussed like game fowl. Darroc's men had made quick X-frames of fallen trees with another log to prop them up. All three prisoners were tied tightly by the wrists. Strong enough to restrain an elephant beast, Zed thought, though he was not flattered.

Three score men who should have been working stood in a large semicircle and stared at the prisoners. None of them had known there were natives on this benighted island, and they were curious to see what king of humans could live here when so many of them had died from so many dreadful causes. The men looked at the small woman and shook their heads, disbelieving. Falling Leaf's wound went untended, and blood trickled down her thigh to drip off her knee into the dust. Zed heard angry mutters about "killed Balka" and "stabbed Toma in the throat."

Darroc stood near Tiger Eye, a spear in his hand. He let it fall from his hand so the point rested in the dirt, but the threat was there. He demanded of her the same question he had asked of Zed. "Do you know the King Under the Forest? Do you know where he can be found? Answer me! Where can I find him?"

The men behind shook their heads. They had a question they wanted answered too: How many highlanders had these tree folk butchered? Darroc's blathering about some mythical king only disgusted them.

At the head of a squad of aides and bodyguards, Cutthroat strode onto the parade ground. He'd been inspecting the work at the head of the trail. Now he walked beside Darroc and stood inspecting the prisoners. He stroked his mustache and beard, unconsciously primping for the women. Since killing the three chiefs single-handed, Cutthroat had done a lot of primping, demanding more respect from his army. He'd enlisted old friends and relatives to be his personal bodyguard of twelve too, for he knew he was now unpopular and was wary of a knife in the back. He'd also made Darroc the Sailor his lieutenant, and the highlanders muttered about Cutthroat rating a "foreigner" over his own kind.

Cutthroat said to Darroc, "All those men to help you, and you only captured two?"

"She's their leader," the sailor retorted, pointing to Tiger Eye. "And a spitfire, a cat let out of hell."

Cutthroat studied Tiger Eye as if she were a prize horse. He frowned at the large swollen purple bruise ripening on one side of her face. He nodded at Zed. "Why is he trussed? He's no enemy. He's nothing."

Zed blinked. Nothing? He'd show everyone who was nothing sometime soon.

Darroc waved the spear impatiently. Compared to the tall stately Cutthroat, the crabbed, ragged Darroc looked like a mashed mushroom. "He's been in the woods talking with these. I've seen 'em. He's a lousy spy! But the girl here knows everything about this island. We can ask her questions till dawn."

Cutthroat stepped closer, ran his eyes up and down Tiger Eye's brown flanks and shapely tunic. "But can she talk?"

"I can speak your language," Tiger Eye snapped. Her words were mushy, for one side of her mouth was swollen. "But—if you are the leader of this invasion—I need to speak to you—privately."

Cutthroat smiled. Some of his bodyguard smirked and elbowed one another. Darroc rolled his yellow-shot eyes. "Don't trust her, Cutthroat. She's more tiger than human."

Cutthroat waved a hand at him. He approached Tiger Eye to speak more softly. "Do you? I thought you might, though I dislike the word 'invasion.' If I remove your bonds, mightn't we step into my tent—"

He grunted as Tiger Eye lashed out with a foot. She made to kick him in the groin, but the big man turned his thigh in time. Tiger Eye wasn't daunted. She snapped up the other foot and kicked Cutthroat just below the breastbone, hard as a mule. The leader staggered back into Darroc, wheezing, his lungs temporarily paralyzed.

Tiger Eye spit at him. "Step up for more, if you want it! I'll snap your breastbone clean into your black heart, you pompous windbag!"

Her attack and insults couldn't have scored better, for the gathered clansmen laughed out loud to see Cutthroat embarrassed. The leader's face flamed dangerously red.

Despite his predicament and his arms pinned overhead, Zed laughed too. But Tiger Eye whirled as best she could and sneered at him with her lopsided features. One eye was swollen shut, and the other squinted. She barked, "And you! You louse! You traitor! You sneaking leech! *You* told them all about us so we could be captured! You stinking snake in the mud! You—" She went on for some time, to the amusement of the soldiers. She called him every vile thing to be found on the island of Aranmor, then some things found in the ocean. She cursed everything about him from the shape of his head to the length of his penis.

Finally she ran out of breath and simply spit in his direction. Zed stared at the distant tree line and tried not to listen.

During her tirade, Cutthroat had regained his wind and limped away. Now he returned with the heavy silver necklace that Zed recognized. Cutthroat started to walk toward Tiger Eye, thought better of it, and came to her from behind. She tossed her white head wildly, but he got the necklace over her neck. He grunted, "This—will save time."

Unable to throw off the necklace, Tiger Eye stopped thrashing and waited for the next move. Most of the army was here now. The men working the trail had heard of the captures and had come to see the show.

Cutthroat stood to one side of the warrior woman. He asked, "Your name?"

She snapped, "Tiger Eye," then looked confused.

"Your father's name?"

"Copper Eye." Again she blurted the answer out. Realizing what was happening—sensing the spell—she thrashed anew but could not get the necklace off.

Cutthroat crossed his arms and smiled smugly. He was back in control. In a casual tone, he asked, "How many of your people are there?"

Tiger Eye struggled, but replied, "Some—f-four hun-dred."

"How many warriors?"

"Th-th-three score."

Zed began to worry. The necklace pulled the answers out of her so hard she'd burst her heart or brain. He reflected she put up a better fight against the spell than he had. But then, she had more to protect. He found himself wanting to protect Tiger Eye, and wondered what she would think of that. Probably she'd kick him in the groin if he mentioned it.

Darroc interrupted. "Ask her about the King Under the Forest!"

"Damn your King Under the damned Forest!" Cutthroat snapped. "There probably is no such thing! This island produces more rumors and legends than mosquitoes! We'll learn—"

He stopped. Tiger Eye had thrown back her head. She sang, or chanted, in a high ragged voice that rose above the clearing and echoed in the tall trees. The language was one Zed didn't know, old and stilted and queerly fluted, with long-drawn notes and many trills. If an eagle could sing, he thought, that would be the sound. Falling Leaf took up the sound. There came from the trees, like an echo, more singing. It was the rest of Tiger Eye's warriors, hiding and watching.

The Fulcrumian men stirred, looked at one another, watched Tiger Eye, turned and looked at the woods. Darroc the Sailor pricked up his pointed ears like a hunting dog. Cutthroat gaped at his prisoners. The high weird singing went on and on, repeating now. Tiger Eye stamped a bare foot on the ground to keep time, oblivious to the enemies around her. Zed found the hairs along his arms prickling.

A man on the outer periphery of the crowd was the first to shout. "Look! There! At the edge of the forest!" Men craned and jostled to see. But the men on the distant perimeter jostled to get out of the way.

"What is it?" demanded Cutthroat. "What's coming? Answer, you cowards!"

Men were pushing one another to get off the parade ground. "He's coming to free her!" they shouted. "Make way! Move!" "Grab your weapons!" Zed thought it was the panic of the Dawn Reapers, the elephant monsters, all over again. He wondered if they were returning. But someone had yelled "he." He who?

Tiger Eye had both eyes shut. She sang to the heavens, as did little Falling Leaf beside her. Cutthroat ran to his tents for something. The three prisoners were temporarily alone on the dust-choked parade ground. Men ran in every direction, but at one point the crowd parted and Zed saw the thing they feared.

Breaking free of the ground, like a shark cutting water, came a green mossy man's head large as a carter's wagon.

Zed watched, aghast, as the giant's head and then shoulders broke the surface of the earth. Though "broke" was not correct, he realized. The giant simply *moved* through the earth without disturbing it: not even making a ripple. He walked through solid earth as a man moved through air, or a fish the depths of the sea. And with every step, as if ascending an invisible staircase, he rose higher and higher. When his breast was above ground, he was already taller than a tall man.

The giant swept through the earth and stood upon it. With mighty strides he reached the edge of the camp. There was no one there to oppose him, for men fled his path. Zed stared. The giant seemed to be made of the earth himself, like an ogre. His skin was gray and shiny, like slate, and it seemed to flicker with highlights like fool's gold. His head was wide and flat-faced, his nose long and gnarled, his chest broad as a small hill. The hair on his head was twisted tight and slightly green, like lichens on granite. He was taller than two men atop one another. Zed could see he was naked and distinctly male. He carried a long twisted staff in one knotty hand and trailed the end on the ground, where it left a furrow deep as a plow's.

Now that the giant was aboveground, his footsteps jarred the soil. He marched, slowly and purposely as a glacier. As he approached the first abandoned tent, he swung up the end of his staff. With a short jab he drove the staff through the tent and collapsed it, as a boy might poke an anthill. Then he flicked the tent up and away. Cloth, ropes, and tent pegs sailed away, far overhead like some crippled bird, and plopped into the canal. A tiny trickle of dirt rained from the tent pegs. Next to the tent was a stack of supplies: barrels of salt cod, crates of hardtack and salt pork, other rations. A giant lumpy foot lifted over the stack and *stamped* it to a jumble of splinters, hash, and dirt. Without stopping, the giant swept up two more tents and rent them to shreds. He scattered a fire without seeming to notice, and embers set fire to another rank of tents. The giant crushed a rack of spears under giant toes.

Men who'd run to the far edge of camp had paused for breath and a look. They saw the destruction of their supplies and howled. Some made to run back, but their friends restrained them. Cutthroat stood in the open flaps of his tent with a number of satchels, jeweled weapons, and other geegaws in his big hands. He stared at the giant's devastation with an open mouth. Darroc, Zed was astonished to see, was actually running toward the giant, waving his hands and calling. But the giant gave no notice.

The giant, or ogre, or god, or whatever he was, warmed to his task. Though he displayed no emotion or outward signs of intelligence, he systematically stormed through the camp, smashing and leveling and grinding into dust every man-made object at hand. He snatched up fathoms of rope and plucked it into fibers that blew away on the wind. He scooped up whole rows of tents and pitched them high up so they caught in the tops of monster trees, lost forever. He batted water barrels and salt casks into loose staves with fractured iron rings.

He twisted steel swords into corkscrews, lifted fires and spread hot sparks across men's drying clothing. As he rounded the camp, he turned to descend on Cutthroat's tent full of valuables.

"Stop him!" the leader cried. He turned to Tiger Eye, snatched the necklace off over her head, and ran into his tent. He dumped armloads of weapons and artifacts into his aide's arms and hefted an iron-pronged spear. "Stop him before he's undone our entire expedition!" The big man ran full tilt at the giant, hopped to set his feet, and hurled his iron spear. The point broke as it struck the giant's flinty side and did no damage at all. Cutthroat called for another spear, but none of his aides would approach. Finally the leader turned and tried to run ahead of the giant and stop the destruction of his tent.

He was too slow. Like a man kicking a tumbleweed, the moss-bound giant waded into Cutthroat's tent. The canvas caught him in midthigh and curled around his body. With both hands, one clutching his long staff, he jumbled together the tent, boxes, portable throne, and all and hurled the lot into the canal with a floppy *swoosh*. The tent canvas sunk in some places and ballooned in others. Boxes floated south or nestled in the reeds. Fish and a giant eel or serpent broke the surface at the disturbance.

All this time, Darroc chased after the giant like a child after a galloping horse. Zed could have laughed, but he was nervous, bound as he was to a man-made X. Suppose the King decided to pitch it into the canal? Zed could picture himself with his arms broken, sinking in the canal and trying to keep from drowning even as monster fish came to tear hunks of his flesh away . . .

"Be still!" a man's voice commanded from behind. "I don't want to cut you!"

Zed turned his head. Behind Tiger Eye a woman warrior—a tree woman—sliced at her bonds with a sliver of steel knife. The man behind Zed was Blackbird, he realized. And another man freed Falling Leaf and threw her across his shoulder so she needn't run on her bad leg.

Zed's arms tingled as the circulation returned. He had to let them hang limp by his sides. The warriors pointed southeast, the shortest space across the camp to the woods. The Fulcrumians had retreated far down the north and south trails to keep out of the King's way. Many saw the tree warriors free the prisoners and dash across the sundered camp, but no one tried to stop them. They were too in awe of the giant.

As he jogged, Zed caught sight of the giant finishing his destruction. What few artifacts remained he either stomped or flailed with his long staff. The camp smelt of mud, spilt wine, cornmeal, and salt rations. Fires burned in a dozen places. Greasy smoke flitted toward the trees and set birds awing.

Then they were among the giant trunks and Zed saw no more.

Huffing, Zed slumped against on oak trunk and let his legs dangle on either side of the branch. From his perch some sixty feet up, he could see easily into the camp, though he doubted anyone below could see him through the canopy of leaves.

Men picked through the camp desolately. The giant had gone. He'd stamped a broad trail one more time through the wreckage, then turned and walked northeast, toward the heart of the Wyr Forest. At each step he sank, a strange and weird sight that made Zed shiver. What must it look like to walk through the earth? What might a man see? Could he pluck gold and truesilver from their veins and bring them to the surface again? For that matter, where had the King come from that he could have heard Tiger Eye's singing and responded so soon? Zed shivered. The last glimpse he had was of Darroc pursuing the sinking giant under the dark trees. What did the sailor want with this mythical—not-so mythical—old god?

"Who—what—was he, Tiger Eye?"

On a lower, wider branch, near the crotch, Tiger Eye tended Falling Leaf's hip wound. All twelve warriors were present: The missing ones had been spread around the camp or had been hunting. Zed was coming to learn their names: Mossback, Morning Rain, Silver Spear, Running Noose. The smaller Falling Leaf had hiked her tunic up to her belly, unashamed of her nakedness, and Zed tried not to look. He concentrated on Tiger Eye's back.

From over her shoulder, Tiger Eye replied, "That was Old Man Malosho, the King Under the Forest. He's an elder god, maybe the oldest god. The only god left on Aranmor too, I suppose, except for Belkor the Cursed. Some say Malosho is part of the Wyr Forest, its heart, though others say he's linked to all the forests of Kulthea and can walk to any one of them in an eye blink."

Zed shivered again. Then he yawned. Evening was coming on, and he'd had a hard day. He wondered about the last rumor. He himself walked the Essence, or at least bored a hole along it, when he jumped, but he'd never heard tell of any Malosho. He wondered if the elder navigators knew about him and kept the secret in the upper levels. Perhaps Zed would spring the name on the High Navigator sometime and see the old man's reaction.

Zed called down, "Can you always summon him with song?"

"If there's a reason. The elder council summons him once every three years and sacrifices to him."

"Sacrifices?"

"That's what I said."

Zed didn't ask what was sacrificed. He didn't want to know.

"And what does Malosho do, just wreak things?"

Tiger Eye finished wrapping a leaf poultice with a ragged bandage and pulled Falling Leaf's tunic down. Tiger Eye wiped her hands on the tree trunk. "I suppose. Sometimes when we summon him, he dances in a circle, though we don't know what it means. Sometimes he doesn't come at all. I guessed he would wreck the camp, since the men are cutting trees at the edge of the forest."

She helped Falling Leaf sit up, then climbed the cracks in the bark to sit alongside Zed. She went to work tending the slice on his arm. She cast her eyes out over the ruined camp. "He's come to our rescue in more ways than one. He's stopped them. Without their dried foods and tools and shelters they can't go any farther. They'll have to run south to the sea."

Zed pursed his lips. Tiger Eye finished his bandage, then sat close enough to his shoulder that he could feel the heat of her body through the many rents in his once-proud uniform. She still wore his black belt and compass around her waist. He said, "Don't count on it. Cutthroat's mad and growing madder. The magic source, whatever it is, is pulling him to the city like an iron fleck to a lodestone."

"His men won't go with him, and something will eat him."

Zed just shook his head. Without looking at her, he said, "Do you see now why I told Cutthroat all about you?"

Tiger Eye dropped her eyes. Zed sneaked a peek at her and realized she was blushing under her tan and black eye. He asked quietly, "Do you see why—"

She turned to him with bright, round yellow-brown eyes. She licked her lips and Zed suddenly wanted to kiss her. "I'm sorry I said—all those cruel things. I didn't know they'd magicked you."

Zed had sat here in the tree, brooding. A little while back, he'd imagined all the fine sarcastic replies he'd make when finally she admitted she'd misjudged him. But now he couldn't think of any of them. He said, "That's all right. I'm sorry too."

Tiger Eye smiled at him. "What are you apologizing for?"

Zed's mind went blank. He didn't know. Women were born with magic in them. They could turn men's minds to mush with the crook of a finger and a smile. Still he smiled back. "I don't know. Being me."

She looked away again. "Don't apologize for that. I—"

It was Zed's turn to stare at her. "Yes?"

"I—like you—the way you are."

Zed's chest swelled at those words. He suddenly felt light, as if he could fly out of the tree. But there had been other words that made his heart drop into his belly with a thump. "Oh? I don't seem to be worth much. You've shown I can't fight, I can't climb, I can't read a forest trail. Your elders said I knew nothing, and Cutthroat said I *was* nothing."

Tiger Eye shook back her hair as if clearing her mind. She still didn't glance at him. "I'm sure you know some other things. Useful things."

Zed grunted. "One or two, maybe. I was counted an excellent student in college. I'm a damned good navigator and I'm going to be a master someday."

Now Tiger Eye couldn't return his gaze. "I'm sure you will."

Zed could say only, "Oh. Thanks."

They were quiet for a while. Then Tiger Eye said, "What will you do now?"

"Now?" He sounded stupid even to himself.

"Now that your work is done. When they return to Fulcrumia, you're finished, aren't you?"

Zed replied, "Only with the first half of my mission. I still have to get inside the city. I've lost the locater focus, but I can make some calculations and citings at the city's center, find an Essence tunnel for the engineers to follow. The guild doesn't accept failure. We're supposed to always find a way, and I will. I'm not going to give up."

Tiger Eye mused, "And we still have to get inside the city. There're still the volcanoes."

"Then we're stuck with each other. Though how I'm going to breach that wall without Darroc's secret word, I don't know. I wish he hadn't run off into the forest to be eaten—"

He stopped, arrested by something out in the camp. The two watched the army assemble. There were not as many as Zed had brought to the island. Only four hundred or so had made it this far. But all of them were present in rough ranks. Cutthroat, hung with some weapons and satchels of artifacts he'd managed to salvage, harangued the men with both arms waving. A few raised their arms in impotent protest, but the rest stood like statues. Cutthroat finished, his face red, and pointed. They marched.

North, toward the lost city.

"And we've still got them to contend with," Zed breathed.

Tiger Eye was silent.

8
Before the Red Gate

In the end, Zed carried a white flag into Cutthroat's camp. He and Tiger Eye had talked long into the night before coming to their decision: They had to parley with Cutthroat. Zed had explained about a "flag of truce" and tied a scrap of bleached leather to a pole. Now he marched from the deep woods to where Cutthroat's disgruntled army hacked at the brush in the trail.

Zed could see the army falling apart in many ways. Since Malosho had destroyed their supplies, they had little food, and not even the most skilled hunters could find much in the dense brush or on the dim forest floor. The land was a jungle with no large herds of animals. The men were hungry. They were tired from slashing at the brush that grew thicker with every step, till it looked as if they were carving into the side of a wooden mountain. They had to sharpen their blades at every fifth stroke. They muttered among themselves and glared at Cutthroat and his bodyguard.

The wild-haired leader swore when the

truce-bearer appeared. Cutthroat put both arms across his chest and boomed, "You bring a flag of truce, you coward? Is that all navigators can do, take a man's money, talk him deaf, and run from trouble?"

Zed frowned and kept his temper. Cutthroat was looking more dangerous all the time. Despite the heat, he wore a wide blue cape that clasped around his neck and hung to his knees. Several satchels were slung about his frame. Zed guessed they contained his various artifacts such as the Necklace of Truth-Telling: Cutthroat had no tent to store them in after Malosho's rampage. And he probably didn't trust anyone else to carry them.

Zed told the leader, "Your troubles will bury you soon, Cutthroat." He didn't butter him up with the title "Lord Aroth" anymore. "Your army is starving and worn out and, if I read the signs right, rebellious. You'll be lucky to get off this island with your head, let alone any magic toys from the bowels of a lost city."

Cutthroat's brow furrowed, and for a moment Zed thought he'd strike him, truce or not. The navigator pressed on with his message. A man of action like Cutthroat needed to be busy. "I come with a proposal, Lord Cutthroat." A little butter now wouldn't hurt. "I come on behalf of the tree folk, the Nureti. They wish to negotiate."

Cutthroat blinked in confusion. Zed wondered if the strain of command wasn't wearing the man down. He seemed stupid these days, whereas before he'd been anything but. The leader asked, "Negotiate? You mean, they wish to swear fealty to me."

Zed grunted. He tried to imagine Tiger Eye or any of her folk bending a knee to an invader and tyrant. "Hardly, my lord. They wish you gone. But if you insist on entering the ancient city, they are willing to guide you to the gate, that you might take what you want and depart forever."

Cutthroat frowned. Zed tried to read his mind. Cutthroat might get half of what he wanted: the magic artifact from the city, but not control of the island. Zed waited. Cutthroat finally said, "You forget something, Navigator. We've lost Darroc to the forest. We've no way to pass the Red Gate without his secret word."

Zed smiled. "We thought of that. Nureti warriors are tracking Darroc now. They'll bring him in."

Cutthroat frowned again, not happy at being outthought. "Then tell your—friends we'll talk. Bring them to the head of the trail under your flag."

Zed picked up his flag of truce. He said, "No tricks."

Cutthroat raised a hand. "On my honor."

Zed nodded and marched off. That honor wouldn't count a lot for Tiger Eye, he thought. Cutthroat was out to become Aroth the Conqueror.

The meeting took place in a hastily widened clearing near the north end of the trail. The Fulcrumian army moved back down the trail to leave the head empty. Cutthroat and his bodyguard stood alone next to a flag of truce. Tiger Eye, with all but two of her warriors, slipped out of the forest, silent as wolves. Zed followed. Tiger Eye stood in her bare feet with her spear resting on the ground. She looked up at the big Cutthroat, but despite the purple ring around her left eye from Darroc's fist, met the man's glare eye-to-eye.

They were introduced all around, Cutthroat's relatives and Tiger Eye's warriors. Zed stood between them as negotiator. Since everyone was eager for something, the discussion went quickly and with only a few lies. Tiger Eye explained some of the history of her people and their ancient claim to the land. She lied only in saying she spoke for the tribe. Cutthroat talked at boring length about his dreams and the siren song calling him to the Lost City of Tarek Nev.

After a long while, the agreement was this: The tree people would guide Cutthroat's men to the city, where Darroc with his magic would open the Red Gate. All would enter the city. They would stay together for mutual protection from whatever fiends still haunted the streets. They would search for whatever called to Cutthroat and try to locate the source of the tremors, if they could. Anyone in either party could take whatever they could carry away, the discoverer being the owner, save for the item that called to Cutthroat. In the event of disputes, the leaders—Cutthroat, Tiger Eye, and Zed—would arbitrate. All was agreed.

Until they got to the definition of Cutthroat's men. Tiger Eye waved a hand at the rank upon rank of men gathered along the trail, each straining to hear. "You cannot take all these men with you. We could never feed this many, not if we scoured the island. There is not much game. You'll have to send them back. Most of them," she amended.

Cutthroat spluttered and swore, waved his mighty hands, but in the end agreed. He knew she spoke true, and in truth, he would be glad to cut his numbers and lessen the chance of rebellion. After more haggling, it was decided Cutthroat could keep his bodyguard and a few more, fifteen men all told. Everyone else could depart.

The group considered whether Zed would accompany the army to Mistroke Channel and jump them across, but they decided against it. It would take him days to reach the coast, and he couldn't jump back to the party without knowing where they were. No one wanted to spare the time. Cutthroat tossed his shaggy head, like a lion his mane. "The hell with them, the traitorous dogs. Let 'em find their own way across on rafts. Let 'em swim with the sharks and the boiling sea."

Tiger Eye picked up her spear. She shifted Zed's belt around her waist and said, "Dismiss them then and pack them off. We'll hunt food for your entourage. Then we'll strike for the city." She gazed at the roiling gray sky. It was still early morning. "We can be there by nightfall."

Cutthroat started. "Nightfall? *Tonight?*" He'd been hacking his way across this island for more than a week, until the city had seemed an impossible dream.

Tiger Eye nodded. "Tonight. We'll be back."

Cutthroat said, "Wait! What of Darroc?"

But Tiger Eye simply nodded to her warriors. They faded into the brush as if they'd turned invisible.

Cutthroat stood next to Zed and stared at the spot where they'd vanished. He turned vaguely north by northwest, the direction of the lost city. He muttered, "Tonight . . ."

Then he spun and bawled at his army, waving his arms. "Well? What are you waiting for? Go on, get out of here! Go home, cowards! You've been whining to do that all along, so go!"

Zed disliked the angry mutter that resulted. These clansmen were not used to being addressed as lackeys. And despite their grumblings and threats, Zed sensed that some of them would have preferred to go on anyway, to see this fabled city and its myriad treasures. Now they had what they wanted and were displeased.

Such was life, he thought.

He watched the trees and waited for Tiger Eye to reappear.

After the dragging, painful progress of former days, events now started to move as if they'd mounted a flying carpet.

Within an hour the army was gone without trace. With no supplies and little save their blankets and swords, the men just turned and shuffled away, grumbling. It was almost twenty leagues to the sea, which would take them three days in this terrain, three days on empty bellies. Zed was glad he didn't have to escort them. Tiger Eye's warriors came from the trees with small red deer, gutted, over their shoulders. Cutthroat and his bodyguard were so hungry they kindled fires on the spot, roasted the meat on sticks, and gorged it half-raw. Having full bellies went a long way to smoothing the friction between Fulcrumian and Nureti.

The highlanders wrapped the leftovers in the deer hides and slung them as bundles over their backs. Except for Cutthroat's satchels and jeweled weapons and cape, no man had much besides a spear, blanket, and short sword. They could be ready to march in a minute.

Tiger Eye explained how the remaining adventurers would travel. "We won't cut trail, but will rather slip through the forest like the other animals. We'll take to the trees where need be. There'll be no talking. If you must talk, whisper and only against one's ear. Stay away from open spots where the grass is yellow at its base, for that means a boiling spring. Do not lean against trees covered with moss, for the drilling spider lives in there. Don't touch any cobwebs you see, but go around them. Avoid razor grass, which has blue lines in it . . ." She went on and on, cataloguing the dangers of the ground. Zed shuddered at some of them, especially the idea of pink larvae that bored into a man's foot and crippled him. Yet, for all the information given, he sensed Tiger Eye was telling them only the basics of survival, and leaving much unsaid.

They were almost ready to go, Cutthroat actually champing at the bit, when a shout sounded from the south. Two tree folk, spears in hand, accompanied Darroc, the ancient crabbed sailor, man or dwarf or elf or whatever he was. He trotted in his rolling sailor's gait. In his hand was a gnarled staff taller than he was. The short man danced like a boy.

"I've gotten it!" he shouted when he arrived. "Look! The

Staff of Old Malosho! I've gotten it! The real thing, taken from the King's hand himself!"

Curiously, wary of the powerful artifact, men gathered to see. Darroc was filthy with cobwebs and sweat and dirt, scratched and mosquito-bitten in a hundred places, yet his face and eyes were smiling. He cradled the staff, which was nine feet long and thick almost as a hitching post, in his powerful craggy hands. The staff was crooked as a dog's hind leg and lumpy, almost warty, as if grown entirely from hardwood burls. Darroc was so excited he set the staff back down and danced a sailor's jig around it like a maypole.

Cutthroat stared at the staff without touching it. "But what use is it? What riches can such a thing bring a man?"

Darroc's eyes went round as a child's. "Oh, more than you can imagine! This staff—the magic in it—it's legend! I come—"

He stopped, hesitating, as if revealing some dark ancient secret. What he did reveal was more surprising than that. He started again in his husky voice. "I come from a fishing village along a rocky coast on—well, far away. The land is poor, nothing but rocks, and all us lads have to go to sea before we grow beards. Most of us spend our lives seafaring, and some of those lives are infernal short. Ever since I was a lad"—he grinned at their curious faces; Zed tried to imagine Darroc as a lad—"ever since I was a lad, I've thought about how—nice it would be if my people could farm. Just grow enough food to survive, so that some of us . . . some of us could stay home and tend the oldsters . . ." He shook his head. "Anyway, I've hunted this staff a good long time, for men say, have said for centuries, that this staff can make greenery grow on the barest flint rock. If that's—but look!"

They glanced down where he pointed. Between his booted feet with his dirty toes poking through the cracked leather, the staff sat in a patch of brown mud. But at the base of the staff, grass had sprouted. As they watched, the greenery sprouted anew and started to curl around the staff. It was good strong green grass, rich enough to eat, Zed thought foolishly.

Darroc tenderly lifted the staff free of the ground. The coiled grass fell back onto the soil and continued to writhe, alive, growing incredibly fast. No one spoke. Darroc caressed the staff lovingly.

Tiger Eye's voice startled them. "We must move." She

hiked her spear and marched for the brush. The others fell into some order, warriors mixed amid Fulcrumians, two tree people in the rear, and traipsed after her. Zed was right behind her, and he saw her touch her bruised face with her fingertips. Maybe she'll forgive Darroc when she's healed, he thought. But who would have believed scruffy Darroc the Sailor had a soft heart? You never really knew a man, not ever . . .

Compared to stomping and hacking through brush with the army in a straight brutal line, following Tiger Eye was simple as slipping into a bathtub. From a lifetime in studying the forest, and centuries of knowledge to train her, Tiger Eye moved through the forest making no more imprint that a shadow. Instead of forcing the forest to yield a path, she rather yielded to the natural paths the forest offered.

She and her warriors rarely walked in a direct line. Tiger Eye slid around the far sides of trees, detoured about small open glades that Zed would have tramped across, tiptoed across roots that Zed would have avoided. In some places, where no threat or even deviation in the forest showed, she would suddenly turn a right angle and walk in a large half circle to get to a point not thirty feet away. Many, many times, she stopped dead, scooted onto her haunches, and insisted the others do the same. Then they would wait for a minute or ten minutes, or longer. Then abruptly she would rise and jog forward for another fifty feet and do the same. Zed never once saw whatever they were avoiding, or watching, but he was glad for the breaks, for she covered country faster than Zed could have walked through a town.

Once, toward midmorning, as they squatted and watched, Zed whispered, "What are we waiting for?"

Tiger Eye leaned her head back to whisper in his ear. Her breath tickled. He liked the smell of her, like a field of flowers. She said, "Do you see any mayflies in that copse?"

Zed looked. "No."

"Where would the mayflies go?"

Zed didn't know.

Tiger Eye leveled her spear and Zed sighted along it. He squinted. Far beyond the glade, something large and green-dappled raised its head and grunted, then disappeared again. She whispered, "Green bear. Eating ants in a rotten log. The flies are after his sweat and the scraps."

"Oh."

They waited some time longer, then Tiger Eye led them in another direction, around the bear. But still later when they waited, Zed distinctly saw flies hovering over a glade. Yet they avoided this glade too. When Zed asked about them, Tiger Eye snorted delicately. "A boar wallow. The flies hover over the droppings. The boars can't be far off."

"Oh." Zed was feeling discouraged again. After having handled the truce negotiations so well, here he was thrown into ignorance again in the forest. Tiger Eye was his master here, and he was glad to let her be. But he had to admit the unspoiled jungle, with its myriad colors and tints and scents and shafts of falling light, was far more beautiful than the glaring slashed path he'd been following behind the Fulcrumians' army. It was a shame, he thought, how deadly this place was, while being so lovely. Like some women he could name.

One thing he did notice was, Tiger Eye never shared any big secrets with Cutthroat and his men. She led them through the forest while keeping them in the dark. They wouldn't be able to get far—nor live long—without her, Zed reflected.

At one point, one of the Fulcrumians stepped into a hole and burst a hornets' nest. A thousand of the insects swarmed over him instantly, plaguing him with stings. The man staggered along the trail, banging into trees, batting at his skin wildly. Two tree warriors went into immediate action. They tripped the screaming man with their spears and rolled him over and over in rotten leaves as if he were on fire. Two more warriors whisked into the bushes to one side of the trail and emerged a minute later with leaves heavy with mud. While two held the man, the other two ripped his clothes off and plastered him with mud. Tiger Eye climbed a low tree and brought a handful of leaves and instructed the man to suck them. Within a few minutes the hornets were dead or flown off, and the man was resting, only mildly hurt. Tiger Eye watched him for a while, then pronounced, "He breathes deeply. He'll live."

Cutthroat, sweating in his heavy cape and satchels, snarled at her, "Why didn't you point out that hornets' nest? You stepped right over it!"

Tiger Eye snorted. "I thought you'd see *that*. Any child would. The hole was lined with yellow faces. Are you civilized men blind in both eyes? If you don't see something simple as that, what *do* you see?"

No one replied. The Fulcrumian men, for all they were tough and enduring, were suffering from the rapid pace and close hot air under the trees. There were fifteen men besides Cutthroat and Darroc, all relatives and much alike, with shaggy golden hair, lean faces, and strong capable hands. Their linen tunics and kilts were plastered to their bodies. Their exposed skin was a welter of insect bites despite the leaves Tiger Eye had instructed them to wipe on. Yet none of the men had complained once. They were brave enough, Zed admitted. But they had yet to see this dead haunted city with its ruby-eyed raven statues.

Tiger Eye took pity on the men and allowed them a short break. "But only a short one, otherwise your legs will stiffen. I'll find clean water. Falling Leaf, come." A push at a fern like a green door, and they were gone.

A few minutes later Tiger Eye returned. She led them off the minute path to a wide shelf whose surface was old black volcanic rock. She indicated they could stretch out here for the midday meal. "A rock floor doesn't yield much except snakes and scorpions." The men sat down gingerly and shucked their blanket rolls and weapons. Tiger Eye pointed to water that bubbled from cracks in the rock shelf. The men drank greedily. Zed found the water warm and strong with some mineral, but decided that made it safe. As he drank, he noticed tiny white insects dancing in the water, but he drank them anyway.

One man built a fire to roast the morning's deer. Darroc lay back and immediately fell asleep. Warriors disappeared, probably to gather more food. Cutthroat stood and stretched his back, as if he were ready for more exercise and not rest. He stamped to the edge of the shelf, dashed some water on his face, and stared at the wall of jungle around him.

"Cousin," called a graying man who'd slipped off his boot to nurse the rot between his toes. "Better not go far. You're not in Serpent Springs's market." But Cutthroat shook his head and marched to the edge of the forest. He looked around again. Zed thought it the look of a man buying property, an assessing look as if Cutthroat were determining what he'd do with the land when he had conquered it. He cocked his head at something farther in the forest and stepped from sight. His older cousin sighed and picked at his toes.

Zed stretched out full on the rock, in wan sunlight for once, and tried to relax. The flat rock shook slightly, making his eyelids flutter. They were moving north toward the distant volcanoes, he remembered, and the seismic activity was more noticeable with every mile. He lay delightfully idle, though he knew it couldn't last. He thought of easing off his own boots, licked his lips at the smell of roast venison, then sat up suddenly, as did others. A thrashing sounded in the woods—in the direction Cutthroat had gone.

A half-dozen Fulcrumians, barefoot and booted, leapt up with spears and swords. They hopped down off the shelf, trotted to the edge of the forest. One called, "Cutthroat! Aroth!" Another burst of thrashing sounded, perhaps a hundred feet into the jungle, though it was hard to tell. Cutthroat's gray cousin barked at them, "Get moving!"

The Fulcrumians set their shoulders, lifted their swords, and hacked at the brush to clear a trail. The remaining men in the glade picked up their swords and came to the edge of the forest. Zed joined them. They could follow the party's progress by the thrashing of brush and their shouts.

In a short while the party fetched Cutthroat out. His hair was wild, his hands and mouth bloody, his tunic torn across the breast, his leg bleeding. He wrapped his cape tight around his shoulders as if he were cold. The six highlanders helped him to the rock shelf and sat him down. They used the warm mineral water to bathe his leg wound, which was only a scratch. "What happened?" they demanded.

"A big cat," Cutthroat wheezed. "With stripes. A tiger. Ran at me. I jumped around a tree, but it slashed me. Kicked it away, got away . . ." He panted, more winded than wounded.

"We told you, Cutty." The gray cousin admonished him as he would a boy, the only man in the company old enough to do it, and Cutthroat nodded. "I know, Eli, I know."

"What's the blood on your mouth?" the man asked.

Cutthroat dabbed as if unaware the blood was there. "Must have bitten my lip. I haven't run like that since we were boys hiding in Cousin Tarn's barn." The old gray cousin laughed and helped mop Cutthroat's mouth clean with the now-tattered corner of the blue cape. They could find no cut on his lip, but the leader shook them off anyway. "Enough. I'm fine. When's dinner ready?"

The men laughed again, loud with relief, and fetched their leader some choice cuts of roast venison. Tiger Eye's warriors returned with round yellow fruits, which when split revealed bright red pulp and a core of many seeds. They ate the tart fruit, finished the venison, and washed it all down with sparkling water.

Tiger Eye frowned when she learned of Cutthroat's tiger attack. "There are better-tasting things than men in these woods. Tigers shun men as unclean." A man joked that Cutthroat certainly smelled unclean. Tiger Eye's frown did not diminish. She asked the Fulcrumians, "Did any of you see this tiger?"

The men shook their heads. Cutthroat dabbed at his mouth where his lip was swelling. He demanded, "Are you saying I lie? That I fled something else?"

The woman warrior ignored him. She looked around the party and asked Falling Leaf, "Where's Blackbird?"

The woman lounged against a tree. With a knife she sawed through a hunk of venison clutched in her teeth. She gulped and said, "I don't know. We separated to find the passion fruit." Disturbed, she glanced toward the woods where Cutthroat had been rescued. Without a word, Falling Leaf, Tiger Eye, and the other tree folk fanned out and entered the woods.

They were not gone long. They dragged something from the brush, much as men had helped Cutthroat return.

Blackbird of the ready wit was dead. His vacant brown eyes stared at the blustery sky overhead. His skin was white, for he'd lost every drop of blood. A swath of hair had been ripped from his skull as if by a wide clawed paw, the blow that had no doubt killed him. The venison in Zed's stomach gurgled and he had to clamp down. Blackbird's guts were missing. He'd been ripped open from breastbone to groin, and all his vital organs—heart, stomach, liver, kidneys—were gone. Eaten by some gigantic cat.

Tiger Eye's eyes flashed at the group. "None of you saw him fall? None of you helped him when he needed it?"

The old gray cousin's voice was quiet. "We saw nothing. We heard nothing. We're blind in these woods. You said so yourself."

Tears ran down Tiger Eye's cheeks, one brown, the other

still purple from Darroc's fist. "Blackbird was too good a warrior to be taken unawares. There is some treachery here." She looked at Cutthroat.

The leader spread his hands in protest, but only said feebly, "He must have been coming to my rescue. I didn't see him. I was running. I'm sorry for him."

The warrior woman's mouth was hard. With a curt nod, she ordered her warriors to grab their fallen comrade. She snarled, "We must raise him to the treetops. We'll be back. Stay here." They hoisted the limp, empty body and disappeared.

They came back two hours later. Without a word, they resumed the trail. Cutthroat's leg wound didn't slow him down. If anything, he had more energy than the others, for he was eager to reach the lost city.

And reach it they did, just as the sun was setting.

Zed was leg-sore and winded. Even he could tell they were marching in a wide circle, and he wanted to protest. But he did not want to be the first to complain, especially to Tiger Eye. And so he plodded on.

Suddenly Tiger Eye halted them, then went forward alone. She returned in a moment and waved them on.

No sooner did they break free of the brush than they saw the city.

Zed blinked. By circling around on land, they'd come to the western face of the city, the only entrance, which he'd been unable to see from the eastern trees. They stood on a stone dock at the edge of the fetid canal that encircled the city.

There was no bridge. Opposite them, set in the city's wall, tall as a church, was an impossible ruby-red demon's face with a dark leering mouth.

Tiger Eye pointed with her spear. "We walk through the demon's mouth, legend tells us. Darroc, let's have your magic word."

9

Ghosts
of a
Dead City

ZED STARED AT THE CITY, WHICH LOOMED higher and higher in his sight, as if he'd walked to Mount Kadaena itself.

From where he stood in the wan evening light, the city stretched up and away, a vast hill rising from a swamp. It rose in tiers that were cut with ancient, often-crumbling stairs. The tiers were banked solid in many places with houses, some roofed, some collapsed, but in other places whole tiers had crumbled and slid down the hill, an avalanche of shattered houses and buildings. Grass, vines, and unpruned trees covered a good half of the city, the jungle taking back its own. At the very top, though, glinting gold in the sun, was the palace or temple. Zed guessed again the city was some five miles across, sloping gently upward in nine tall tiers so the peak was a hundred and half feet above the swamp. Half the height of the Wyr Forest giants, he thought. No wonder he'd been able to see so much of it from the treetops.

The city looked unhealthy, uninviting,

and it took him a moment to realize why. It was dead, deader than any usual abandoned house or barn, for not even birds could light in the city—the raven statues saw to that. Seeds might blow in and root and grow, but there would be precious few animals to frolic among the shrubs and trees. It was uncanny to see a monument of man's, an entire city, without a breath of life, silent as a petrified forest in the middle of a salt desert Zed had once visited. The thought of entering made the hairs on his neck stand up, and he shivered in the open air and oppressive jungle heat.

In the distance, in sight once more, a volcano chuffed smoke into the gray sky.

Tiger Eye startled everyone again. Her voice was steeled to cover her own nervousness. "Well, Darroc? Have you the word to open the gate?"

Zed shook his head. The Red Gate. He noticed now they stood on an ancient cut-stone road that crawled from the forest behind them and terminated, square-cut, at the swamp's edge. The neatness of some spots and the overgrown chaos of others left him disoriented. Zed turned a circle trying to place everything. Ah. The Tradeway Canal was easy enough to pick out, though it was a mere trickle amid the reeds and cattails and lily pads. The ancient road that Cutthroat's army had tried to follow was awash, reclaimed by the swamp, but it had traveled to the east of the canal, then spanned it to land on the west side. Zed could just see three tall, carved granite posts that had marked the bridge. The road then hooked through a stretch of hardpan and came here, under his feet, to form both a dock for the canal boats and the foot of a drawbridge. But everywhere the forest had crept forward, burying man's efforts. Smaller trees had grown three quarters of the way around the city, and the Elder Swamp had risen to flood part of this road and raise the level of the canal until it lapped at stretches of the city wall.

And the demon's mouth gate.

The demon had fat round cheeks, pop eyes, spiked teeth, and tall pointed red ears. His mouth was wide open, as if saying "Ahhhh . . ." but inside his mouth was only blackness. Zed didn't like the implication. If the gate was truly a gate, then why couldn't they see through the demon's mouth into the first tier of the city? Where went the darkness, and what did it hold? The more he looked, the more curious he became.

The gate did not look carved from red stone or even painted. It looked like living flesh, although cherry-red. And he noticed something else. The red of the demon, its skin or blood, extended into the city wall itself. Between the worn, cut gray stones was mortar red as rubies, as if the city had been built with blood. Zed blinked. There was only one conclusion . . .

"That gate is alive."

"Hunh?" asked a dozen tired people.

Zed pointed. "It's alive. It's not a carving of a demon, it *is* a demon, bound into the city walls. Look at its skin. Every other stone surface is weather-beaten, but his skin shines like ours, from sweating. Very clever."

Men muttered and fell silent. Tiger Eye stared at the gate and then Zed, as if recognizing new properties in him. Even the gate itself seemed to be looking at him. And laughing.

Darroc thumped his new staff on the stone dock. "But we have to go in anyway."

"Through his *mouth*?" asked a young Fulcrumian.

The sailor shrugged. "Aye."

"It's the only way in," agreed Zed. But he frowned at the raven statues atop the wall. He disliked them. Now that he could see them closely, he noticed they were not stone but metal, jointed and hinged like a suit of armor. Most definitely machines, then. The statues stared at the sky, but Zed had no doubt they could turn and lower their red eyes. Better be quick, he thought. He said, "Come on. People did it in ancient times, we can too. Go ahead, Darroc. And hurry."

The sailor nodded. He stepped to the very end of the stone dock, thumped the staff once more, and bellowed, *"Tero-glu-strod!"*

They waited. Nothing happened. Cutthroat tugged at the cape around his shoulders and throat. Men shuffled their feet.

"Teroglustrod!"

Now something happened. Zed went cold. The nearest raven statues began to swing in their direction. Creaking and squeaking, they nevertheless turned. Rust trickled from between their iron feet. And just as Zed had feared, they began to lower their beaked heads.

Darroc hollered, "TE-ro-GLU-stroooooood!!!"

The demon almost chortled with evil delight. A raven fixed its gaze, and another. Zed thought he heard a rising hum in the still humid air. "Get it right, would you!"

Darroc fairly danced in place. "It's the demon's secret name! It gives you power over him! It's supposed to work! Te-RO-glu-STROD! TERO—"

Zed shouted, "Look out!" He dove at Tiger Eye and knocked her sprawling. Men and women jumped all over the dock.

Two pairs of raven eyes sparkled. Red beams flashed across the canal and scorched the stone dock. Smoke wafted from burnt earth and weeds. Zed heard creaking. The birds were tracking again. "Keep moving! Keep moving!"

Another sparkle. A man cried in pain. Others scurried for the woods. Zed smelled smoke and burnt flesh. He shouted in Tiger Eye's ear, "Say it! Say it!"

She pushed at him to get clear even while crawling frantic as a crab. She snapped, "Say *what*?"

"The name! The name!"

Tiger Eye lifted her head and called, *"T'ro-gl'strud!"*

The ravens froze. A rumbling sounded, so deep and low the dock under their feet trembled. They stared. The blackness in the demon's mouth grew dimmer, faded to gray, became clear light. They could see houses and shops inside the dusty ruined city. People picked themselves up, dusted off. Some Fulcrumians bandaged a man's scorched hand.

A long red tongue, entirely flat and pointed like a spear blade, rolled out of some unknown depth and across the murky canal. Without a click or thunk it touched the stone dock.

Zed wiped his forehead. They'd come within inches of being incinerated. "It needed to hear the name in a familiar accent. Who's first?"

Everyone stood eyeing the tongue drawbridge, except one. Cutthroat tossed one end of his cape over his shoulder, stepped onto the red smoothness, and marched across. One by one, the Fulcrumians and tree folk tiptoed across. The bridge was dry and smooth, not tonguelike at all. Zed wondered what alchemist or sorcerer had fashioned this spell. Someone powerful enough to pass for a god, he reckoned. Imagine this type of extravagant magic being commonplace when the city was populated and prosperous.

As they approached the giant face, the bug eyes rolled downward to watch them. If the adventurers had had any disinclination to enter the gaping mouth, they seemed to forget it now, and Fulcrumian and Nureti pelted the last few feet and leapt from the tongue onto the city street.

Only Zed lingered. As he approached the mouth, he paused to lay his hand on the demon's cheek. It was indeed living skin, sweaty and smooth as his own. The fat cheek twitched under his hand. Zed asked aloud, "How long have you been here?" But there was no answer. The rolling eyes had regained their blank stare.

A gurgle sounded below the bridge. Zed craned to see what caused it. Something golden lay in the water close by the gate. It looked like some sodden lump, but as he watched, it rolled. It was a man, a golden man, trapped below the surface among slimy eel grass along the wall's foundations. It stuck out a melted hand that broke the water's surface. Reaching for Zed. He galloped through the mouth and landed among the party.

Behind him the light faded. The gateway grew impenetrably black again. A rumble sounded. The tongue retracted.

Zed dusted his tunic tails. As a joke, he muttered, "In the belly of the beast."

As one, the party stared at him with round eyes. Zed looked back at them curiously.

Tiger Eye asked, "How is such a thing possible?"

"Hunh? Oh, it's a simple binding spell. Someone, someone good, very powerful, summoned that demon eons ago and put him to work guarding the gate. Demons are like horses or dogs, you see. They like to serve, though they might grumble about it. It's good to keep them busy, actually, for otherwise they get into mischief. But this is nothing compared to some of the things you can do with demons." He asked Darroc, "Where did you learn its name?"

The sailor's mouth was dry. "Oh, around."

People continued to stare at Zed, horrified and fascinated. Ah, he thought, they're not used to magic, either for good or ill. But Zed was. He almost grinned. "What's wrong, Tiger Eye? Is there anything else you'd like to know?"

Numbly she shook her head. He stepped through the party and took Tiger Eye's elbow in one hand. She let him.

"Follow me," he said easily. "I'll lead."

Zed led them out of the small gateyard. It emptied onto a street wide enough to drive three wagons abreast—a working street, used for large loads, that curved away in both directions to encircle the city. Warehouses, both standing and collapsed, lined one side of the street and backed against the red-laced wall. More warehouses, counting houses, and chandlers' shops lined the other side, with circular streets behind them that eventually reached the first tier wall. The tier walls were also cut stone, banked back at an angle. The houses on the next tier looked finer, and Zed supposed the richest houses would be near the top. It was that way in most cities. Wide stairways with thick balustrades cut the tiers. As they'd noticed from outside, in many places the walls had broken and flowed down, burying lower tiers in dirt, stone, and shattered dwellings.

The road under their feet was gray flagstones. More often than not, the flagstones were blackened, glazed, and cracked, as if by fearsome heat. Dust lay thick everywhere, and not a few crisped bones and skulls could be seen in alleys. Greenery ran rampant. Vines crawled up and across buildings, trees grown outsize had pushed aside flagstones and driven branches through walls and windows, grass filled cracks. But the plants gave no impression of life. Rather, they emphasized how dead and desolate and peopleless the city was.

The party huddled close together. Zed looked in both directions. "Which way goes up, do you think?" When no one answered, he strode off to the left, north. The stairs on that side had seemed more often intact.

They walked. Ashes sighed, bones crunched under the feet. The Fulcrumians and tree people glanced everywhere nervously. Zed looked around too, but he was studying. When he spoke, people jumped.

He asked, "How long ago was the city abandoned, Tiger Eye?"

"Hunh? Oh. Thirty generations."

Zed nodded. He strode so coolly, so confidently, the others had to almost trot to keep up with him. "Six hundred years or so. Yet look, there are still bones in the streets. There must be some time-slowing spell in place. The work of the city gods, probably. Gods like to slow things down whenever they can. It keeps 'em young and in power longer."

Tiger Eye murmured, "Perhaps you shouldn't scoff at the—them—so much. They might—hear."

Zed waved a hand. "I'm not scoffing, just trying to understand them. If we meet any, we'll pay them appropriate homage. They'll love us for it. But I don't think we'll run into any."

Cutthroat rasped, "Why do you think they're gone?"

Zed waved another hand to take in the ruins. "There are no people left to worship them, so they have nothing from which to derive power. It's people who make gods powerful, not the other way around. And if they lived here and created all this grandeur, then let it fall to ruin, what does that tell you? Would you live in a house with a leaking roof and vines on the floor?"

Darroc muttered, "Gods work different than men. That's what makes 'em gods."

Zed shrugged. "They still need food, water, and shelter. And this city has none of it. It's an empty nest." He squinted at the gray, darkening sky. "We'll need a place to camp the night."

Tiger Eye whispered, "Not in one of these houses."

"No. Ah, here we are."

They had reached the bottom of a stairway. It was some sixty feet across, of granite so old and oft-used the risers were polished smooth and the edges dished in the center. Across from the stairway was a small park. The oak trees around its edge were hung thick with old grapevines. Flower beds had turned to weeds, but there were still some pale pink flowers in bloom that Zed recognized as roses. At the center of the park was a stone fountain, once a center where women had gathered and gossiped and washed clothes. Zed could make out grooves on the edge of the fountain where generations of washboards had rested. Now it was dry, choked with dust and old rust. Zed scanned the buildings to either side. Prosperous houses, probably of merchants who'd owned the warehouses. Empty now, a wooden one fallen, a stone one gutted by fire. Probably thick with ghosts, he thought. But silent.

"We'll camp here."

The soldiers and warriors slashed at the vines for space and firewood. Before long they surrounded a fire, roasting more venison and sucking fruit rinds. They set a guard and bedded down early. They were weary from long walking and tight terror. The tree folk curled up like dogs on one side, the Fulcrumians wrapped in blankets on the other. Zed sat between them by the fire. He watched Tiger Eye scoop a hollow in the ground for her hip, and curl up like a big cat at a hearth. She nodded at Zed and smiled. "Good night."

Zed stretched out on his blanket. He pointed to her middle, where she still wore his belt and compass. "When will you give me that back?"

She closed her eyes as if to shut him out. "When you need it."

He frowned, "This is a dangerous place. I might need it in a hurry."

Eyes closed, she smiled. "Then you better stay close to me."

Now Zed didn't know whether to frown or smile. He supposed it was safe enough with her, but he felt naked without it. Maybe she liked him and the attention it got her, or maybe she still didn't trust him. There was no telling with women, he thought, savage or civilized. And he certainly couldn't force it away from her . . . He studied her for a while longer. He liked the way her side rose and fell, and the way the firelight sparkled on her white hair. He wondered if she'd ever dreamed of leaving the island . . .

With a final frown, he curled up in his tunic, as close as he could get to Tiger Eye without rousing her.

He was awakened by a woman's scream.

He sat bolt upright, struggling in his confining shirt, grabbing at his belt and compass that weren't there. He struggled to his feet and rubbed his eyes.

Fog lay all about. It shut off everything except the park itself, the ashy road, and the first few stairs. A tree woman held her spear cocked in its atlatl, screaming the while. Zed peered to see what attacked her.

At the fountain stood an old woman, eerie in the fog. With her hand, she was sluicing out a wooden bucket at the empty fountain. Then she bent and dipped nonexistent water. She turned and said something to a neighbor who wasn't there. She laughed in reply. Zed walked slowly to the woman, then through her.

Everyone was up now, and staring. Zed spread his hands. "A ghost. A woman who came to the fountain every morning all her life, and still does."

Other people relaxed, somewhat. Tiger Eye asked, "Do you think there are many ghosts in this city?"

Zed shrugged. "With all the long years this city stood, and

the sufferings it endured in its last days, I imagine there are"—people hung on his every word—"a few, but all harmless. Ghosts can't hurt you."

The old ghost turned and walked off into the fog with her bucket.

Tiger Eye looked at Zed with something like wonder in her eyes. "How know you these things?"

Zed smiled. "I spent years studying. Something had to sink in. Knowing the ways of ghosts and demons and gods and magic portals is my work, the way you know trails and plants and the beasts of the forest."

The warrior only nodded. Zed said, "Let's go. We don't want to stay here longer than necessary."

People hustled to eat and break camp. Without much trouble, but with much trepidation, they mounted the dished stairs. Zed found himself in the lead again. He called to the party, "We're going, I take it, to the palace?"

Cutthroat nodded. "The Temple of the Burning Night."

Zed turned as he climbed stairs. "How do you know that?"

Cutthroat flipped his cape back over his shoulder to free his legs. "I just know."

Zed asked, "What else do you know? Is this more knowledge gleaned from your dreams?"

The big man didn't answer, just marched.

A Fulcrumian called, "Aren't we going to investigate some of these buildings? What about all this treasure we were promised?"

Zed regarded the man. Like most of the fifteen relatives who accompanied Cutthroat, he resembled him slightly, in looks and temperament. These were quiet men who grimly followed their famous leader without asking questions, usually. This was the first query any had made about getting rich.

Cutthroat answered, "Shut up, Valimere. We're mounting to the temple to find my—destiny. You'll have your riches there. These houses are full only of ashes and death. They were pillaged centuries ago."

And how does he know *that*? Zed wondered again. It seemed Cutthroat the Conqueror had returned. The navigator reminded himself to keep a close eye upon the clan leader, while staying out of sword's reach.

In silence, as the fog diminished, they mounted stairs up one tier, crossed the cracked debris-filled streets, mounted more stairs. As they climbed, the houses grew larger, longer, more ornate, with bigger and fancier gardens, but all ruined and overgrown. Whole tracts had slumped to lower levels, revealing red clay or lead pipes and undercut bridgework. Occasionally they had to follow a street around a tier to find an unbreached staircase. Often they had to detour around vast holes in the street. Some were only big potholes, ten feet deep, but others dropped so deep they couldn't see bottom. Zed guessed much of the hill was honeycombed by sewers and aqueducts and storehouses. He wondered if the artifacts found underground would be intact and valuable. Zed would receive a percentage of any moneys the scavenger teams found, plus a bonus for unique magic items. But on this first scouting mission, he was to avoid pilferage and concentrate on his work—finding a spot for a locater focus.

And keeping an eye out for Cutthroat's dream-object. And seeking out the source of Tiger Eye's volcano tremors. It was a lot of looking, he told himself.

Finally, after some rests, they reached the plateau that was the city's cap. The stairs exited directly onto a vast plaza that was also shot full of black holes. There was a stone banister with balconies all around the rim. Zed counted twelves breaks for stairways, and each was connected by a path of gold bricks (or something that looked like gold) to twelve sides of the only structure up here, the temple of the Burning Night.

It was immense, at least five stories high. It looked even bigger, for it stood alone against the sky and the distant smoking volcanoes that belched fire and ash. Red streaks flickered across the dome of pure gold. Each gold path led to a pair of gold doors. Across the doors and all sides of the temple were disturbing glyphs of people fleeing something in mortal terror. The image was supposed to conjure a sense of awe, Zed knew, but the building only looked sad now. It had seen hard times. There was a hole in the gold dome where fire had melted the gold. The walls were riddled with cracks, and whole patches of the frieze had fallen to shatter on the plaza. The doors they looked at were crooked but jammed tight in their frame. Rainwater had stained the walls and presumably seeped inside. The glory and terror of the gods of Tarek Nev was long over.

Cutthroat marched directly to the doors. He proceeded to

thump them, testing. Zed was startled by a tentative hand on his arm. It was Tiger Eye. "Do you think we should enter?"

Zed shrugged. "Why not? It's a temple, meant for people to enter and worship long ago. If we behave, are respectful enough, there shouldn't be any danger. Or much. I'll protect you from the magic," he added.

She didn't respond. She stood in her bare feet and leather tunic, clutching her wooden weapons, looking very small and primitive against this soiled grandeur. Zed looked at her face and then back at the fleeing-people montage. Yes, there was a resemblance there: the shaggy hair, the wide eyes, the firm mouths. The tree folk really were descendants of this city. Zed mused they were better off now. They might live in trees, but they were their own masters. They didn't cower in their gods' shadows.

Cutthroat and his bodyguard had gone out of sight around the building, and now four men headed for the stairs. Zed and the tree folk walked around the building. Cutthroat stood before a pair of doors that sagged but were melted together. Cutthroat explained these were the most promising doors for breaching, and he had sent his men to find a stout post for a battering ram.

Zed and the others nodded and waited. Tiger Eye stood at the distant rail and gazed at her tall forest in the east. Zed skirted a large square hole in the plaza floor and joined her. Under his hands on the rail he could feel the trembling of the volcanoes.

He heard her murmur, "I wonder if I'll ever be able to return to the trees."

Zed didn't know what to say. He pondered how alone she must feel, having made herself an outcast, risking death to pursue a hope for a tribe that might kill her if she returned. Zed offered, "Tiger Eye, I wanted to tell you—just so you'd know ... If you have to—stay away, you could always go away with me. I'll be leaving the island once I've completed my mission here."

Tiger Eye looked at him, and her eyes were blurry with tears. "I don't want to go away. I love my home. I wouldn't fit anywhere else ..."

Zed tried to smile. "You'd succeed wherever you went. Prosper, even. I could show you—"

They were interrupted as a voice shouted, "Lend a hand!"

Cutthroat's relatives had returned with a long post they'd ripped from some fallen building. It was long enough for everyone in the party to grab hold. Zed found himself between a tree woman's brown back and a Fulcrumian's bearded front. Cutthroat took the head. At his count, they backed from the door and rushed it. The thundering blow shook them all to their bones, but the door had creaked. Another long rush, a stouter blow, then another, and the weld cracked. The door struck the inside wall of the temple with a mighty *crash*.

They dropped the heavy post. Their ears rang as Cutthroat called, "That's done it! Let's—"

Something whirred and chittered in the black interior. Metal glinted, as if an armored knight marched upon them. A knight tall as the doors. The party backed away. Daylight glittered on a polished knife blade fully six feet long. A tall metal leg, thin and sharp as an insect's, stepped through the doorway. The knife stabbed out of the doorway and just missed impaling Cutthroat.

Then the door was filled with whirring, slicing death.

A man wailed, "It's coming after us!"

The thing that stepped through the doorway was like nothing Zed had ever seen or heard of before. It was ten feet high and made of metal. Its body was egg-shaped and plated. Atop was a glass dome with apparently nothing inside. From a ring around its neck a half-dozen arms protruded, each with a different-shaped cutting tool: a sword, a scythe, a halberd blade, even a square blade like a vegetable chopper. Another ring around its base sported six jointed legs like a spider's. It's a machine, Zed thought, unless there's a demon or soul trapped inside. Just a contraption. From its mismatched design, he guessed its purpose was to intimidate more than actually kill. But the blades on the front face were all moving, cutting, chopping, jabbing the air. They'd kill a man easily enough.

The thing took small mincing steps, again like a spider, careful to keep its balance. It came through the doors, just clearing the lintel, and aimed for the thickest knot of adventurers. Men didn't wait, but turned and scattered.

All except Cutthroat. He flattened himself alongside the building, trying to hide. As the whirling cutting machine took another step, he tried to slide behind it through the doors. But the idle blades in back sprang to life and whipped at him. Then the machine stepped his way. Cutthroat turned and ran, his cape flapping, all dignity gone.

With no one near at hand, the machine stepped back into the doorway and stopped its flailing. It stood poised and alert, like a hunting dog on point.

People stopped running, turned, watched, waited.

"Now what?" a Fulcrumian asked.

"It's only a machine," Zed explained. "A mechanical guard to keep us out of the temple. It can't think, it can only react."

"Clever of you to identify it," Cutthroat snarled, "but how are we to get past it?"

"Hush. Let me think . . . Ah! Tiger Eye, you stand here and distract it. You others, grab that beam . . ." Quickly he outlined his plan. Cutthroat grunted, but didn't disagree.

Tiger Eye's warriors edged toward the metal monster and the fallen beam. As they drew near the sundered door, the machine marched out at them again. Tiger Eye cocked her arm and tossed her atlatl knob-first. The wood got past the front set of blades and bounced off the glass dome. The machine gave no sign it was aware of the attack, but by then her warriors had snatched up the post and dragged it away.

They called to the Fulcrumians, who ran up to lend a hand with the heavy beam. Using the tree folk's rope, they wrapped coils around either end of the long beam and tied them down tight. That gave them a rope to haul on, fifteen feet long, at each end. Under Zed's directions, the two parties lugged the beam to lay it along one wall next to the doorway. The machine moved to track them, shoo them from the door. They retreated.

But not before Falling Leaf cast one rope behind the machine to the opposite wall. Trotting in a wide circle, half the party ran around to the other wall and tailed onto the rope. Both groups were now far enough back that the machine merely turned in their direction without advancing. By lifting, so as not to scrape the rope across stone, they hauled the beam across the doorway, in front of the machine.

Tiger Eye stood directly in front of the machine, then slowly stepped forward. The machine rattled forth. Long odd blades began to jab, slash, and mince the air. Zed, holding a rope, held his breath for Tiger Eye. The machine took a step, then another, then stepped over the log with three legs.

"Now!" shouted the navigator.

Ducking in quickly, the two parties rushed along the wall and grabbed either end of the beam. Squinting, mentally ducking the whirling blades, they hoisted it shoulder-high with a massive collective grunt.

It was high enough. The solid beam caught the machine under its egg-shaped bottom. The three back legs came off the ground. The machine flailed the air. Blades thunked into the wood, chopping white chips loose. The three front legs were not enough to balance on, and as the beam slid higher, the machine toppled forward.

Various blades chipped and clicked and skittered on the plaza flagstones, then the glass head struck. It exploded with a crash. The metal arms went limp and sagged to the ground with a metallic whine.

Zed stood over the wreakage and dusted his hands. "Good enough." Tiger Eye beamed at him in obvious approval.

Falling Leaf pointed inside the black temple where lights suddenly flickered. "Argamanthol's Valor! There are *people* in there!"

10
Below the City, beyond Life

ZED, THE ONLY MAGIC-USER, WAS THE FIRST to enter the black corridor. He'd disliked Aranmor's gray red-shot skies from the first minute he'd set foot on this cursed island, but suddenly they seemed friendly and embracing compared to the sickly darkness inside the temple. But someone had to go first and see these people that inhabited a decrepit temple built for dead gods.

The doorway opened onto a dark hall with a ceiling so high it was lost in the darkness. The walls were lined with some dark gray-streaked stone carved with more images: glyphs of dog- and lizard-headed men, gladiator battles, and parades of crowned kings. Scorch marks showed black on the walls, and high up, the ragged remnants of tapestries were curled and dark. The air was cool inside the temple and smelled of rust and stagnant rainwater. Ashes and wood fragments crunched underfoot.

Far down the corridor, in the blackness, people flickered as if lit by candlelight.

Zed watched for a while. He could see someone dressed in gold robes waving his arms, shouting. A woman with crow-black hair sobbed on a purple couch, then lifted her head and gave orders to a slave. A fully caparisoned horse cantered by. Zed strained his ears until they rang in his skull. All this action, but no sound.

He kept his voice calm. "Follow me." Then he marched off without waiting. He'd show them courage in the face of ancient magic.

The corridor ended in a hall with twelve walls and twelve corridors ending in twelve doors. Zed peered up at the gloom. There was no sign of daylight above, though he knew the dome had had a hole melted in it. The darkness seemed deeper than could be natural. He wondered if, as the city was slowed in time, the quiet had been somehow intensified here, in the physical and spiritual center of the city.

The centerpiece of the temple was an enormous pearl fully six feet high. On the milky surface of this pearl flickered the images of ancient peoples and ancient times. One by one, the Fulcrumians and Nureti crept forward, stood behind Zed, and watched.

They watched a story coalesce on the misty rounded surface. An old man with gentleness in his face walked through a wildflower meadow under a sunny sky. In the distance was the city of Tarek Nev, bright as a new-minted penny and bustling with sailing ships at the docks and strange soaring machines in the sky above it. Suddenly a black-haired woman thundered into the meadow in a chariot made in the shape of a dragon's head. The wheels scorched the grass, setting it afire. As the old man turned, the woman lashed out with a silver-tipped whip. The man was transformed into a phantom that blew away on the wind. The image faded . . .

"V'Rama Vair," breathed Tiger Eye in the stillness. "Ancient Queen of the Nureti. A cruel goddess. But who is the old man?"

Another image formed. A beautiful and tall man lay dead on the stone flags. By his slack hand was a crooked lance. Both the man and the lance shone with a golden inner light. Seven high priests drew a pentagram around the man's corpse and chanted. From the air suddenly appeared a bony, scaly red demon, all spines and venom, held fast by their magic. With hands that defied the spines, the priests seized the demon and drove it like a handful of knives into the dead man's body. By and by the man sat up, but his eyes were empty.

"Argamanthol-Raz, Lord of the Amarrishi," said the leader of the tree people. "He fell at the Last Battle. But I didn't know the priests brought him back to life."

"That's not life," Zed corrected. "That's demonic possession. Worse than death."

The image faded and Zed walked farther around the giant pearl. There seemed to be twelve sides to the pearl, one for each corridor and door. Zed imagined the pearl was a storytelling device, imbued with magic and historical lore to teach the history of the city and its people. The parade of gods and humans mingling, fighting, loving, bargaining, and more went on. Skeletal hands donned a black helmet with a closed visor. A jowly man with red hair beheaded a troll with a double-bitted war ax. A primitive fur-clad female, more ape than human, was killed by elven archers in the depths of the Wyr Forest. Her body was carried away, and her mate left to howl at the moon. A white-haired man blew a silver-bound ram's horn that made the temple shiver and crack. A golden god was sucked into a black sword in the hands of an ogre, to leave no trace behind . . . There were many more stories, enough to make Zed's head ache.

He walked farther around the pearl and almost bumped into Cutthroat. The man stood still as a statue. He was wrapped tight in his ratty cloak as if cold. His face was white in the reflection of the pearl's images. Zed studied the story that had arrested the Fulcrumian's image.

A cat-headed man striped like a tiger was dragged into a hall littered with battle dead. Guards restrained him, and an old man in red robes condemned him. A wizard stepped forward, incongruously holding a pair of blacksmith's tongs. Clasped in the tongs was a silver collar that smoked from the heat of a forge. As the cat-man struggled, the collar was fixed around his neck and welded shut with two copper hammers wielded by dwarfs. The cat-man screamed at the burning pain. When the guards let him drop to the floor, the old man barked a command and pointed to a distant door. The cat-man, branded a criminal and outcast by his collar, scampered for his life through the door and raced for the forest.

Tiger Eye startled both of them. "The branding and banishing of Belkor the Betrayer."

Cutthroat shook himself. Zed sighed. Watching so much misery and pain and destruction made him sad. Cutthroat said, "We must move on."

Zed hesitated. "If we watch long enough, we could learn a lot. We might see how to proceed, where to go." Though inwardly he wondered how many of these stories were true.

"I know where to go," said Cutthroat.

Zed looked at him curiously. "How?"

The big man shook his head like a lion's mane. "My dreams tell me. We go down. To the crypts."

He stooped and pressed a hand against the base that held the pearl. A flagstone along the wall sank out of sight. Zed stepped closer and peered in. By the wan light of the pearl he saw steps descending. Dust glittered in the passageway.

He looked around at the Fulcrumians and tree folk. He took a long breath. "Let's go, then."

There was a delay as men left the temple to fetch materials for torches. They split green tree limbs and wedged aged wood into the cracks, then got them burning with much difficulty. They made fitful torches but were all they had.

Again, Zed led. Cutthroat followed, then Tiger Eye, then the others, and finally Darroc. Every other man or woman carried a torch. The stairs were wide enough for three men to walk abreast. They spiraled down around a central column. Zed had to watch his footing. The signs of destruction were more common here, as if the fire had rushed up these stairs and only licked into the temple above: that the pearl had gone undamaged reinforced the theory. On the third riser he had to step around a full suit of armor without an owner. Some warrior had fallen on these stairs and died here, boiled in his suit like a lobster in its shell. The metal had been heated so severely that when Zed nudged it, it crumpled like an old eggshell. A scalloped helmet rolled off the step and bounced down the stairs, losing pieces along the way. It made an empty, lonely clatter.

The stairs dropped for thirty steps, then flattened to a landing. There were more dead on the landing, a heap of them in armor of two different designs, but all burned a uniform black. Some teeth were all that remained of the owners. The walls were as thick with soot as the depth of a man's hand. The air grew thicker, hard to breathe. No one talked, and Zed descended again. Another thirty steps brought them to another landing with more collapsed armor. He descended farther, wondering when they'd find something other than stairs and debris.

Walking, walking, walking, Zed began to curse. Still more stairs descended at his feet. This was taking a very long time. He was growing hungry, though he'd eaten just a while ago. More stairs, another landing, more burnt armor. Zed frowned when he saw this batch. More stairs, another landing, more . . .

Zed had begun to descend when he stopped short. Cutthroat thumped into his back. Tiger Eye just missed ramming him. The Fulcrumian barked, "What are you waiting for? Get moving! I want to find—"

Zed cut him off. He shoved the leader back up the stairs to the landing. "We're not going anywhere. Back up!"

The party demanded to know what Zed meant. The navigator crouched, lowered the torch, examined the fallen suits of armor. A helmet, a breastplate, a dagger with a broken blade, some greaves. He was sure he hadn't seen this batch before, yet he had. He told the group, "We're not going down, or if we are, we're just coming out on the same landing. This is the same place we've been, uh, four times so far."

"What are you blathering about?" Cutthroat demanded. "These are not the same scraps as before."

Zed shook his head. "Yes, they are. Now don't argue. I have to figure this out." He stood silent for a while, rubbing his chin, studying the stairs and the walls. Finally he said, "All of you, go and sit on that landing up there. Tiger Eye, you scooch down and watch me. When I return, call."

The woman warrior held a guttering torch that shone on her white hair. It had a streak of soot that made her more tigerlike than ever. "Return? Return from where?"

"Just watch me." Zed waited for the people to ascend. They grunted in surprise one flight up. Cutthroat sent a cousin up one more flight and he hollered. He'd found the trapdoor. Zed nodded. It was only two flights up when it should have been six or seven. He called, "Tiger Eye, watch me!" The striped woman scooched and nodded.

Zed turned and descended the stairs. Thirty steps down, he encountered another landing with a random assortment of crisped armor. A voice called, "Zed!"

He looked up the stairs. Tiger Eye crouched above him. Her long shapely legs were poised on the stairs. The navigator asked, "What did I do?"

She called, "You went down, then came back up, then turned to go down again."

Zed's mouth hung open. "No, I only went down . . . No, you're right. I see . . ."

"What is it?"

Zed turned back to the lower stairwell. "Something on these stairs is spelled. When you get to a certain point, it places a geas on you. You turn around, walk back up the stairs, see the landing and this junk slightly differently, then turn back to descend again. Clever. With this spell in place, a man would walk up and down the stairs all day, or else give up and return to the hall above."

Above in the torchlight, Tiger Eye's eyes were wide. "Can it hurt you?"

"Oh, no. It's just a simple protection, like that cutting machine."

"That was simple?"

Zed shook his head. He disliked carrying on a conversation at a distance, and he was tired of climbing stairs. "The cutting machine was simple, yes. Look at how easily we defeated it with the beam. And this spell is simple. They all are. When this temple was full of priests and novices and gods and whatnot, their numbers were the best protection. A few simple diversionary devices completed the security. But now, with only a few things left to stop us, they'll be easy to defeat."

"But—" the jungle woman asked, "why do we see the armor differently each time?"

"So no one can draw a chalk mark on the floor to mark their passage. When you returned, you'd see the mark as something different, or not notice it at all. Now hush and give me a minute to think . . ."

Tiger Eye watched him. Zed sensed she found none of this easy. Well, he thought simply, I get to show off my talents after all. He said, "Watch me again. Or rather, just stay there. When you don't see me return, I'll have made it to the next real landing."

With that, he hoisted the torch and went down. He went slowly and studied the left-hand wall all the way down. At the next landing, he looked up. Tiger Eye sat there. He went down again, this time studying the right wall. Tiger Eye smiled thinly at him from the stairs above. "Loremaster's ballocks!" he grunted. Fabricating a magic puzzle was fun: solving someone else's magic puzzle was a pain. He studied the ceiling this time. Same landing. He swore some more and rubbed his chin. It became black with soot from his filthy hands. He was sweaty and dirty and breathing hard from the close air. He sighed and started down again. This time he stepped over the first riser. He came out at the same landing. He went down, skipped the second riser. Same landing.

He was a lot more leg-sore and worn out before he found the step. When he stepped over the twenty-first riser and kept going, he found himself at a different landing, one with only a shoulder bone on it. He looked up. There was no woman peering down at him. He let out a satisfied grunt and skipped up the stairs.

He tried to mark the trapped step with soot, but when he blinked, the mark was gone. He gave up and called the others down. Tiger Eye came first. "You solved it?"

Zed tried not to smirk. "Easy."

"You're very clever, Zed." Her eyes shone in the dimness.

Zed nodded his head down. "Don't step on the twenty-first riser."

The party soon stood on and below the next landing, the one marked by a shoulder bone. Only one man accidentally stepped on the twenty-first riser, and the party had to wait as the man completed the geas. Struck dumb, he turned mechanically and marched up the stairs, turned and looked down the stairs again. He suffered some ribbing from his nervous companions, then sheepishly climbed down, avoiding the magicked step.

Zed set a foot on the next lowest steps. Behind him, Tiger Eye said, "Why did it send us all back when just you, in front, stepped on the trap?"

Zed shrugged. "Obviously, the spell triggers and everyone behind that person on the stairwell is affected."

"Oh. Will there be any more tricks?"

Zed nodded slowly. "No doubt. And understand this: The traps above are intended only to keep the uninitiated and thieves from wandering into the crypts. Harmless traps to befuddle. But down here is the high priests' territory. The traps will be meaner. Deadly."

"Oh." Tiger Eye said no more as they went deeper into the earth.

After one more landing, they reached the bottom. The stairwell opened into a catacombs either hewn by hand from rock or cut long ago by water. The corridors twisted, the ceilings were low, sloping rounded to the walls. Zed stopped. The catacombs split as irregularly as veins in a man's body. There were five paths leading off from the stairwell.

The signs of destruction grew thicker. Almost blocking the stairwell was a whole pile of bodies. To judge by the profusion of swords and scimitars and round shields, the men had died fighting, probably blocking something from ascending the stairwell. Zed tried to picture the final moments. Had some king or lesser god fled up the stairs, and these guards prevented some assailant from following? Had the assailant carried fire like a dragon, or fireballs like a wizard, or something else? He would probably never know. But fire had scoured these passages clean of all life.

The ground shook slightly, then stilled. Zed reflected grimly that the three volcanoes might scour the island unless they could find some way to arrest them. But how? Zed knew nothing about volcanoes. He wondered if they were merely erupting according to nature, as unpredictable and unstoppable as a tidal wave or earthquake. He hadn't said as much to Tiger Eye, but if there was no source of the tremors down here, the island was doomed.

"Which way?" someone asked.

Zed minced around the armor and bones and studied the ash-heaped floor. It was hard to tell what the trail was like down here.

Cutthroat brushed past him. "This way." He set off down the central artery. His followers looked at one another.

Zed shrugged and followed, as did the rest. Tiger Eye was just behind, and he asked, "Are your feet suffering? I can cut a swath from my cloak if you'd like to wrap them."

The woman glanced at him. "I've never worn a boot in my life. I can walk over hot coals, kick through briars. But— thank you for asking," she added shyly.

Zed called, "Cutthroat, how do you know the way?"

The leader plunged ahead, eager to lead now. He called, "It's the most well-used path. It stands to reason." But farther

on he turned from the central artery and darted down a passageway so low he had to duck. Zed wondered anew: What
told him to deviate from the well-worn path?

More crisped corpses, feet toward the doorway, lay on the
ground. The iron door had been blasted from within, bubbled
from the doorjamb to run like black rainwater and harden in
rivulets. Zed stepped over the brittle threshold. He hesitated a
moment, then moved forward to make room for the rest. They
hesitated too.

They had entered a crypt. A half-dozen stone sarcophagi
filled the low room. Another dozen sat in niches in the walls.
On each coffin was an effigy, a carved replica of the person
entombed. Many men, four women, a child in a full-sized sarcophagus. All the statues bore the circlets of royalty around
their brows. All the caskets and walls were smoked with soot.
Some of the caskets had been cracked by heat or hand.

"One is false, I know it." Cutthroat was dancing around
among the caskets now, like a child on his birthday. "In my
dream, I saw myself lifting a lid and finding riches. But I
know not which lid to lift."

"That's a shame," said Zed, "for I won't be party to
graverobbing. They told me in school, 'Don't disturb the dead
unless you want to join them.' "

One or two of the younger Fulcrumians muttered about
"buried with gold and jewels," but the older men ordered
them to hush. Cutthroat wandered around again, touching a
stone face here and there, but being careful not to shift any
lids. A dead king—or god—had powers no one could dream
of. He said, "But one is not a sarcophagus. It's a—"

Zed perked up his ears. "A what?"

Cutthroat tugged at the cape still wrapped clumsily around
his throat. He muttered, "It goes to another cellar, I think. It's
a blind, you see, a secret passage. Ah, I know!" He fumbled
in a satchel and pulled out something that chinked softly. He
stepped to Zed and put the heavy platinum necklace in his
hand.

Zed weighed it. "The Necklace of Truth-Telling?"

"And True-Seeing. It will let you see the false entrance. We
can leave the room, get out of your way, and you can don it
and ferret out the truth."

The navigator frowned at the clan leader, sure he only

wanted to leave in case Zed triggered a trap. "I've had to wear this one time too many. Why not you?"

"You're the magic-user. You'll understand what you're seeing. Here, we'll leave." And Cutthroat shooed his men back past the melted iron door like a mother hen. Zed scratched his head. The deeper into this hill they descended, the flightier Cutthroat had become. Maybe the source of his dreams was close by and scattering his thoughts. Zed looked at Tiger Eye, then shooed her folks out too. He draped the necklace over his head, laid the cool links around his neck.

He looked around. Nothing was different.

Slowly he circled the room, holding the torch high, then low. He walked between the sarcophagi. Nothing had changed.

Zed turned back toward the door to tell them of the failure when something caught his eye. He stepped to the side of a coffin near the center that bore a queen's effigy. She lay serene and beautiful, with her arms folded over her small bust. Her stone hair flowed from her head to spill over the edges like ice. A faint smile lingered on her lips, a sardonic smile. Here was a minx, Zed thought. Then he realized what had caught his eye. There were carvings around the stone lid, but square reliefs on one side of the coffin were larger than the others by a fraction. He caught the opposite edge of the coffin lid, held his breath—if he picked up the lid and found a mummy, he'd scream—and lifted.

The coffin tilted easily to one side. The square reliefs were concealed hinges. He shucked the necklace and called to the party. "Found it!"

All the Fulcrumians crowded back into the tomb. The Nureti came too, though more slowly. They were not a materialistic people, nor did they wish to offend their ancestors. But they were curious.

Cutthroat came last. "What's inside? What do you see?"

Zed stared into the sarcophagus. "Nothing. Nothing at all."

Their fear of the dead subsiding, men crowded around the coffin. Some of the taller Fulcrumians leaned over the open lid. Inside, there was nothing to see, only blackness in the bottom of the coffin.

Zed tried to think what this meant. An empty coffin? He held a torch high and peered low. The bottom of the coffin couldn't be that black, he thought. He put his free hand inside to feel the bottom. There wasn't one. His hand disappeared into the blackness as if into a bucket of black paint.

Men gasped. The tree people drew back. Only Zed and Cutthroat kept their place. The navigator leaned back and lowered the torch into the coffin. The flaming head dipped into the darkness and the light went out. Zed snapped it back up. It was still flaming.

"The darkness . . ." he murmured, "sucks up the light . . ." He couldn't help adding, "I don't like this."

Cutthroat leaned over the coffin and dipped his arm into the darkness. He fished around blindly. "There's nothing to fear. It's like a well."

"A well into darkness," Zed said. Folks nodded.

The leader straightened up. "Nonsense. It's just a well. We'll put someone on a rope and lower him. He can tell us what's down there. Aldar, you go."

The Fulcrumian, one of the youngest men and the lightest, jumped at his name. Other men moved away from him. "N-no, Aroth. I don't want to. I don't want to go down there."

Cutthroat grabbed a coil of rope from his older cousin Eli. "No argument. You go."

The boy backed away. Eli caught his elbow. "It won't be bad, lad, we'll just dip you and bring you right back."

"No!"

The boy turned to run and a large man tripped him. He kicked and screamed, punched and writhed with all the strength of his young frame, but the men managed to pin him and rope him. Still hollering, he was hoisted above the open pit, balanced on the edge, and jerkily lowered down. His shouts and curses were abruptly shut off when he passed the edge of darkness. The Fulcrumian men looked at one another with fear in their eyes, but Cutthroat paid out the rope without a qualm. After some twenty feet, the rope went slack, having hit bottom. A man almost shouted, "Bring him up!"

They crowded around and hauled hand over hand. The boy, his face pale now, with tears on his cheeks, came clear of the darkness. They pulled him from the coffin and propped him on the edge.

As they untied him, he gibbered and quailed, but got out, "Just a cellar. Just like this. But so dark. And cold."

Cutthroat gave orders. "Get to work, then. Fashion a rope ladder." Men demurred, but worked. Zed watched Cutthroat and thought long and hard.

Before too long the men had assembled a rope ladder and dogged it securely to a neighboring coffin. The men waited for Cutthroat to lead, to descend first, but their leader hung back. "No, I'll go last. I want all of you down there. Go."

Grumbling in their beards, the Fulcrumians glanced around. Zed stepped to the ladder. "I'll go first." He swung a leg over the coffin's edge and dipped his legs into the pit. It had no feel, no temperature difference he could sense through his clothes. He didn't like it, but he couldn't avoid it. He gave Tiger Eye a tight grin and hooked his feet on the rungs of the ladder.

He groped his way down. The darkness enfolded him, darker than any night, darker than the inside of his own head. Then he saw light, a red blistered light from close at hand.

He stepped to the rock floor and let go the ladder. It twitched and slapped him in the shoulder as someone else grabbed hold above.

Zed cast about as other men and tree folk descended and assembled behind him. The tunnels down here were similar to the ones above, like the arteries in a body, gray rounded walls. The ceiling was high, too high. Zed measured the twenty-foot drop and calculated that this ceiling was in fact higher than the floor of the tomb above. Not good, he reflected. There was nothing in sight in the corridors but more lights. The red glow came from ruby domes set in the walls. Very not good.

Tiger Eye stood so close behind him her spear touched the back of his knee. She grabbed his upper arm. "What is this place?"

The navigator wished right then he knew nothing of magic. "This is no subcellar. This is another plane. It reeks of Unlife. We can't stay here long."

A man shouted. A woman screamed. The gray walls were moving, flowing. Blobs elongated and popped free of the walls. They grew arms to enfold the humans.

They were surrounded by men made of dirt.

11
Duel with the Gods

THE DIRT MEN OVERTOOK THEM IN THE SAME way an avalanche sends a man tumbling, pummeled, suffocating, helpless. Zed saw more and still more sand or dirt men form from the walls all around. They were seven or eight feet high, shapeless as stones with blunt arms and legs. Around him, in a swirl of dirt and hurtling bodies, he saw a tree woman jab her spear through a dirt man. The spear point exited, doing no more damage than a pitchfork through a haystack. Cutthroat roared and split a dirt man with his sword, only to lose it out the creature's back. Men went down under smothering waves of sand or else were pinned between hilly bodies.

Two dirt men slapped themselves together around Zed. Stale dirt covered his face, blocked his nose and then his mouth. He beat and flailed at the dirt men frantically, but it was the same as fighting a mine cave-in. He gasped for air, panicking, heard a roar build in his head like a windstorm . . .

Then he was being hauled by both arms. His boot tips dragged on the stone floor. He shook his head and tried to think. He'd only passed out for a moment. A mound of walking dirt held either arm and pulled him through the stone subcellar. Zed sucked air and kicked and got his feet under him. His arms were enfolded in dirt from elbow to fingertip, but at least he could walk. By craning his neck, he could see the others, Fulcrumians and Nureti and, far behind, Darroc, all being hauled similarly.

The queer parade tramped down the central artery. The lights in the walls painted everything bloody in their dim glow. Then the floor began to rise, suddenly so steep Zed's boots began to slip. A new gray light shone down the tunnel. They passed out of the tunnel into the open, and Zed closed his eyes rather than look.

We're dead now, was all he could think. People gasped behind him as they were dragged from the tunnel.

They stood on a humped plain that extended so far to the horizon its edges were lost against the gray sky. The sandy soil was gray, like coarse frozen ashes. Clouds scudded across the sky like tattered sails of a ghost ship. The tunnel mouth behind them was a raised tube of stone that burrowed into the ground. There was nothing else in sight except a ruin of stone columns in the middle distance. The dirt men dragged them that way.

Zed craned his neck, but there was nothing else to see. The sand crunched under his feet. The air was cool, sterile, and dead, with no wind, despite that the clouds shredded themselves across the sky. There was no smell. Even the air tasted dead, like something inside a tomb, yet even that had once held life, and this was Unlife. Zed found himself sweating heavily. This place was more than a desert. It was a blasted wasteland that had never felt the touch of life. It was no place for anything alive. Just staying here would drain them of spirit and flesh, as the sun in the desert sucked the juices from a stranded man.

The ruins drew closer. A circle of standing stones, some tilted or fallen. Behind Zed, Tiger Eye called, "What *is* this place?"

Zed choked on the answer, then spit it out. "H-Hel, or some bit of it. An outworld."

"What do they *want* with us?"

Zed licked his lips and looked at the ruins. "Maybe she'll tell us."

"She" was a silver or steel statue, standing atop a stone box in the middle of the canted stone columns. Some had toppled into the sand and been half-buried. The woman represented by the statue was eight or nine feet high. God-sized, thought Zed. Her hair was long, down to her waist, but the ends turned up everywhere and were tipped with flame like so many candles. If she wore any clothes, they were obscured by more flames that wreathed her body. Her eyes were blank, her smile knowing and nasty. Zed realized she was the goddess whose effigy adorned the fake sarcophagus that disguised the shaft to this outworld. A trick, and a signal. He couldn't imagine this smirking, flaming goddess doing any man good.

The dirt men dragged the captives bodily over two fallen columns and positioned them around the silver statue. Even though he was terrified of losing his life—and Tiger Eye's—part of the navigator's trained mind could still function. His curiosity alone might get him killed, he reflected. He noted Cutthroat stood facing the statue. Zed wondered if this destination were the culmination of the Fulcrumian's long-vaunted dreams.

Once people were in place, they waited. They could shuffle their feet, clear their throats, watch, but do little else. One of the Fulcrumians asked a question, but Zed hushed him. The navigator noticed about half the party had lost their spears or swords back in the tunnels. Darroc still had the Staff of Old Malosho. He'd tied rawhide to it and hung it on his back, but where the point touched the ground, no grass or vines rose from this dead soil.

Time dragged. Zed's terror eased somewhat—if these sand men had brought them here alive and unharmed, it must be to some purpose. Maybe once whoever was responsible for their capture, a god or devil or whatnot, arrived in his or her flaming chariot or from a flying ship or on the back of a giant sand lizard, they could negotiate. Gods always wanted something, if only worship. Zed watched the ragged clouds lift above the misty horizon, scud across his line of vision, and disappear. How could there be so much sky underground? Were they underground? Zed pondered a long time, then found himself growing sleepy. That was the other problem in dealing with immortals (he'd heard): They took forever to get things done.

A flicker of yellow light got his full attention. Had he imagined it? No, there it was. Flames flickered on the statue. They came and went, like a grass fire dying. Then the flames coalesced, formed a ring around the statue of the goddess, until she was fire all over. Zed could feel the heat on his face, the first sensation he'd experienced in this outworld.

The statue gave a sigh, the silver muscles twitched, and the goddess opened her eyes.

Stretching like some glossy cat, she tossed back her flaming hair and stepped off the stone box. Her eyes were still disturbingly blank, as if she were blind. Her hair was now jet-black, yet her skin remained silver. Zed saw she was naked beneath the writhing flames, but she was too scary to be sexy. Zed was glad she turned her attention immediately to Cutthroat.

The Fulcrumian leader stared at the tall goddess with a mixture of wonder and fear. Cutthroat looked anything but lordly. His shaggy hair was awry, his face sweat-streaked and sooty. His clothes were torn, his weapons tarnished, his traveling gear askew. The ridiculous blue cape was twisted around him so he had to lift his bearded chin over the folds. But he was rapt. Zed thought the man's face revealed a sense of purpose, as if here all his questions would be answered.

The goddess stepped closer to Cutthroat. He writhed in the grip of the dirt men, trying to retreat from the searing flames. The goddess chuckled and raised a hand, and the flames dimmed to mere flickers. With another half gesture the goddess shrank until she was no taller than Cutthroat. She waved a hand, and the dirt men released him.

"So," she chuckled, "you've finally come." Zed disliked her dry laughter.

Cutthroat threw back his shoulders, straightened his soiled clothing as best he could, and answered in kingly fashion, "I've come. Be it you who bid me? Be you Orgiana?"

Zed glanced at Tiger Eye off to his right. Her lips formed the words "Mistress of the Underworld."

Another dry chuckle, like logs crackling in a campfire. "For a long, long time have I sown dreams through the Essence. And they've found fertile soil. A fine champion." Zed noticed that even the goddess's words had no ring in the still, dead air. Rather, they seemed to be sucked dry of meaning or power.

The goddess made a circle in the air with her finger. The dirt men holding Zed let go, but he found he still couldn't move. Some power gripped him and the others. Only Cutthroat could move. Four dirt men shuffled forward and pushed at the box Orgiana had stood upon. A stone lid was shoved off to sough into the sand. Zed could just see black somethings inside, like insect shells.

Cutthroat reached into the box with both hands and plucked out a black wine cask. No, a closed helmet. The eyeholes and mouth hole were mere slits. The metal was blacker than night, actually seeming to absorb light. The brow pieces were sharp and fluted. Pointed earpieces stuck up almost past the top, like an elf's ears. If there were any rivets or seams, Zed couldn't spot them. A triad of two emeralds and a larger ruby decorated the brow. Silver chasing held them fast. With trembling hands, Cutthroat lowered the helmet over his head. It rested full upon his shoulders and covered his throat almost to his breastbone. The stone men stepped close and pawed Cutthroat, but he took no notice. Their rough stone hands stripped away his cape and tunic and kilt and gear in shreds. They drew more black fluted armor from the box and clumsily fit it around his naked form. Yet the armor seemed to know its owner, and straps and buckles bonded magically. Breastplate and backplate, shoulder guards, leather skirt with metal flanges, greaves for his calves and feet. Wide arm braces with matching rubies and emeralds were fit around his forearms. Cutthroat stroked his arms through the still air as if swimming, getting the feel and fit of his new skin.

Finally, a dirt man fumbled out a black baldric and scabbard. Cutthroat took the pommel of the sword, long enough for two big hands. He drew the blade from the scabbard, and the steel was black as the rest of the armor. Cutthroat took a step, cut the air, took another step, made a bigger cut. Zed gulped. A man with a new sword lusted to test it, and there was nothing to sunder here but frozen prisoners.

Tiger Eye hissed, "Soulcrusher! It holds the trapped form of Solus, beloved of the Nureti!" Zed wished she'd shut up and keep the history lesson to herself. Attracting the attention of fire goddesses and men with swords was risky.

Orgiana shook her shoulders and flames quivered on her

body. They licked higher until she was ablaze again. Zed could smell smoke, a dry, frightful smell like a raging forest fire. She approached the armored man and he did not flinch from the flame. She put out flaming hands and stroked his shoulders. Fire rippled along his armor. Though the armor was polished as volcanic glass, it still reflected no light. The goddess caressed him again and chortled, "You are ready."

Cutthroat's voice came as if from far away, way deep under the black metal helm. "Aye. I've waited a long time to regain the Helm of Kadaena."

The goddess cooed. "I've waited a long time for my champion. Tilak. You are risen. We can go complete our plan. The rest are all gone, long dead." Her voice rose with excitement. "Nothing can stop us now! We'll conquer, island after island, continent after continent! All of Kulthea shall be ours!"

"ALL KULTHEA!" boomed the man.

Then the two were shouting, bawling to one another like drunkards, a harsh hash of rapid words in a forgotten language. Zed, who knew several languages, didn't understand a word. He watched these lesser gods with growing uneasiness and mounting curiosity. He tried to piece together their story . . .

Cutthroat had become Tilak? He wracked his brain to recall what Tiger Eye had told him. In her mishmashed recounting of the city's history, she said Tilak the Defiler had been Orgiana's lover before the city was destroyed in the final cataclysm. Tilak had been slain by . . . wait now . . . Argamanthol, the Nureti champion with the Lightning Lance. No hint of what happened to Orgiana. Now . . . Orgiana was here and whole. She must have retreated to this outworld and turned herself into a statue to survive the city's destruction or the retribution of its survivors. (Had she even engineered the city's destruction herself?) She'd brought Tilak's sacred armor with her, encased it in this box, put herself over the top as guard. After six centuries (or *for* six centuries?) she'd sent forth dreams to find a new champion. That was Aroth Cutthroat, leader of the Fulcrumians, and probably a descendant of the scattered Nureti. A strong, ambitious man, he'd had the will and the means to assemble an army and penetrate the forbidden island of Aranmor. Under her guidance, armed with mental pictures and maps, he'd traced a route through the

Lost City of Tarek Nev, down into the catacombs and through the sarcophagus to here, this outpost of the outworld.

Zed squirmed in his invisible bonds. He was watching history become legend. Infamous legend. Two mad gods who'd helped destroy a fabulous city had now regained their powers. They faced no opponents that Zed could see and were bent on conquering all of Kulthea. And, he gulped, Zed had personally helped Cutthroat every inch of the way. He'd have a lot of explaining before the Guild of Vurn-kye, and they'd have a lot of explaining before the world.

If he survived the next hour, he amended.

Something else was bothering him too. He worked to pin it down. It didn't seem as if the two gods—Orgiana and Cutthroat, or Tilak now—actually talked to each other. Rather they were talking to themselves, talking past each other like two strangers. Wouldn't two lovers long separated be quicker to express their love? Or did gods view love differently?

A man's voice interrupted the gods' jabbering. Darroc the Sailor, held tight in invisible bonds and shorter than the rest, was almost suspended in air and obviously in pain. He bellowed at the armored god. "Cutthroat! Aroth! Can you not let us go? You've gotten what you wanted! Can't we be free?" His voice, once so haughty and sure, was almost a whine.

The armored god swung his blind gaze at the sailor. The black helmet fitted his head so tightly and came down so low on his shoulders and chest, he had to turn his whole body to see. His eyes were hidden inside slits. He stepped toward the dwarf, or elf, or man. "Fool! Cutthroat is gone! I am the reborn Tilak, the Defiler! I am the mightiest and sole-remaining champion of Tarek Nev, and none oppose me!" And with that statement, he raised high the black sword.

The moment Zed had dreaded arrived. Tilak whipped the long blade through the air and, with one stroke, sliced the sailor in half. Still suspended in air, the body popped apart. Zed saw half a gray brain fall from its pan, half a row of yellow teeth clamp shut, pink guts with open ends spill out onto the coarse gray sand. Blood fell like rain and soaked the soil. The ancient staff of the King Under the Forest fell neatly between the two halves and thudded on the ground. Men and women around the circle moaned.

Zed had the oddest thought: So much for the hopes of a

rock-bound fishing village that wanted to grow food and keep their sons home.

Tilak held high the black sword, which showed no trace of blood. "All, *all* must join my cause! All must join—or die!"

Orgiana laughed, the way a silly woman might laugh at her lover's simple joke. She shrieked, "More! Every death increases the sword's power! Sacrifice them all! Let the blade drink deep!"

Tilak replied in his own language. He turned and surveyed the captive audience. There were dirt men, Fulcrumian soldiers, tree folk, and Zed the navigator. One of the green emeralds on the helmet glowed. Tilak puffed up his chest. From out of the helmet's slit of mouth, the resurrected god blew a black cloud that wafted out and engulfed the nearest dirt man. Zed heard a creaking, squeaking sound like unoiled armor moving. The black mist vanished, and where the dirt man had stood was now an armored soldier. He wore a simpler, slimmer copy of Tilak's armor and sported a shorter, slimmer sword. But the dirt man could move as easily as any live thing. He cut the air experimentally with his sword, as he'd seen his master do. Zed marveled at the god's magic that could fuse a pile of sand into a fully armored mannikin.

The god Tilak turned to the next being, a Fulcrumian, and spit a black cloud around him. In seconds, there stood another armored mannikin. It too cut the air with its sword.

The remaining Fulcrumians and tree folk sent up a howl that emptied into the outworld sky. Zed tried to imagine what it would be like to be transformed. Would a man retain his native intelligence, yet be trapped in the form and helpless, a slave to Tilak the Defiler? "Defiler" was the proper name, Zed realized. This god didn't just kill men, he perverted them to his own form and enslaved them. Would a man lose his mind and thought forever, irrecoverably? Where had Cutthroat's mind gone? Had he, in the last moment before the god's soul overpowered his, realized his dreams had brought him to disaster? Or did he revel in the ascent from manhood to godhood?

Mostly, Zed wondered, would the transformation hurt?

Tilak turned and breathed life into another dirt man, transmuting him into an armored warrior. Then another, and a tree man, then another dirt man and another. He skipped over the spot where Darroc's guts lay on the sand and breathed again, each black cloud as large as the last. He turned around the circle. There were more armored mannikins than people now. Zed clenched his teeth. Tiger Eye was next.

Zed groaned and yanked at the nothingness holding him. Tilak puffed up his chest. A voice called out: Tiger Eye's. She shouted, *"Argamanthol,* help me!"

Zed blinked at the name. He blinked again as something flashed far off to his right. A striped streak, like a tiger fresh from the woods, slipped behind the animated black warriors. Tiger Eye, he realized, had loosed her invisible bonds. Then he got it. She'd invoked the name of her ancient champion, the warrior who'd defeated Tilak and killed him, once. That ancient name held some power over Tilak. Zed nearly burst his throat calling, *"Argamanthol!"*

His body tensed; he spilled over backward as the invisible bonds winked away. He shot a glance at Tilak. The god had been so surprised at the name of his old enemy he must have swallowed the cloud. Orgiana laughed and clapped flaming hands as if at a great joke.

Two other tree warriors, a man and woman, shouted their hero's name and were freed. They dashed to hide behind dirt men or mannikins. Three Fulcrumians—all that were left—shouted a garbled form of the name. One came free, and he ran pell-mell to get behind a stone column. The other two writhed in the air until Tilak blasted them with the black cloud and transformed them. Then he turned to find the missing people.

A stone no bigger than an egg bounced off his helmet, hurled by a tree woman. Tilak turned that way. Orgiana laughed again, then pointed a finger. Flame sprayed from her finger and engulfed the tree woman. She shrieked as her hair and tunic ignited, then her skin. She fell to the sand and writhed, screaming and dying. Zed smelled scorched flesh, a sweetish cloying stink. Orgiana shivered all over and laughed, "Yes! Yes!" The screams trickled to a stop.

Zed had ducked behind a dirt man. He cast about frantically for Tiger Eye. She had dashed around the circle behind an armored mannikin, near Darroc's dead body. She tore frantically at the armored gauntlets, trying to wrest away the man's black sword. But the hands were locked as tightly as if welded. The armored warrior turned and tried to shrug her off. Tiger Eye's back was exposed to Orgiana, who smiled and pointed another finger.

Zed's mind spun so fast he felt it must be shooting sparks. A weapon. He needed a weapon. An effective weapon. Rocks were no good. Swords were no good. Then he remembered one thing that might help, a magic artifact, and a friendly one.

Before he had really thought it out, the navigator slid around the dirt man and dashed straight across the circle, between the two villains. He slapped an arm against the smiling Orgiana. The goddess rocked at the blow and lost her smile. Zed's sleeve ignited, but he didn't have time to beat it out. He dove across the sand and scrambled on elbows and knees. The fire on his sleeve extinguished. But he knew an enraged goddess was probably pointing him out.

The hideous form of Darroc lay sprawled on the sand, split asunder and empty like a doll without its sawdust. He grabbed for the staff that lay among the gutted remains and got it. It was slippery with gore, knotty and lumpy to the touch. Zed prayed for some idea of how to use it. Beside him, not an armspan away, Tiger Eye wrenched at a mannikin's sword.

Tilak had blasted his hellish black cloud into a knot of humans, transforming all the people still alive except for Zed and Tiger Eye. The warrior wouldn't give up on grabbing that sword, hopeless as it might be. Zed spun on his buttocks in the sand, clutching the staff in front of him. Orgiana, her face a steel mask of rage, aimed an arm in his direction. Tilak faced them, sword out, chest puffed. The navigator didn't have time to think.

He jammed the end of the staff into the dead soil and shouted, "Protect us!"

With a scream, Orgiana let go a sheet of flame wide enough to ignite a house. Zed stared past the staff and watched the fireball boil at him. The center was white-hot, so intense it filled his vision with purple spots. He wondered if Tiger Eye would be caught in the blast and hoped not. Though she'd only outlive him by a moment. He wished—

The fireball never reached him. The sight of Orgiana and Tilak was shut out as a huge wall of sand welled up in front of Zed like an ocean wave. Sprouting from the ground where the staff rested, the soil coalesced and rolled into a shield fully six feet high. An odd sucking noise sounded all around as the coarse sand flowed. Zed had time to shut his eyes as the blast-fire heat struck the sand. As it was, the intensity of the blast showed yellow through his eyelids. He smelled burnt earth as the sand fused into glass. He also heard Tiger Eye shriek.

Without thinking, Zed scooted up and dove to his left. The fireball had hissed against Zed's earthen shield and spilled around it. Tiger Eye had been scorched by the heat. She was down on the sand, writhing. Zed had time for only the briefest look. Her hair seemed to be gone, burned off, with her rope and a swath of her clothing. And—his heart jumped—most of her skin. He could see the bare bones of her shoulder and ribs. Brown skin was charred black all down her side and thigh. She stopped thrashing suddenly, as if she'd stopped breathing. Zed's stomach dropped, his vision blurred. For a moment he didn't care if he did die, now.

But he couldn't quit, not while she might be alive.

Orgiana and Tilak stepped closer. They had been momentarily confused by the display of magic and the dirt shield the staff had thrown up. But the goddess pushed off with her toes and floated a dozen feet into the still sky, high above Zed's dirt bunker. The flames on her body fluttered like bird feathers. She aimed both flaming arms from on high and sighted along them. "Die, friend of the Nureti!"

Zed clamped onto Tiger Eye's bleeding shoulder. She was hot as roasted meat. He jammed the staff in the ground again and shouted, "Remove us!"

He had no idea what would happen—any more than he could have guessed the sand shield would arise—so he was as surprised as the two gods when the earth parted to dish around his feet. The dish spread to encompass the two of them within the protection of the staff, and suddenly the dish began to move.

The dish rippled across the surface of the land like a dimple across a pond. The staff in Zed's hand was its center. The navigator glimpsed an upright column flash by as the dish surged past the columns and out of the circle. For the first time Zed felt wind pluck at the back of his neck and ears. Orgiana and Tilak receded at a speed faster than a galloping horse, like something out of an interrupted dream. In seconds the two gods and their mannikin army were the size of insects, then they were gone, out of sight behind a low dune.

"Circle to the tunnel mouth!" he shouted. He wasn't sure if the staff could interpret such a command, but they changed direction and surged around the rim of an imaginary circle. The

horizon and landscape were so blurry and featureless he wasn't
sure they were going the right way. He could only hope.

Then he saw the exit to the catacombs, a bump on the desert surface like a sandworm's tunnel. His heart leapt, then fell.
Orgiana, Tilak, and the mannikin army were flying toward the
entrance as if on an invisible wind. There were more than two
dozen warriors, as alike as ants. As Zed watched, they flicked
into the tunnel like bees returning to the hive. No sooner were
the heels of the last man-thing passed through than the tunnel
mouth crumbled and collapsed. It fell with a huff, and a jet of
dust spewed into the air.

There was no sign left of the enchanted tunnel, not even a
depression. More of Orgiana's destruction, he cursed. She was
good at that.

Then the full import of his plight struck him. They were
trapped in this outworld, this bit of hell. They were probably
the only living things in this sphere. And the only exit had been
closed. How the hell would they get out? Which way was out?

He muttered, "Stop," and the dish slowed. The sand rim of
the disk flattened, trickled away, as if it had never been. Zed
laid the staff down and looked to Tiger Eye. He couldn't
imagine what he'd do to help her: She was the one with the
clever medicines, not he. Nor did he relish telling her they
were trapped, cut off from the living world.

Zed started at the amount of blood fluids pooled around
him and her. There was too much, too much. The fluid
clumped on the sand without soaking in, as if this Unlife
world wouldn't tolerate living matter. Zed waved his hand ineffectually, unsure where to begin. She was burned over more
than half her body. Even his navigator's belt and compass
pouch were scorched: he saw the wink of jewels on his gold-
chased compass. He could have cried. She had thought it such
a grand joke to keep his compass hostage.

He laid a bloody hand alongside her singed cheek, atop
what remained of her white hair. She was very still. Zed knelt,
frantic, and put his ear to her back, charred as it was.

There was no sound, no murmur. Nothing.

He'd have nothing to tell her.

She was dead.

12
Through the Essence

ZED KNELT IN THE BLOODIED SAND BY TIGER Eye and wept. Tears ran down his dirty cheeks and itched in his beard. He wept for the woman he had grown to love; he wept for their lost chances; he wept for the emptiness inside him. Tiger Eye lay cold and still. Zed cried to the ragged dead sky, the only living thing in an outpost of the damned. He was so tired, so exhausted, so alone. He dropped his head on his knees and wept himself dry.

And as he sobbed for breath, his hand touched the wooden staff.

Zed jerked upright as if he'd been stabbed. The Staff of Old Malosho, the King Under the Forest. An ancient, ancient god, maybe the oldest one on Kulthea. A god of trees and flowers and brush, of wilderness and growing greenery. A god of life.

Desperately Zed snatched up the staff. He held it so tightly his knuckles went white and his hands shook. He held the staff as if it were his last link with life, and indeed it was. He whispered to the wood, "Please. Please, spirit of Malosho, King Under the Forest. Please use your goodness and power of life over death to bring back one of your devoted subjects. Here is Tiger Eye, one of your faithful tree folk, the Nureti, a woman one with your forest. *Please* restore her this spark, that she might live and see the trees again, and worship you forever."

Zed waited for some reply, but found none, not that he knew what to expect. Shaking all over, he touched the knotty end of the long thick staff to Tiger Eye's back, above her still heart. He strained his eyes for some sign, some spark or glow or other sign of magic working. But there was nothing. The staff did not even grow warm under his hands. He touched her again, thumped her even, but there was nothing.

The lone navigator sat back on his legs and closed his eyes. What, he thought, what was he to do now? Did he even care to do anything? A blasted dead plain like this was as good a place as any for a man dead inside—

He started at a noise. It had sounded like the sough of the wind, though there was no wind here. He heard it again. A sigh. He snapped his attention to Tiger Eye.

She was still—no. Zed bent close over her head. Her unburned cheek lay against the sand. Her mouth was open and sand speckled her lips. But as he watched, a grain of sand blew off her lips. She was breathing.

And there was more. As he watched, the exposed bones in her shoulder were shrinking. No, being covered. Her back muscles were knitting like red threads, closing the wound. The white bones disappeared under a layer of healthy muscle, then the muscle thickened. The black skin around the wound began to move. It too thickened, and the burnt, charred portion sloughed off like snakeskin to trickle onto the sand. Gradually the red muscle disappeared under a solid sheet of healed skin. All down her back, along her side, and down her thighs the process continued. The charring on her face dried up and fell away like black powder.

With another tiny sigh, Tiger Eye opened her eyes and moaned. She groaned, fumbled her arms under her, and pushed herself up from the sand sleepily. Zed helped her. No sooner did she have both eyes open than she clutched at the tattered remains of her leather tunic. Most of one side had been burned away. She looked at the ruins of the clothing with more wonder than embarrassment.

She felt her side and thigh. She croaked, "I thought I was burned."

Zed's voice croaked too. "You were. Burned to death."

Tiger Eye looked around blankly at the pool of clumped brown blood she had lain in. "How?"

For answer, Zed hefted the staff.

Tiger Eye blinked sand off her lids, wiped it absently off her face. "Old Man Malosho. So he does have wondrous powers we don't know. I always thought he was our most powerful god . . ."

Zed helped her sit up properly. Dazed, she took his hand. He looked her over critically, anxious to find anything wrong. But she was healed and whole. The only thing that hadn't grown back was her singed hair: she was almost bald on one side. The new skin was a curious sight. It was untanned, white as a baby's bum. Tiger Eye's new stretches of skin were plain as white paint on a cedar boat. A round patch on her cheek looked like cheap makeup. She ran her hand over them in wonder. "I was really hurt . . . He saved me . . ." Suddenly she glanced up at him. "No, you saved me!"

Zed shook his head. "No, I only wielded the staff. It was Malosho's power. I'm surprised it reached this far, or there was that much power stored in the staff . . ."

He couldn't continue. She looked at him with new wonder in her eyes. "You thought to use the staff to save me. Others wouldn't have thought of that. You really do know wondrous things."

Zed stood up and offered her his hand. She took it and arose. With the other hand she clutched at her tatters, not very effectually. She blushed, the white patch on her cheek flushing pink.

Zed turned away and yanked his tunic over his head. He handed it around his shoulder. "Here, don this. And give me my compass. It's time. I have work to do."

He stood in his tight chemise and waited. He should have felt cold, he reflected, but there seemed no temperature in this dead land. Hel, or this piece of it, was neither hot nor cold. It was nothing, and nothingness.

The woman said, "All right. You may look." Zed found her wrapped in his voluminous tunic, looking like someone's daughter playing in her father's clothing. She blushed again and avoided his gaze. She rolled the sleeves up past her wrists, brushed the hood back. The tails hung below her rump. She'd tied the leather tunic on underneath. She handed him his wide black belt with the scorched compass pouch.

Zed strapped on the belt and settled the pouch. He was glad to wear it again, he found. It was like finding an old friend in the wilderness.

Tiger Eye asked, "Why do you need your compass? Oh . . . Where's the tunnel that leads back to the catacombs?"

Zed pointed ahead at the wasteland. "The spot where the tunnel stood is up there, but there's nothing now."

Tiger Eye peered around. "Can't we dig? Did the tunnel collapse?"

The navigator shook his head. He took her shoulder, hefted the oversize staff, and pointed toward the distant circle of ruins. They struck out over the coarse sand. "There's no point. That wasn't a tunnel, really. It was more of a—hole in a net. One spot is the same as any other spot on this desert." He saw he'd confused her, so he added, "If we dug we'd only find sand."

Tiger Eye let him hold her arm. Recently resurrected, she arose from the sand like someone from a sickbed. Her legs were wobbly, her feet clumsy. She leaned on him, almost staggering. "Do you mean, we're *trapped* here?"

Zed didn't bother to soften the answer. He had too much to think about. "Yes. That passageway is gone for good. We're going to have to navigate our way out of here. I am, anyway."

They reached the circle of stones. Still unsteady, Tiger Eye leaned a hand on one. She looked around at the wreckage. The stone box that had contained Tilak's armor was scorched black in spots. One of Tiger Eye's comrades, a woman, lay dead, burned alive, a charred lump almost unrecognizable as a human. Darroc the Sailor lay in pieces like a spilled jigsaw puzzle. Otherwise there was little to see.

Tiger Eye nodded to the circle. "Could the staff bring them back to life?"

Zed sat on a fallen column. He had taken out his compass and was dusting it with a chamois cloth. He picked up the thick staff and handed it to her. "You can try. But there isn't much to resurrect. And I never heard of an artifact—even a god's—that could bring back more than one person. There may not even be any magic left in it."

Tiger Eye used the staff as a crutch. She picked her way across the circle, touched the staff to the charred ruin, prayed quietly. Zed kept busy with his polishing. After a while, Tiger Eye sighed. "Morning Rain, I've failed you twice. I'm sorry."

She gave Zed back the staff. He told her, "Don't be hard on yourself, Tiger. We've been dragged into Hel at the mercy of savage gods. It's a wonder any of us are still alive."

The woman didn't answer. A line in the sand caught her eye. She tottered to it and pulled up a lightning spear someone had dropped. "Ah. I feel stronger with a weapon in my hand. But, V'rama's Whip, I'm so *hungry!*"

"That comes of using all the food in your system to rebuild the muscle and skin. If we had a fire, we could cook up part of Darroc." He hoped a joke would distract her from their plight.

But she studied the sailor's remains in a way that disturbed him. She murmured, "We could eat him raw. But his liver's spoiled, I expect. So are his sweetbreads."

Zed looked up quickly. "Sweetbreads?"

"Brains."

Zed blinked. She was serious. He asked in a quavery voice, "You folk really eat—other folk?"

Tiger Eye yawned and patted her mouth. "Not so much now. We were cannibals early on, when we first took to the forest and life was so hard. Now we only have ritual feasts. We drink blood at the sacrifices. The elders eat the brains of any elder who dies, to preserve the knowledge. I hope to be an elder someday . . ." she finished dreamily. "Maybe I should just sleep . . ."

"Do that." Zed polished his lenses and changed the subject. "I'll be a while calculating. This will be some jump we're going to make."

Tiger Eye slid off the column, leaned against it, and wrapped herself in Zed's tunic. She laid her spear across her stomach. "You can do it, Zed. You can do anything, I think."

Zed chuckled. "A few days ago you said I could do nothing."

She murmured. "Not now. You're . . . wonder . . . ful . . ."

The navigator sat still and watched her sleep. He worried for a moment if she were relapsing, sinking into sickness or even dying, but her breathing was regular and healthy. Malosho's magic did thorough work.

Now it was Zed's turn. He breathed on the telescope lens, polished it once more, then put the cloth away. He moved all the settings to their middle positions. The instrument resembled a sailor's sextant. A triangular frame supported a folding telescope, all chased with gold on steel. Set into the frame and along the telescope were various slides and levers mounted on jewels, with some other lens set sideways. Odd demarcations marked the legs. A circular box held a clockwork mechanism with an ornate key.

The navigator stood up, then plumped his bottom on the edge of the stone box that had contained Tilak's armor. The box was at the center of the standing stones, which must have marked some sacred function long ago. Perhaps they were in the center of an Essence flow.

Zed sighted through the telescope section of his compass. The distant murky horizon stayed murky. Bringing it closer couldn't clarify a blurry line. He stuck out a foot and turned slowly in a circle, still squinting. Gray scraps of cloud rolled by. Zed knew exactly what he was looking for. He'd seen it often enough. The telescope filtered normal light to reveal Essence flows. They usually showed as one of three phenomena: either bands of white light, or disruptions in the atmosphere, "cracked" lines in the sky or alongside an object, or else as narrow violet rainbows. Essence flows covered the planet Kulthea, more common than clouds and rain. They were fluctuating paths of magic, invisible and fitful as the wind, and almost as hard to grasp. But navigators had mastered them, just as sailing masters could harness wind to drive their ships. Navigating skill involved deciding which flows were safe, which had an actual destination, which were solid and big enough to ride. There were endless considerations. A usable Essence flow had to touch the ground at some point: one in the upper atmosphere was useless unless you could fly. A band that flickered was dangerous, since it might wink out at any moment and leave you stranded in limbo, or only partly arrived. A flow near a lightning storm might disappear. One too deep in the ground might be a dead end. Directions and angles were important too: you couldn't expect a party to drop down a "mineshaft." And so on.

Given normal circumstances, a navigator could find a

dozen Essence flows in a matter of minutes. Within a hour or two, he or she could assess them, calculate their width and stability and end points, determine the safest path. Within another hour he could complete the spells to open the portal. Traveling the tunnel was then the simplest part, a matter of minutes. But that was all under normal circumstances, somewhere on Kulthea.

This was not Kulthea. It was outside the world. And what Zed saw through his telescope was exactly nothing.

He licked his lips and turned another circle, staring harder this time. No bands, no rainbows, no distortions (though those would be very hard to spot).

He left off the telescope and turned the compass sideways. Set in the frame toward the bottom was a large fish-eye lens. He held it up and scanned the horizon again. This lens gave a cruder picture, but it would amplify any distortions out there.

There were none.

This is what he had been afraid of all along. Without an Essence flow, he had no way to get out of this outworld.

He tried again. He removed the main lens from the telescope, put it directly over his eye, and closed the other one. He turned a circle. Nothing. He replaced the lens and inserted a red filter behind it. That would make the darker colors stand out. There were none. A blue filter. Again, none. He slid the settings to their farthest marks and looked again, slid them all the way back and looked yet again. Nothing.

Zed began to sweat in the still air. Below him, Tiger Eye snored gently. He hoped he wouldn't have to wake her with bad news, but this was the baddest he could imagine. No Essence anywhere, of any kind, at all? It wasn't possible. The *world* was created of Essence!

But this wasn't the world. It was beyond, somewhere outside the world.

He bit his lip and tried not to panic. He forced himself to sit down, breathe deeply, reset everything, and calmly go through the entire process again. Work would keep him from despairing for the moment. But the repetition was over too quickly.

Nothing.

Suddenly Zed jumped up from his seat and stamped on the soil. He swore bitterly and long. He could have hurled the compass against one of the standing stones for all the good it did. He actually cocked his arm to throw it when something caught his eye. A hairline crack in a milky piece of stone.

Carefully, without moving the compass in the air, he twisted his head and peeked. Set into one of the back legs of the compass was a cylinder of quartz, or quartzlike stone. These stones had been discovered by the Northmen of distant Quellbourne. They used the stones—a common, natural substance—to steer by in the everlasting fogs of the north seas. A sailor could put his eye to the quartz and turn a slow circle. He would suddenly see a faint black streak in the stone. That streak meant he faced south, no matter the weather. The navigators had found another use for "Quellbourne Quartz." Near an Essence flow, they would reveal a black streak at any crosscurrents or "leaks": places where the Essence was disrupted by another trace or line, usually an old, fading flow. The quartz was more of a diagnostic tool for purists than anything. It allowed a navigator to measure the purity of a flow, not that most cared: as long as they could ride the flow, who cared how "pure" it was? Yet as Zed had whirled the compass in the air, he'd seen a streak of black.

He thought. He put his eye to the quartz and turned slowly. That revealed nothing. He tilted the compass and turned again. Aha! He had a black streak.

He marked the position of the compass in his mind and looked around. He was within the stone circle. There was nothing remarkable to see. He stood stock-still, thinking.

Tiger Eye sensed something amiss and woke. She grasped her spear and asked weakly, "What is it?"

Zed shushed her. The stone box, he mused . . . The stone box had supported Orgiana and protected Tilak's armor for six hundred years. The armor was magically charged, fantastically so. The box would have absorbed some of the magic over the ages, as a stone grew warm in the sun. And Orgiana had sent messages from this stone out into the world of men, dreams to Cutthroat . . .

He checked again. There was a leak of Essence, just a trace, from the box, pointing downward at an angle. He marked the spot in the sand with his toe. The trace, the leak . . . should be . . . pointing toward the armor . . .

Zed grinned. That trace of Essence was a flow, no matter how weak, back to Tarek Nev.

He boasted to Tiger Eye, "I've got it!"

"What? A path?"

But he ignored her. What to do with this information? He'd located a flow of Essence, but that was supposed to be the easiest part. Could he open the trace wide enough for them to slip through? Usually the process resembled parting curtains and assuring the hole was big enough or long enough. Here he had only a crack in a wall and no prybar.

Or did he?

"Tiger Eye, give me the staff, please."

The woman struggled up, handed him the long staff. He said, "Thank you. Are you feeling stronger?"

She tossed her head and almost staggered. "Stronger in some ways, weaker in others. I'm so hungry I might faint."

Zed's voice was tight. "Don't. I need you to stay close by me, as close as possible. I'm going to try something, and we'll have to be quick. That is, if the staff has any power left . . ."

"What are you going to do?"

He didn't answer. Balancing his compass in one hand, the navigator carefully drove the end of the staff into the spot at his boot tip. He consulted the compass, then adjusted the angle of the staff a fraction and sighted along it. "Hang on to my belt with both hands. Tight. Better yet, stick a fold of the tunic through and tie yourself to me as best you can."

The woman's hands were busy. She hugged the crooked spear between them. "But what's going to happen?"

Without moving the staff, Zed carefully folded his compass and slid it into the pouch, buttoned it securely. He concentrated on his work as he talked. "Normally . . . I find an Essence path, part the vale, and I and my clients march through, sometimes on horseback even. It creates a tunnel between the spheres. The walls are colored light. You've never seen me do it, but I'm quite good. But this . . . is different . . . We don't have a proper Essence flow to follow, just a hint of one. So . . . I'm going to hold the staff in the 'crack' and begin my parting spell. I'm hoping . . . that if the vale parts . . . the Essence in the staff will be drawn into the void, creating a path solid enough and wide enough for us to travel . . ."

Tiger Eye now clung to him, her arms locked around his waist. He liked the sensation. Her voice was more curious than afraid. Perhaps she was not yet fully back from the realm of the dead, and death no longer frightened her. "But what if it doesn't work?"

Zed flexed his fingers. He held the staff in place with his chin. "Oh . . . we'll be sucked down a rathole and ground up like sausage. Or cut in half. Or we'll get only halfway to where we want to be and will be turned into phantoms . . . There are all kinds of stories about the navigation failures, but most are just theories. The ones who fail don't come back to talk. Hold close. I've never done this before . . . I usually have people stand back too, in case there's a thunderclap. But we can't hang back now . . ." He wondered for a moment if he did fail, would anyone find any part of him to know it. Then he stopped worrying. He was too busy.

Zed put his hands in front of him, above his head. He turned them over so the backs touched. He wet his lips and began his chant.

"Essence flow, blood of the world,
   Open here, secrets unfurled,
   The path we make you shall not pall,
   We'll bring home safe . . . one . . . and . . . ALL!"

A simple enough spell, more for focusing attention and impressing a client than anything. But here it made all the difference. As Zed shouted the final word, he ripped his hands downward toward the sterile ground. The Staff of Old Malosho dropped from his chin to fall across his shoulder, almost rapping Tiger Eye in the face where she peered over his shoulder. Zed's hands ripped the fabric of the dead air with a hideous hissing noise. He saw a flash of whirling lights and knew he'd succeeded, at least in opening the proper rent. Another whistling hiss sounded by his feet: the Essence leaving the staff and disappearing into the depths. The hole Zed ripped was a wavery one, and it wanted to snap shut. As soon as his hands moved, it immediately began to close at the top.

The navigator didn't wait. He reached behind with one arm, hugged Tiger Eye to him, and yelled, *"Hang tight!"*

With a hop and a grunt, he leapt into the rent in space.

There was something else he hadn't liked about this Essence trace, and that was its angle. Almost straight down.

With Tiger Eye clinging, the two of them dropped down a

shaft of whirling lights. The "walls" were a blur of every color imaginable, as of a normal countryside passing at high speed. Zed suspected that was exactly what it was. Sometimes there was no light at all, as if they passed through a mountain. Other times there was too much light, as if they passed the sun. Unlike other Essence flows he'd navigated, where there was a "floor" to stand on, here there was nothing. They fell, at a crazy angle, through a mist of melted colors. Clinging together, they plunged head over heels, yet there was no "up" or "down." The shaft seemed to twist, and Zed even felt invisible humps shunt him from side to side. There was a whisper of wind to their passage, an ethereal nicker around their ears that seemed to impart secrets just too low to hear. Zed spun, lazily, trying to hold his stomach steady. Tiger Eye's clutching his middle so tightly didn't help, either.

Mostly Zed wondered: Where the hell will we come out? *Will* we come out? They'd been traveling a very long time, he guessed. Maybe there was no exit, and they'd fall through limbo forever.

A blind jump was always dangerous. Jumping to a focus was the best, for the black obelisks anchored in permanent Essence flows had been tested and used again and again. Jumping blind shouldn't be done without a good map or verbal description of the countryside you sought. They shouldn't pop out inside a mountain, for the Essence flow exited in the least dense space around—usually. Lacking open air, the charm would settle for exiting in soft stone over tough stone if the flow petered out. The spell Zed muttered as they fell, an anchor spell, should allow them to pop out somewhere close to the earth, but again there was no telling if he'd exit ten miles up. As he muttered spell combination after combination, he prayed too. It couldn't hurt. He should have reminded Tiger Eye to pray too.

Suddenly he noticed a different quality of light below his feet. About the same time, he landed. Solidly.

Dirt stung his hands, then Zed hit the ground face first. Tiger Eye, tight behind him, slammed atop him and nearly broke his collarbone. She grunted painfully as she rolled off him. Zed spat dirt, tasted blood from a cut lip, flopped sideways and onto his back. His neck ached as if he'd broken it . . . Then he noticed something hanging above him.

Like a hole in the sky, the exit hole was fading. Usually a

hole would remain open for hours unless a navigator closed it. Now he watched, fresh with icy sweat, as the hole sealed and faded. That, he pondered, had been close. Another minute in transit and they'd be partially or fully lost in the Essence, absorbed by it, giving it power as they ceased to exist. Death, or something very like it . . .

Yet even as reaction set him shaking, he noticed the dirt under them was good honest soil with weeds. A slanted cut-stone wall covered with green vines was to one side of them. His heart leapt. He grabbed Tiger Eye and hugged her. He shouted, "We did it! We made it!" Tiger Eye clung to him, weak. Giddy, Zed tried to clamber to his feet but stumbled. There was something wrong with his left foot. He peered at it dizzily. His toes poked through his boot tip. The nails were bloody, as if he'd stubbed them. What? Then he knew. He'd lost his boot tip when the portal slammed shut. It could have been his whole leg. He shuddered and had to sit down again.

Tiger Eye rose in a crouch, Zed's tunic wrapped tight around her torso, her spear ready. She cast all about them, taking in their surroundings. She whispered, "It's all changed. It's returning to what it was."

Zed finally groped back to his feet. One glance told him where they'd landed.

In the distance, the Three Masters of Aranmor smoldered as dismally as before. Columns of smoke rose to be ripped apart by the sea breeze, and red lava bubbled in cracks hundreds of feet wide. The earth under him shook in the now-familiar way. A distant screen of trees, impossibly tall, he recognized as an outthrust arm of the Wyr Forest.

Zed nodded. He guessed from their height they were on some lower tier of Tarek Nev, about a third of the way up the nine levels. That made sense. He'd followed the Essence trace of Tilak's armor, and the god and Orgiana should be somewhere nearby, yet he saw no sign of them. What he did see was curious.

On one hand was the wall of vines, and white flowers with yellow centers speckled the greenery. It was strange, he thought, because the only flowers he'd seen earlier were tiny roses. He could smell their perfume. Across from them was a small park. It was overgrown and brambled, but the plants looked green and fresh. Tangled peach trees in need of pruning bore waxy leaves and ripe round fruit that made Zed's mouth water. He hadn't seen any fruit before, either. The park's fountain gurgled merrily, bubbling out a silver cascade that made his throat ache for a drink, and that was the first working fountain they'd seen. Before, everything in the city had been dead, decayed, dusty, or fallen. Something was queer . . .

A gabble, a half-human cry sounded above them. Tiger Eye snapped into a fighting stance. The stone wall stopped at a wide flight of stairs. Zed blinked. Then he recognized them. They were the stairs he'd walked up a day before. In fact . . . the park was where they had slept and seen the ghost in the morning. But the fountain and plants had been bone-dry. What was . . . ?

The gabbling cry echoed again. Along the top rim of the staircase, a squad of monsters galloped into sight.

Men and women, naked from head to toe, gaped and howled like animals. They were animals. They had brown furred jackal heads or scaly green lizard heads. One man had the head of an octopus, with writhing tentacles hanging about his naked chest. A boar-headed woman drooled slobber onto her dirty bare breasts.

Tiger Eye hissed, drawing air for battle. Zed just stared.

The animal-men leapt down the stairs to attack them.

13
City
of
Fiends

ZED HAD THE IMPRESSION OF AN ALGAE-brown green-flecked tide, then the monsters were upon them.

The jackal-headed man never reached the bottom step. Tiger Eye planted her feet, grunted sharply as she shoved, and drove her spear through the monster's neck. He dropped a long knife he'd been carrying. Blood sprayed across Tiger Eye in Zed's tunic.

"Close!" she shouted.

Zed remembered then that Tiger Eye was one of the best fighters of her tribe, that she commanded a squad of her own and was used to giving commands.

Unfortunately, he didn't know the commands. He called, "What?" even as he ran to her side.

Muscles bulged in Tiger Eye's arms as she whipped the dying jackal-man off her spear. She dumped the body at her feet to form a partial barrier. She spat monster blood off her lips. Zed jumped behind her and asked again, "What?"

"Close with me! Back to back! Grab that knife!"

Zed scrambled past the bleeding corpse for the knife. The boar-headed woman and lizard-man were circling around them on two sides. More monsters barked and whooped and howled on the stairs. One had a tiger head, he noted. Another a snake head, and horse. Most of them carried crude butcher knives or tomahawks in filthy hands.

Tiger Eye didn't wait for another attack, but moved. She half stepped backward, in a circle, stabbing her feet down firmly. She crouched with her weight balanced forward. Zed thought she looked more dangerous than any tiger. She barked commands at him all the while, and shouted and snapped war cries and bullying remarks. The cacophony confused Zed as much as the animal-men. "Back now! Don't trip! Hyaa! you filthy scut! Got the knife? Hoo, monster! Watch my feint! Moving left—"

Zed was almost bowled over as Tiger Eye moved. She slashed air with her spear, jabbed her spear point at the lizard-man's eyes, then spun on both feet and sliced at the boar-headed woman. The wooden spear pinked the round snout and elicited a squeal and blood. Then Tiger Eye spun back to face the main of the crowd.

Zed couldn't get over the horror of these man-things. A magician and scientist by trade, even now he wondered how they'd come into being. Had some sorcerer beheaded a man and a beast and switched their heads? Might there be animal bodies with human heads? Or had an alchemist infused men with animal blood and grown their heads that way? These beast-things combined the worst traits of man and animal. The animal heads simply ended around the neck, with coarse brown fur or scales running next to dirty tanned skin. The bodies were filthy, dirtier than natural animals, caked with grime and cockleburrs and stains. Their stench was overpowering, a stink of the slaughterhouse and dungheap and prison combined. Worst of all, for Zed, were the female bodies. Below a bleeding snout and slobbery red jowls were a pair of small dirty breasts with protuberant nipples, arresting and disgusting at the same time. As he recoiled both physically and mentally, he had to wonder: For what purpose had these things been created other than to act as mankillers and nightmares?

He pondered all this in a second, then Tiger Eye was shout-

ing at him again. "Watch the boar! We'll move north, run
when we can! Watch it—"

With a snarl, the tiger-man leapt full length at them. Tiger
Eye bumped Zed forward—toward the boar-woman—as she
backstepped. The tiger-man lashed with grimy cracked nails
for her face, but she stooped and stabbed upward at the exposed belly. She had time for only one deep jab, then she had
to rip the spear free or lose it. The tiger-man snarled again,
this time in rage and pain, and made a fumbling landing on
the stones of the street.

That attack told Zed one thing: These creatures had the
original brains of the beasts and not of men. Even a civilized
man like himself could see that had been a true tiger's leap,
but without a tiger's massive legs to power it, it was a clumsy
failure. The tiger-man rolled on the cobblestones clutching a
leaking hole in his belly.

Zed saw that from the corner of his eye, for as he was
shoved into the boar-woman, she lowered her head. Her jowls
retracted to expose yellow tusks long as Zed's fingers. She
meant to duck and rip and disembowel him. He pushed wildly
with one hand at her snout and swung the knife with the
other, hoping he didn't lop off his own hand. The knife was
a hatchet with a heavy blade, a crude square of steel sharp-
ened along one edge with a rawhide-wrapped handle. The
blade thunked into the boar's chest just above her right breast.
It didn't stop her lunge.

Zed cursed. Apprentice navigators, mostly young men, had
asked their instructors time and again for instruction in fighting, if only to protect themselves. And always they were told,
"If you want to learn to fight, go to gladiator school. A navigator's weapon is his mind, his sword, negotiation." Zed fervently wished he had one of those pompous old instructors in
front of him right now.

As the slashing tusks sliced toward his vitals, he ducked
out of the way, then threw himself backward, stumbled over
some impediment, and went down.

Tiger Eye tussled with the lizard-man. When she'd exposed
her back during the tiger attack, the lizard had leapt forward
and clamped his teeth at her neck. Zed's tunic and hood,
bunched around her neck, confounded him, and he snapped
instead on her shoulder. Tiger Eye snarled and writhed sideways. She smashed the butt of her spear into the lizard-man's

brisket, then again. He let go with a dry rasping wheeze. Unable to turn fast enough, she aimed high and clonked him in the throat with the shaft. Gagging, he staggered back.

She saw Zed pitch backward over the jackal-man's corpse. The navigator thrust out a hand but slid in blood. The boar-woman pressed her attack, swinging her tusked snout like a flail. A tusk caught the side of Zed's boot, tore a furrow in his trousers and calf. Tiger Eye hopped, stamped a solid one-two cadence, and drove her spear into the boar-woman's side and up. The thing dropped in her tracks.

Tiger Eye glanced behind, but the lizard-man had fallen, still clutching his mashed throat. No threat there. The other monsters were poised on the stairs in two ranks, screaming and yipping but not pressing their attack. Zed was fumbling to get his feet under him. The injured leg gave him trouble. Tiger Eye snagged his stout black belt and jerked him bodily. "Get *up*!"

She spun him around and planted him next to her, facing the monsters. "Knife up! Come on, you half-things! Who's next? Hoo, cowards!"

Zed counted wildly. The snake-man flicked a forked tongue. The horse-man rolled its lower jaw as if chewing cud. There was the octopus-man, two more jackals, and something like an owl. Too many, he thought. His heart was pounding so fiercely the bloody knife in his hand jumped to its pulse.

Tiger Eye nudged him with her spear butt and he started. She hissed, "Smartly now, retreat. They won't attack our front." The warrior edged sideways, careful of her footing, skirting the gagging lizard-man. Zed crabbed along with her, keeping close as he dared. They crept a dozen feet away. The monsters stepped after them, but stopped on the other side of the fallen enemies. Tiger Eye grated, "Watch what they do."

They retreated sideways, spear and knife out, down the wide stone-cobbled street, away from the park. Zed wondered what they waited for. A jackal-man cast them a last look, then jumped onto all fours. He opened a slavering jaw and sank his teeth into the bloody wound in the boar-woman's side. With a wrench of saw teeth, he ripped loose a hunk of flesh and swallowed it. The snake-man snuffled his muzzle deep into the wound, bloodying himself to the eyes, then hissed as the jackal-man snapped at him. Another jackal-man dove onto the writhing lizard-man, butted his arms aside, and sank teeth into his belly. Another ripping sound made Zed gag. Even the horse-man gnawed at flesh. The octopus-man writhed his tentacles and dipped a yellow beak to nip out the boar's glazed eyes.

Zed grabbed for his mouth, but Tiger Eye pulled him off-balance, stumbling away. "We must make time while they feed."

Then the two were running, Zed's boots clumping, Tiger Eye's bare feet padding, off down the haunted empty street. The growling, slurping, rending noises were left behind.

"That reminds me," Tiger Eye panted. "I'm still starved."

Zed groaned and ran.

They zipped into a park long enough for Tiger Eye to grab some pears. She wolfed half a dozen, pointed him at the tree. "Hurry and eat. We must keep moving."

Zed grabbed two pears and tried to eat, but his stomach was a knot from the recent battle. "Because of those beast men? They're busy eating, aren't they?"

"There are others." Tiger Eye chomped down half a pear, tossed away the rest, and plucked at Zed's sleeve. "Can't you hear them, smell them? They're all over the city."

"What are?" But she was off, almost skipping down the curving road.

Tiger Eye scurried along in short bursts, as do animals in the jungle. She'd take five or ten quick skips, then freeze in a crouch and listen, all senses alert. Zed plowed along behind her, finding the uneven pace tiring. The woman hugged the tall stone wall of greenery and the stone faces of houses and empty shops. They moved along the inside of the curving road, it being the shorter route.

At one point the warrior paused and sniffed the air, shot a peek around the corner. She blinked, thinking a moment, and took another look. Zed, breathing like a bellows, leaned past her and peeked himself.

Down the next curving stretch of road was another staircase and park opposite. The park sported tall, bushy maple trees, bright with new leaves. Standing amid the trees, shoulder high to their lower branches, was a giant hairy elephant. "A mammoth. Or mastodon," Zed whispered. "I thought they were extinct."

Tiger Eye looked again, signaled. They bolted across the

foot of the staircase and ducked into brush on the far side.
The mammoth cocked a tiny ear at their passing, but then returned to stripping leaves and stuffing them by the bushelful
into its pink maw. Zed stared at the great beast, wondering
how it had been used in this city in ancient times, and where
it had lain. Had it been released from some hidden barn, frozen in ice? Had it been resurrected from bones?

Tiger Eye gurgled a curse and shoved Zed deeper into the
brush with one brown hand. Down the road, coming toward
them, were two black-armored mannikins, walking in tandem.
Their right hands on their black hilts caused their arms to jut
out at a jaunty angle. "We'll probably meet more of those before we're through," Zed whispered. "They'll be the eyes and
ears of Tilak."

Tiger Eye didn't answer. She turned and slipped up the
stairs faster than Zed could keep up with her. She flattened at
the top, poised on fingers and toes, and Zed got a good look
along her firm shapely legs. Then she was up, dashing to the
protection of the stone balustrade at the corner, hissing for
Zed to catch up. He plodded after her and stamped to a halt.

She gave him no time to rest, but suddenly scurried across
the stairs again to the opposite balustrade and faded behind it.
Zed panted, "Why can't you stick to one side?"

For answer, she pointed to a disturbance on the road Zed
hadn't noticed. As he watched, a section of paving stones rippled and flowed forward, like a gray puddle oozing along.
The edges of the section rippled again, flowed over a pile of
fallen brick, edged toward the stairs. The squarish thing was
almost impossible to see, for it was the exact color of the paving stones, and even had sunken dividing lines like grass-
filled cracks. Zed wasn't sure, but he thought it looked like a
giant manta ray, even dragging a long stinger. "What *is* it?"

"Flapper," breathed Tiger Eye without looking at him.
"They live on the forest floor too. They change color to
match the ground. They eat anything that stands still."

Zed shuddered. He would have walked right onto it, been
tumbled and knocked down. "Where are we going? Do you
have any specific place in mind?"

The woman scanned the street ahead, and the buildings
above it. She was sweating, and she puffed. "Just
someplace—to hide and rest."

Zed was so tired and hungry his voice shook. "What are we

going to do next? I mean, providing something doesn't eat us?"

"You tell me. You're a man of the city."

"Not like this one," he grumbled.

Tiger Eye grabbed his wrist so hard it hurt. Zed looked over the top of her head, fine-haired on one side, bald on the other. Around the distant curve shambled something tall and shaggy as a haystack. It stumped along on feet broad as millstones. A face like a sleepy dwarf's looked out from under bushy brows. It wore only wheat-colored hair. Perhaps an ogre, thought Zed, a hairy one. It filled the roadway and brushed against houses on either side. Zed wondered idly what all the monster traffic was about. Were they simply walking around, stretching newly resurrected legs? Or were the intelligent ones hunting him and Tiger Eye? Could Tilak and Orgiana know they were in this plane? Hel's Gate, he thought, we have no way of knowing what ancient gods know.

Tiger Eye pressed him backward onto the stairway. But a yip sounded at the bottom. Zed cursed. Spread along the bottom were the animal-headed men. The snake and jackals rattled to one another in some gabbling tongue and loped up the stairs two at a time. Tiger Eye pointed Zed along the street to where the flapper lay. Behind them, the ogre gave a snort and picked up its feet, pounding the paving stones as it trotted after them.

Zed ran, though how he'd get past the flapper he didn't know. It filled the street too. Then Tiger Eye surged past him. She skipped to one edge of the flapper, which was no thicker than a rug, and pinked it with her spear. The edge curled up, then curled sideways to wrap around the spear. Tiger Eye held on tight, tugging, and waved Zed to go on. Staying as close as possible to the edge of the house, he gingerly stepped up onto the flapper's back. It felt spongy under his feet, as if he were walking on a down comforter. With three long steps he dashed across the gray sectioned back to the true paving stone beyond. He steered wide of the stinger tail and looked for Tiger Eye.

Down the street the ogre gained speed, rolling along like a boulder down a mountainside. The jackal- and snake-men had vaulted to the top of the stairs, but hung back to let the ogre pass. Otherwise they might be crushed. Tiger Eye certainly would be, in another moment. Zed started to yell her name.

But the woman had seen that Zed was clear of the flapper, and now she acted. She jabbed down with her spear, stinging the flapper and causing it to momentarily recoil. Lightly, she hopped over the raised rim onto its back. Immediately the raised rim shot higher. The creature proceeded to roll onto its back to catch the woman in its folds. But by then she'd dashed across the monster's back and joined Zed. Catching his arm, she hollered, "Run!"

Zed did, down the curving street, but he paused to look over his shoulder. The flapper was rolled up halfway like a carpet. Evidentally it would take a while to realize it had not caught its prey. Meanwhile, the ogre stopped at the barrier. The animal men hung back in wary fear.

"That was wonderful!" Zed panted. "How did—you know to do—that?"

She loped along easily. The folds of his tunic bounced around her body. "A game we play as children. Loser gets eaten."

"Oh. Oh, shit."

They had trotted past dead buildings, between leveled lots, past another cavelike hole in the tier wall where ancient aqueducts sagged crumbling and broken. They reached the next open space of parks and stairways, only to be met by another jackal-, owl-, and octopus-man. The jackal snarled, baring fangs and clawed fingernails. The owl-man raised a rusty tomahawk. Tiger Eye thudded to a halt. She lifted her spear and took her stance, but with a weary curse. Zed doubted she could fight another round. He certainly couldn't.

He grabbed her shoulder. "Back here. Follow me."

She shot him a query, but followed as he turned and ran. He still clutched the bloody knife he'd taken from a fallen jackal-man. He paused to throw it now at the monsters pursuing. He pulled Tiger Eye past another building front and pointed to the hole in the tier wall. They scrambled up tumbled stone and broken masonry, then over curved sections of sewer or water pipe baked from red clay. Zed pointed above their heads.

Above was one of the aqueduct pipes, six feet through. When the wall had collapsed, it had sundered the pipe, which now had a break in it five feet wide. There was no sign of dripping water. Past the pipe, behind it and above inside the hill, was darkness. They couldn't see more than fifteen feet with their outdoor-light vision.

Zed didn't need to. He slapped his stomach, chest, and shoulder, then made a cup of his two hands before his waist. Tiger Eye didn't hesitate. Clamping her spear in her teeth, she hooked her foot in the stirrup of his hands, stepped to his shoulder, grabbed two sides of the great pipe, and disappeared inside.

Zed turned at a growl. Silhouetted in the cave mouth was a monster-headed, pointed-eared jackal-man. Then a smooth-headed snake-man appeared at his shoulder. Jagged weapons swung in their hands. They spread out and slipped through the rent. After Zed.

He looked up but saw nothing. Where the hell? A snuffling sounded in front of him and he wished he'd kept that crude knife. The jackal-man crept through the dust-moted air, stalking him. It raised its head, sniffing.

A hunk of red clay pipe banged on its snout and it fell howling.

"Hist!" Zed glanced up. Tiger Eye's head popped out. She dropped an arm, he grabbed, and she pulled him bodily up into the pipe mouth.

In almost total darkness, she pushed him past her. "I'll take rear guard. They can't get around us in here."

Zed put both hands on either side of the pipe and started into blackness. "I'll guide."

Zed shuffled along for what seemed like miles. It was black inside the pipe, blacker than any night he'd ever seen, blacker than being blind. He borrowed Tiger Eye's spear to prod the floor of the pipe before him. He knew enough about engineering to know there might be unexpected drop shafts anywhere. He chose the most direct branches he could find, and they traced a curving route, curving like the hill itself. Sometimes a branch tilted up sharply, or down, and they had to backtrack. Once he almost pitched through a rent in one side. But he kept on, selecting this or that branch, ducking his head until his neck ached, with the warrior woman close behind. He hoped he could find a resting spot soon, for despite her good fight she must be dead tired. She'd been dead not a few hours ago, and that was no rest.

Eventually he spotted light ahead, though at first he thought it was merely dancing lights inside his eyes. But the light came from a grate overhead. By bracing his back against it, he shoved the rusty grate up and aside. It slid off the pipe and slammed down on stone with an awful clank. He gripped the edges and pulled himself out, helped Tiger Eye along. The two sat on the curved pipe and looked around.

They were in a vast square cavern like the bottom of a well. They could see by the light of another grate high up in the rounded ceiling. Many huge pipes along the ground and smaller ones along the walls converged here, at a central platform of rusty iron that sported some valves and lock mechanisms. Zed helped Tiger Eye down, and they found an actual man-sized bench to rest on. A ladder climbed one wall, up to a half-round black hole.

"I think we're safe here," Zed panted. He whispered, for their voices and every movement echoed in this stone chamber.

Tiger Eye nodded. She was too weary to talk. Zed got up and hunted around. By feeling various large and small pipes, he located a moist one and then a valve. Leaning on the valve, he creaked it open and loosed a spray of water. He washed his filthy hands in the spray, then cupped them and fetched Tiger Eye some water. She put her face into his hands and sucked the water up like an old dog. The navigator smiled. It pleased Zed that he could help her even in this tiny way. He fetched her more water, then drank himself. Then the two collapsed anew on the corroded bench.

"How," Tiger Eye gulped. "How do you know of these things? These pipes and—circles that open the water?"

Zed shrugged and stretched his shoulders. Now that he sat still, he felt his myriad cuts and bruises. "Navigators have to study how things work, especially anything we might have to trace. Aqueducts are one path. Sometimes we jump to beneath cities, when the ruling class doesn't want it known they employ navigators."

She laid her head back on the bench, pulled up his hood to pillow her neck. "How did you know which way to go in the pipes? I am lost underground."

Zed shrugged again. "Instinct. We're trained to always know north, our height, which way is up. One exercise was to encase a student in a bag of wool, then other students would carry him anywhere in the city or country, for however long, and spin the bag at intervals. We are supposed to know where we are at all times."

She smiled weakly. "And did you?"

He smiled back. "After a while."

The light of the grate high above threw a checkerboard pattern on their feet. Zed sighed and returned to business. "What do your legends tell about Orgiana?"

Tiger Eye closed her eyes. Her spear again lay across her stomach. "She's a bad one. A trickster goddess. Sometimes she killed for fun, the stories say. But all our gods are bloody. Even V'Rama Vair, of the dragonhead chariot, the ancestor of women warriors, could be cruel to friend and foe. Only Solus was a good god, and he's imprisoned in Tilak's sword, Soulcrusher. And Argamanthol was a good man turned god. He was a follower of Solus. That's where he gained the name The Golden."

Zed nodded wearily. Talk of cruel gods made him feel small.

Tiger Eye asked, "Why are there monsters in the city again? And water in the fountains, and fruit on the trees?"

The navigator pursed his lips. "I'm not sure. It's either a direct wish of Tilak or Orgiana, or else it's just some manifestation of their return. Perhaps things once under their command have been renewed, as flowers react to the return of the sun in spring. They've stirred up the Essence flows, loosed it. It flows downhill sometimes. Did you notice the plants grew greener as we climbed? The monsters will be thicker too near the top. Tilak and Orgiana must be in the temple. Maybe this is more marshaling of the forces. Eventually they'll move out from the city, go after your people for more slaves, then move out from the island, overtake Fulcrumia ... "

Tiger Eye sat bolt upright. "Then we must get to work. We must protect my people, now before the gods grow stronger."

Zed shook his head. "I'm just guessing. I don't know anything for sure."

But the warrior was vehement. "I'm guessing you're right. We need to get close to Tilak and Orgiana, and stop them."

"Easy to say."

Tiger Eye snapped, "Are you afraid of them?"

Zed didn't rise to the bait. He shifted his butt and settled back. His left leg ached where he had dropped out of the Essence flow. His chipped toes were dirty and black where his boot tip had been clipped off. His right leg ached where the boar-woman had gouged him. The wound had bled clean, but the threads of his torn trouser leg plucked at the clots. He was too tired to fuss with it. "Yes, in plain language, I'm afraid of them. They're gods, damn it! Lesser ones, to be sure, not sky gods. Ones you can poke with a spear and knock on their arse, but gods still, more powerful than any human sorcerer. Or elven sorcerer, even. I'm very much afraid of getting killed, and getting you killed too. You were, once. Remember?"

Tiger Eye sat back. She made no noise, but her wide staring eyes spoke volumes.

The navigator stroked her shoulder. Looking at this side of her, he could see her patchwork white and tanned skin by the checkerboard light of the grating. With her eyes glowing, she looked more tiger than human. "I'm sorry. But we can't get close to them without some effective weapons and a simple, workable plan."

The warrior woman nodded. Dealing in practicalities kept her from musing. "What did you do with the Staff of Old Malosho?"

"I dropped it in the—other place. I couldn't grab it and you. Anyway, I must have drained its last Essence cracking that flow open. It's just a stick now. Ho! Could you sing your song and summon Old Malosho here to battle the gods? He would be a match for them."

Tiger Eye shook her head. "He wouldn't leave the forest and come into a city. I shouldn't, either. I miss the trees. But I'll never see them again if we don't succeed . . ."

Zed cursed himself. He'd forgotten about her reasons for coming to the city. She sought the source of the tremors that shook the island. Now that he took note, he could feel the vibrations through the iron frame of the bench. It seemed they were increasing, both in duration and intensity, but it was hard to tell. They'd become part of him since he arrived on this benighted island.

Tiger Eye muttered to herself. "And all my warriors. Blackbird dead in the woods, eaten by a tiger. Falling Leaf and Mossback and Silver Spear transformed into armored slaves. Morning Rain burned to death ... I'm a miserable leader ..."

Zed poked her. "We need to stop counting the dead and look to the living. We need to assess what we have for weapons. You have a spear. I have—nothing."

She pointed to his belt where the compass peeked through the burned pouch. "What about that? Couldn't you transport us directly into their presence, or somewhere near them, out of sight?"

Zed slapped the pouch. "Not likely. We could ride the Essence, but not close to them. Gods throw off Essence like grinding wheels throw sparks. They disrupt the flow all around them, warp it. It's good for them. Prevents sneak attacks by their enemies."

"Like us."

"All two of us, one without weapons."

Tiger Eye suddenly began to shiver violently. She squeaked, "I'm frightened."

Zed put his arm around her, pulled her head onto his shoulder. She didn't resist. She mumbled, "I'm frightened. Everything's going to die. My people enslaved, my home destroyed, the whole island split and sunk into the Sea of Fire. There'll be nothing left, no place for me to go, unless I'm killed again. Oh, V'Rama, it was so dark, so cold, so lonely ..." She cried silently. Zed felt tears hot on his bare shoulder.

He rocked her and patted her, and crooned things his mother had crooned. She shuddered and cried some more, then stopped. She reached out and toyed with the chest hairs that showed above his chemise. There were not many left. The Nureti elder had burned away most of them when she dumped hot coals on Zed. That seemed a very long time ago. She said, "You're not frightened, really. You understand all this magic, and this city."

"No, no, I don't. I'm just used to viewing magic and gods' power objectively, that's all. Too objectively, sometimes. I find myself standing still and thinking when some Essence-charged monster's about to bite my face off. You, you're brave. You leap at monsters and spear them. No one has bitten *you* yet."

She sighed. "That's nothing brave. That's just training. But we make a good team."

He sighed and kissed her white hair. "Yes, we do."

They sat awhile longer without talking. Then the silence was shattered by the growling of Zed's stomach. Tiger Eye perked up her head, then laughed. Zed laughed too.

Gently he pushed her away and stood up. He shook his limbs, which had stiffened again. His myriad wounds throbbed, but moving around quieted them some. He told her, "Come. We'll journey up to the top of the hill and see how close to our quarry we can get. Maybe the fates will send us some opportunity. And maybe some real food."

Tiger Eye stood up and straightened his tunic around her. "I'm not taking very good care of your handsome uniform."

He took her hand. "You look lovely in it."

She brushed at her patchy skin, her choppy hair, the dirt on her nose. "I must look like a old warthog trampled by mating season. Where shall we go? I don't know where we are."

Zed pointed to the ladder. "You don't need a guide to follow that."

He stepped to the ladder and leaned his weight on it. It was scaly with rust, but bolted to the stone wall and sound. He hopped on and climbed, upward, toward the gods they opposed. Tiger Eye, bare feet silent on the rungs, came after him.

Zed stepped through the ladder's uprights into the domelike black hole. A few steps inside the light failed and the blackness was complete. But he put his hands on the rounded ceiling, felt the stones. He whispered, "Recognize the stone?"

Tiger Eye crowded behind him. She frowned. "No."

"These are the same passages as the catacombs. Remember the branch tunnels we passed on our way to the tomb? This is one of them. We follow this back and find the main passage, then we can climb that spelled stairway and come out at the story pearl."

Tiger Eye only nodded. "Lead, then. But I don't like this dark."

Zed suddenly recalled they were marching toward bitterly strong enemies and possible hideous death. But he hitched up his black belt and marched into the dark. "Keep your spear handy."

He stepped forward carefully. It was outrageously dark in here. He wondered why there weren't torches set in sconces on the walls. Surely the men who worked down here—

He stepped on something soft, spongy. Like a down quilt.

Warm blackness hit him in the face. He shouted, *"Flapper!"*

Then the smothering, pliable flesh enfolded them both. They were wrapped all over, knocked to their knees, curled up, squeezed tighter, tighter. Zed tried to shout Tiger Eye's name, but he had no breath.

He discovered an even deeper blackness.

14
Fire All Around

ZED GROANED, REACHED FOR HIS ACHING head, and fell out of bed.

At least that was the feeling. He twisted to catch himself but only revolved in the air, slowly, like a feather. A dry, familiar chuckle made him open his eyes.

He was back in the Temple of the Burning Night. The giant story pearl was gone. The twelve tall pairs of doors were shut tight, so he didn't know if it were day or night. The great hall was lit by chains of fire that chased up the twelve walls. They burned and flickered and writhed with no fuel, nor did they scorch the friezed walls. Armored mannikins encircled the room, all still with their right gloved hands on black hilts. At the center of the room, where the pearl had stood, was the black-clad Tilak the Defiler and flame-wreathed Orgiana. Zed and Tiger Eye lay hovering four feet in the air before them. Obviously, the flapper had not digested them, but brought them to its masters in the temple above.

Zed wanted to close his eyes again.

He tried not to revolve in the still air, but the least movement spun him. Drifting, with nothing to stop him, he couldn't face the goddess's blank-eyed stare, and that unnerved him. His stomach didn't like it either. He clamped down.

Orgiana walked to Zed's feet. With a flaming hand she gave his boot a twist. Helpless, Zed spun like a top. Dark ceiling, stone floor, walls of flames spun around him. He really was going to throw up. He hoped he could hit the goddess when he did.

With a snort, Orgiana dropped him to the stone floor. He landed with a grunt. She asked, "How came you back from that outworld?"

Zed shook his head, sat up, and told her. He talked slowly, trying to think all the while. Tiger Eye was awake next to him. She suddenly dropped to the stone also, but she lay still, watching and waiting.

The goddess listened to Zed's technical recital. Her lips were still curled in that cruel half smile that Zed wanted to slap off. When the navigator finally ran out, she said, "It interests us, this walking along corridors of Essence. That is not how we immortals manage." Oh, no? echoed the scientist portion of Zed's mind. "It's clever, for a worm. I wonder if I shouldn't make use of you."

Tilak the Defiler, who'd once been Aroth Cutthroat, a man like Zed, growled, "No. He knows nothing. Destroy him. Both of them."

Orgiana looked half-amused at his vehemence. Zed found the conversation interesting. It looked to him like two old lovers quarreling, carrying on a quarrel they'd started centuries ago. But again he had the sense that Tilak was not giving Orgiana the right answers.

The goddess stepped lightly and high, like a cat in water, turning a circle around Zed and Tiger Eye. Zed thought her long silver-clad legs and woman's curves revealed by flickering fire interesting. He wondered what Tiger Eye thought. The goddess murmured, smiling more brightly. "Mightn't we use his power in our campaign of conquest? A route jumping from island to island would be sure for the worms. It would allow humans to enslave more humans. I may weary of watching men slaughter one another and wish—"

"No, I say," Tilak interrupted her. He tilted his sword hilt, slid the black blade free of the scabbard. It was hard to see, Zed noticed. Black and reflecting none of the firelight, the blade was next to invisible. He might not even see the blow that severed his neck. "I'll kill them now."

Orgiana's voice grew frosty. "Not enslave? How shall our army grow? And how can you say me nay, when *I* say we may have use of his Essence walking?"

Tiger Eye spoke for the first time. Her voice was hard. "He's afraid."

Everyone in the room turned eyes on the warrior who lay on the floor. She went on, speaking hurriedly. "He's afraid of what we know, and that's why he wants us dead." She rose to her feet, and kept them under her. Zed knew that crouch. It was her fighting stance.

Orgiana stopped wandering, stood with silver hands on shapely hips. "What do you know?" Zed wondered the same thing.

For answer, Tiger Eye leapt straight at Tilak. She came off her toes and dove with both hands out. She moved so fast even this lesser god was taken aback. He swiped with the sword too late, only thumped her in the back with his gauntleted fist. Zed wanted to cry out. Tiger Eye looked small and frail against the gruesome black armor. Ignoring the sword's danger, she rammed the heels of her hands against the lower edge of Tilak's magic helmet, the Helm of Kadaena that gave him his power and his identity.

The man-god howled as the helmet was peeled from his head. It struck the stone floor with a clang as the man recoiled. Zed saw Cutthroat's broad, tanned, homely face, but it was twisted now in rage and madness. The two humans and the goddess saw why.

Tiger Eye, daughter of the Nureti, follower of Argamanthol, wielder of the Lightning Lance and slayer of Tilak the Defiler, had exposed the god's secret.

At his throat was a silver slave collar.

Orgiana hissed, "Belkor!"

The truth stabbed through Zed's mind in a flash. Now he knew what had really happened to Cutthroat. In that afternoon's rest stop, in the jungle, he had wandered off, cocky as a king, and they had heard thrashing. Cutthroat had staggered back into camp, wild of hair and eye, scratched and bloody, especially about the mouth, his clothes in rags. But his blue cape had been tight around his throat. The Fulcrumian had babbled about a tiger attack, had joked with his relatives about old times and boyhood memories.

Yet now Zed knew the truth. Belkor the Cursed, the Tiger King, had killed Cutthroat and taken his guise, just as he'd taken the guise of Tiger Eye to lure Zed into his lethal embrace. Somehow—by eating Cutthroat's brain? by sucking up his soul?—Belkor had gained Cutthroat's memories as well as his form. The Cursed One had even fooled Cutthroat's cousins.

But Belkor couldn't hide the silver collar that branded him an outcast. The collar foiled even his masterly powers of disguise. So Belkor, posing as Cutthroat, had wrapped the cape tight around his neck.

But not for long. Because of his ancient knowledge, Belkor had known the city, known the secret door below the story pearl, known the proper tunnel to take, known one of the sarcophagi hid the passage to the outworld.

Zed could have slapped himself. Cutthroat had given *Zed* the Necklace of True-Seeing to ferret out the hinged lid of the sarcophagus, and then had slipped out of sight. Had Zed looked at "Cutthroat" he would have seen through Belkor's disguise!

Belkor, as Cutthroat, had even fooled Orgiana long enough to don the helmet and only *then* had torn off the cape, since the helmet hid his slave collar.

Zed wanted to curse aloud. The real Aroth Cutthroat was a pile of moldering bones at the edge of the Wyr Forest, and Belkor the Betrayer had the power of Tilak's armor!

"Belkor!" hissed Orgiana again. The flames around her body burned white-hot, and she lifted clear of the ground in her indignation. Her heat made Zed sweat and he had to back away, almost to the ring of armored mannikins, who never moved. Tiger Eye too had fallen back.

Cutthroat's face split in a snarl, and all could see Belkor's pointed tiger teeth, the other feature he could not disguise. He rasped in a hungry tiger's voice. "Aye! Belkor! Cursed! Betrayer! Loathsome one! Cast out of the circle of the gods who ruled Tarek Nev! But I've survived, all these long centuries, living as an animal on the forest floor! I've had a long time to plot revenge, and now I *have it*! Tarek Nev shall *not* rise again, *nor* her armies conquer! It is *dust* and *dust* it shall remain! There will be no glory for Orgiana, Mistress of the—"

His rantings were cut off. Orgiana, rising and glowing like a star, loosed a fireball so bright Zed had to turn away. He caught at Tiger Eye and clutched her head to his breast, dropping them both to their knees. They scurried behind a pair of mannikins.

The fireball scorched the air, actually whistled like a comet, and struck Belkor full in the chest. The black paint of the armor bubbled and burned in a swirl of smoke. The god's beard and hair ignited. Zed could smell scorching all over the temple even as sweat ran into his mouth. Yet the magic armor protected Belkor from substantial harm. Knocked backward, he fumbled for the helm and pulled it on, snuffing out the flames on his head. He clambered to his feet and hefted the great black sword.

Fifteen feet in the air, Orgiana screamed like a harpy. *"You've taken my lover!"*

She slung out an arm and fashioned a long hissing whip of flame. It cracked like a thunderbolt against Belkor's armor, yet he kept his feet. The stone floor where the flame-whip touched smoked. The tiger god inside the armor snarled and whisked his sword through the air, dispelling the flame.

Belkor stooped and, with his free hand, caught a paving stone by one charred edge. He wrenched it loose from the floor, scattering crumbs of stone, and tossed it at the hovering, sizzling Orgiana. The goddess flicked out a silver-steel hand and shattered the stone. Chunks as big as Zed's head ricocheted off the friezed walls and pattered on the floor. A chip of stone drew blood from Zed's hand. He clutched Tiger Eye under him, covering her. Sweat from his brow dripped onto her half-bald white head. He shouted, "I think we should get out of here!"

She screeched, "Let's!"

Yet they lingered a moment, curious. It was not often one saw a battle between gods. The room was bright with light from the flaming Orgiana. She had descended to the floor again, and now she breathed like a dwarf's forge. She grew hotter, and hotter, until the stones under her feet began to pool and melt. Zed suddenly couldn't breathe: Orgiana was consuming all the air. Clutching Tiger Eye's arm, he crawled across the floor and into a corridor. He hoped the doors had been unstuck. Otherwise they would cook in this temple turned oven. They staggered to their feet and ran hand-in-hand to the tall gold doors. Zed pushed and the doors opened without resistance, as if enchanted. Natural light washed over them, and fresh air. Even the tropical heat was cool compared to the temple.

A slapping sounded far behind them, and Tiger Eye turned. "Look!"

Down the corridor, between two mannikins, they saw Belkor's and Orgiana's final moments. The goddess, mad with fury, glowed so hot her outline was indistinct. She had locked fiery hands on Belkor's shoulders. Even in the fierce brightness, they saw she was hurting him. Her hands were melting the shoulder guards and must be burning the skin within. Belkor was shaking as if in an earthquake. He was howling like no man ever could, Zed thought. But he could still lash out, and he did.

As Zed watched, Belkor shoved the black blade Soulcrusher through Orgiana's molten body. Mortally wounded, the goddess put back her head and screamed, a long, high piercing death cry that shook tiles from the temple ceiling. Then the fire goddess fell upon Belkor, enfolding her in molten arms, and clung.

The fire raged too hot to see. Heat blew down the corridor at Zed and Tiger Eye like the breath of a dragon. The navigator grabbed the warrior and stumbled outside. They crawled across rough gray paving stones, rolled out of the way of the door, and sucked fresh air.

Flames licked out of the door behind them. A whistling roar hissed inside, loud as the distant volcanoes. Then, gradually, it fell silent inside, with only the whisper of ash settling.

The two adventurers flopped on their backsides and mopped sweat off their faces. Zed was about to congratulate both of them for surviving a duel between gods, but Tiger Eye hopped to her feet. She ran across the pockmarked plaza and pressed her waist to the stone rail that overlooked the city and jungle below. She had run to the north side. Zed, uneasy, got up and trotted after her.

"Oh, my."

The Three Masters were finally erupting.

* * *

Zed rubbed his eyes at the vision, for the mountains quaked so vigorously the volcanoes seemed to dance. Long cracks, new this past hour, snaked up the faces of the mountains. Red lava bubbled in a dozen spots. Steam gushed from fissures in the wasteland of ash and glazed rock that led to the foothills. Rocks were shot out of the flaming mouths thousands of feet into the air. Boiling water along the ocean shore created tall rollers of fog so thick the sea breeze couldn't whisk them away.

"This is the end," squeaked Tiger Eye. Her face was wet with tears. "My home is going down in the Sea of Fire."

"It must be the helm," Zed muttered. "The Helm of Kadaena must be linked to Mount Kadaena. It's more than just a name. It must have been forged there from something in its heart. Orgiana must have destroyed—"

Tiger Eye cut him off. "The sword!" She pushed off from the rail and ran for the temple doors that stood open.

Zed sprinted after her. "What sword? What about it?"

Tiger Eye ducked between the tall doors and into the corridor. Zed noted the door faces were partially melted. Tiger Eye stood just inside, hopping from foot to foot, trying to see inside. Zed unthinkingly touched the doors and almost seared his hand. He grabbed Tiger Eye by his own hood and jerked her back. "You can't go in there! It's hotter than your damned volcano!"

The woman was frantic. She opened and closed her hands uselessly. "We must get the sword! Soulcrusher! Solus is imprisoned inside! He's a favored god! He'll help us if we release him!"

Zed dragged her back from the doors until it was cool enough for her to stand without flinching. "Maybe. It's an idea. But we can't go in there just yet. We must wait."

She batted him on the chest with a fist and rocked him. "There's no time!"

Zed just walked away, out onto the plaza and around some sinkholes. The gutterings of the volcanoes were loud as a battle. After a time Tiger Eye joined him. "When do you think we can go inside?"

The navigator stared at the doors. "In a few hours, I think. Maybe. I'll open the doors to let it cool off, if they'll open. We can get some rest, and some food. Then we'll see."

Tiger Eye stared at the silent temple. "I just hope—"

In the distance the volcano belched a column of ash a thousand feet in the air. The blast drowned out her last words.

Zed circled the temple, prying doors open. Most worked. The hole in the roof of the temple had been repaired too, or healed. Even the cracks in the temple walls were gone. Yet the potholes in the plaza remained. The wreckage of the egg-shaped, blade-spinning monster still lay outside one set of doors. He wondered how the gods inside had decided what should be fixed, and how they'd gone about it. If at all. Maybe the sacred temple had enough Essence to repair itself, given the chance. The heat inside the temple was still fierce when he'd opened the last pair of doors, but the ever-present breeze whistled through the passageways, flushing out the heat.

Tiger Eye, meantime, had descended a few levels and found some beets in a garden. They ate them ravenously, walked down a level, and slaked their burning thirst in a fountain. Zed saw no sign of monsters. He wondered if they'd disappeared when their masters were immolated. It seemed to him the greenery was fading too, the leaves on tree and vine yellowing and curling at the edges.

The rumblings from the volcanoes grew more pronounced. Occasionally there was a jolt that threw them off their feet. They imagined they could feel the heat of the lava when they faced the north side of the island from the plaza wall.

Tiger Eye kept checking the temple interior, and finally she insisted they venture inside. Zed insisted he go alone. With no shoes, she had to give in. Red-faced, he asked to borrow his tunic to protect him. He turned his back and she handed him the garment over his shoulder. He stepped between the doors and entered the Temple of the Burning Night for the last time.

The walls and floor were covered with a fine ash, probably the remains of the paint that had adorned the walls. The floor was hot through his boot soles, but not unbearably so. He padded down the hall, slipped between two armored manni-kins, who still held their hands idiotically on their hilts, as if ready to serve the dead Tilak.

At the center of the room were two objects. The Helm of Kadaena lay on the floor, unmarked, the three gems still bright. An armspan away was the black sword. Nothing else was to be seen except some ash and tiny flecks of rust or

metal. Zed used the tail of his tunic to pick up the two artifacts. He slipped back down the corridor.

Tiger Eye stood naked as a baby to receive the sword
Soulcrusher. Zed shucked off his tunic and insisted she don it.
They stood face-to-face on the plaza. The smoke from the
volcanoes filled the sky now in the north, and would soon oc-
clude all the sky. The warrior hefted the sword as if ready for
a practice swing. "What do we do?"

Zed juggled the warm helmet. "I'm not sure. I think the
Helm of Kadeana controls Mount Kadaena, and it's causing
the eruption, maybe to destroy the island if its mission can't
be completed. But I'm just guessing. I don't know."

"But what do we do?"

The navigator sighed, exasperated. "We can try to shatter it
with the sword. Usually when you break an enchanted item,
the spell breaks. But these are both tough items to sustain that
fire unscathed. I don't know what will happen."

"Try anyway. I'm sure you're right."

"We'll see." Zed set the Helm of Kadaena down on the
plaza stonework, then took the sword. It was surprisingly
light for its length. Probably enchanted so the swordsman
won't tire in battle, was his thought. He waved Tiger Eye
back some distance, spread his feet wide, and tilted the sword
far over his head. This was not a job for finesse, it was one
for brute strength. He stood as if once again chopping firewood on the farm. He forced himself to keep his eyes open
and prayed that nothing exploded.

He swung with a *swoosh* that ended with a frightful *clang*.

It was the sword that shattered. The helmet didn't even
nick, but the long blade sprang away and bounced far off on
the plaza cobblestones. Zed dropped the hilt from numb
hands. His wrists and arms tingled to the shoulders. He hissed
and swore, then stopped abruptly.

Issuing from the broken end of the sword, like steam from
the ground or a genie from a bottle, rose a golden glowing
mist that fluttered into the air higher than the navigator's
head. The mist widened, thickened, slowly took on the form
of a man. Then they could make out details. A thick golden
mane of hair, a broad kind face, a sturdy jaw and shoulders.
A young man, or godling, with a long but kind face, clad in
a golden tunic and kilt such as the Fulcrumians wore.

"Solus!" whispered Tiger Eye.

The god nodded. He was clear as spring water, ethereal as any ghost. Zed would have sworn a good breath would blow him away. His ghostly feet didn't touch the quaking plaza. The god opened his mouth and spoke, but they heard nothing.

Tiger Eye snatched the black helmet and offered it to Solus. "Good Solus, Beloved of the Nureti, God King, please, *please* destroy this helm! Save our home! Please!"

The god, who was ten or twelve feet tall, reached massive hands toward the helmet, but the hands only passed through the helmet and Tiger Eye. The god shook his head. There was infinite sadness in his golden eyes. Zed could only imagine how he must feel, to be freed after centuries only to find himself a helpless phantom while his old home disintegrated. To be a powerless god must be a terrible thing.

Sadly, the god raised one thick arm, pointed to the helmet, then to Tiger Eye and Zed, then out toward the crumbling volcanoes. He dropped his own ghostly hands in despair. Then, with a final nod, he wafted away on the breeze.

Tiger Eye dropped the helmet and wept in bitter frustration. Zed gnawed a knuckle and looked to the north. The lowering cloud of smoke and ash now obscured the top of Kadaena. The bitter cloud would be infiltrating the city soon. Maybe the island would be poisoned before it was rent in half.

Zed unbuttoned his pouch and quickly unfolded his compass. He checked the settings, then scanned through the telescope. He told Tiger Eye, "Pick up the helmet."

"Where are we going?"

He refined a setting on his telescope without removing his eye. "Back to Hel."

Zed tucked away his compass, then braced his feet, facing empty air. He had to shout over the noise in the distance, like a thousand drummers pounding in a frenzy. "I've found some hole on the far side! A cave, I think! Let's hope it's one of the old dwarven caves where they forged that thing! Are you ready?"

Tiger Eye nodded. She'd cut strips from the tunic's tail and wrapped them around her feet. She clutched the jeweled helmet to her breast. Zed said, "We'd better be quick!"

He rattled off his opening charm, grabbed two spots in the air, and ripped a doorway straight down to the plaza floor. Instantly they were blasted by a wave of heat that shriveled

Zed's mouth dry. A wisp of smoke trickled from the ragged portal and spiraled into the air. As if in answer to this intrusion, Mount Kadaena in the distance pulsed and loosed a torrent of rock down its quaking sides. Zed poised before the portal. Winking, whirling lights lined all four sides of the magic corridor. The far end, not very far away, was an angry orange-red. He grunted in the blasting heat, "Maybe this isn't a good idea—"

But Tiger Eye slipped under his arm and ducked into the tunnel. Taking a deep breath, Zed dashed after her flying brown legs.

The tunnel was very short, for the true distance was short. Zed hadn't made a jump this small since leaving school. Navigator theory frowned upon short "lazy hops." If they'd frowned on that, he wondered, what would they say to a portal into a live volcano?

In an eye blink he'd traversed the tunnel and emerged onto solid, if shaking, rock. This cave was immense, high as the temple. The floor had once been polished smooth, and Zed took heart. Only dwarfs would go to that much trouble. There were stone workbenches carved from the wall of the cavern, and niches, and doorways leading into tunnels. His portal exited in the center of the huge irregular room. One big tunnel, tall enough for a dwarf but not a man, went due north, deep into the heart of Mount Kadaena. That would be where they did the actual forging, he thought, where they could channel lava and generate temperatures high enough to forge magic metal. The room was lit by hellish light that streamed from apertures in the upper walls. The light was blocked by low-lying, evil-colored smoke.

Zed's heart gave a lurch as Tiger Eye skipped straight into the vast red-rimmed maw. They'd agreed he would wait by the portal to keep it from closing. With the Essence flows being warped by this seismic activity, the portal might suddenly shift five or six hundred feet in any direction, or open onto another destination, or simply wink out. Zed was to guard it while Tiger Eye found some way to pitch the helmet into the heart of the mountain. Zed sweated and tried to breathe shallowly. The heat squeezed water out of him as if he were a sponge, and he felt it sear his lungs at every breath. He hoped Tiger Eye would hurry.

He waited. And waited. Once the portal flickered along one

edge, and he recited a quick stiffening charm. The earth jumped under his feet and so did the portal, till it was clear of the ground a tall step, and he rapped out a lowering charm. Loremaster's Love, where was Tiger Eye?

He waited, counted to ten. He barked a standing spell at the portal, but it quivered dangerously. Zed turned and ran, stooped, down the north tunnel.

Smoke obscured the top half of the tunnel and he had to stoop even lower to stay below it. He banged his head hard enough to strip hair and skin. He put one hand overhead on the ceiling and another before him, for now the smoke had thickened and he couldn't see ten feet. His eyes watered like fury, but the tears dried instantly on his parched cheeks. He stubbed his toe on a fallen rock, then narrowly missed having another drop on his heel. Where was—

His foot bumped something hollow that rolled away. On all fours, he fished with his hands in the dark. He coughed so hard he almost fell. Then he found the object. It was smooth, polished, and it sported three precise bumps.

The double-damned helmet.

Zed clutched it to his heaving chest and stumbled forward. After three more paces he stepped on something soft. He groped. It was Tiger Eye. Above her forehead was an open sticky gash. She'd either brained herself on the low ceiling or else been struck by a falling rock. Zed couldn't tell if she were alive or dead. At this point, he swore, it almost didn't matter. They'd both be poached in minutes.

Sobbing for air and sorrow, he left her body behind and fumbled down the tunnel. Abruptly the air cleared, though the heat intensified. He could see, somewhat. This was a ledge with an artificial raised rampart. A monstrous forge fed by pipes and valves was poised near the rampart. On an anvil big as a table lay an iron hammer, as if the dwarven smith had stepped outside for a breath of air. Zed couldn't bring himself to look over the rampart. He'd be cooked through, blinded as his eyeballs baked. That was a drop to the center of the earth.

With a prayer to the Loremasters for luck, he swung his arms three times, then pitched the helmet over the edge. It sailed up and away, and down.

After three seconds, a hissing roar threatened to lift the mountaintop into the sky.

Zed turned and bolted down the tunnel, blind again in the

swirling smoke. He scrambled on all fours down the passage, desperate not to miss Tiger Eye. His blistered bleeding hands found her soft hot flesh, and he pulled her close. Hoisting her across his shoulder and back, he scrambled pell-mell down the passage.

Smoke, heat, more smoke, fallen rocks that bashed his exposed left toes through the cut boot. He coughed fit to break a rib, blind with tears, wheezing like a bellows from smoked lungs.

Behind him came a roar, a river of lava and ash.

He broke into the workshop cave and ran desperately for the portal.

It was not there.

Stunned stupid, Zed rubbed his burning eyes and cast about. Had it winked out or—

There! It had drifted across the shaking floor and stopped at the far wall. But one side was bulging inward, and the other was ragged, ready to break.

Zed felt fire lick at his heels. A stream of lava was boiling down the tunnel after him. The back of his trouser legs began to smoke. The navigator ran.

The portal walls squeezed closer. One wall flickered out of existence, flickered back. Zed tried to shout a stabilizing spell but broke into a wracking cough. He concentrated on running. He stumbled on a rock that dropped in his path and almost dropped Tiger Eye. Blind, confused, he spotted the sagging portal, took one long step, and dove headlong into whirling lights.

15

Forest of the Burning Night

ZED BOUNCED OFF STONE YET AGAIN, BUT this time it was the paving stones of the plaza. The stone ripped his elbows open and stung like fury. He didn't manage to shield Tiger Eye very well, either, and skinned her knees as he dropped her. He did manage to stop her head from striking the stone. He thumbed back her eyelid, panic making his hands shake. He hadn't had time to tell if she was alive or dead back there—

One red-rimmed yellow-brown eye stared at him fishily. She rasped, "What are you doing?"

He answered with a hug.

She hugged back, faintly, then put her hand to her head. Her white hair was clotted with brown blood. She asked, "Did I do it? Throw the helmet?"

A rumbling blast shook the earth. The two heroes leapt up as one and faced north.

Mount Kadaena was collapsing. Three of the largest cracks that ran up its face had become yawning chasms filled with red lava. Crumbly and shaken, the sides of these canyons began to fall in upon themselves. Slabs of stone large as hills dropped into lava beds with a splash that sent gouts to the sky. Zed and Tiger Eye could feel their impact through the soles of their feet. The cracks widened, then closed upon one another until the intervening sections were gone. All this time, the three mountains quaked, loosening stone, splitting their fire-rimmed mouths, expelling jets of steam and ash as newly exposed pockets of water and mineral were ignited and evaporated in seconds. Finally, some fissure at the back of Mount Kadaena, the side overlooking the ocean, gave way. In one great rush, the heart of Kadaena split. A furious avalanche of molten rock and lava poured from the center of the volcano and thundered into the Sea of Fire. Steam vomited into the sky, wreathing the Three Masters in cloud upon cloud that piled into the heavens.

The heroes held their breath. The rumblings quieted, quieted, quieted, then slowly, very slowly, subsided. The eternal tremors stopped.

Tiger Eye looked down, wiggled her toes, knelt, and put a hand on the paving stones near the rail. She breathed, "This is the first time in my life I've felt the earth lie quiet."

Zed took her hand and pulled her upright. "Then it's really over," he said. And he kissed her.

She kissed back.

They were interrupted by a squeak and crash from the temple. One of the tall golden doors had fallen from its hinges and crashed in the plaza, raising a square outline of dust. Zed and Tiger Eye waited in sudden fright. They had no weapons at all now and were too spent to put up any fight.

But the folk who tumbled through the doors were friends. Blinking in the light, out staggered the tree folk and Fulcrumians who'd been transformed into armored mannikins: Falling Leaf, Mossback, the oldster Eli, the boy Aldar, and the rest. Zed and Tiger Eye ran to them and took their hands.

To their questions, Zed replied, "You were released from the enslaving armor when the helmet was finally destroyed. The dwarfs who forged the Helm of Kadaena did better work than they know, for the helmet and the mountain were joined in spirit. As the helmet lay in its tomb and muttered its dreams and hopes for a master, it roused the volcano too.

When we pitched the helmet into the heart of the volcano, the one consumed the other. Of course, this is all just guessing."

"I'd say it's a bonny guess," wheezed Eli. "Look yonder."

They turned north. The steam clouds had dissipated, pushed away by the tremendous sea winds. For the first time, they could see blue ocean water between Mount Orso on the east and Mount Kirsil in the west. Mount Kadaena was gone. In its place was a black-mouthed cleft.

"You could walk across there now, I'll bet," muttered Eli, "and throw a fishing line off the cliff."

"Bet you a tall ale you can't," retorted Aldar.

The old man cracked a smile across his dirty face for the first time. He hit his cousin in the chest with a knotty fist and laughed. Then they were all laughing, Fulcrumians and tree folk alike. They laughed until they had to hold on to one another, so weak they became. Zed hugged Tiger Eye and they laughed too.

It was some time later, after rest and water and some more scrounged food, that Zed noticed the temple had lost its shine. The gaping hole in the roof had reopened, and most of the doors sagged anew. The fruit they picked from the trees was the last of it. Most had dropped to the ground and rotted. Greenery was wilting everything. "This city will be a ruin again by nightfall," Zed told Tiger Eye.

"Let it be so. As a ruin it caused us no grief."

Zed stood at the rail and looked down at the tiers ringing the city. "I suppose so. It had too many monsters for comfort. Though there must be treasure and magic items aplenty buried here. Unless they're buried in time too. I doubt our exploring teams will find much . . . We'll leave in the morning."

Tiger Eye was quiet beside him. "And go where?"

He put an arm around her shoulders. "Why, back to your tribe, of course. You're a hero now, the stuff of legends. You've saved the island."

Tiger Eye shivered and clung closer to Zed. "I hope the elders see it that way."

"I'm an outlaw. I defied the elders," Tiger Eye told them. The adventurers, Nureti and Fulcrumians alike, sat in council around a campfire and ate the last of their fruit for breakfast. She went on, "I was ordered to watch the Fulcrumians struggle toward Tarek Nev and make sure all were destroyed by

the forest." She nodded an apology at Eli and the other highlanders. "We were not to reveal ourselves. Yet I actually negotiated with the enemy, then guided them to the gate. And I
was supposed to toss you from the branches," she said to Zed,
"but instead I spared you. I contradicted every order they
gave me."

Zed laid a hand on Tiger Eye's shoulder and shook her
gently. "But you were trying to find the source of the tremors
and stop them if you could. And you did. You saved the island. They can't condemn you for that. The situation changed,
got all turned around, after you received your orders."

Falling Leaf put in, "The elders don't accept change easily.
Tiger Eye opposed their orders. And we helped. According to
their lights, we should have deposed Tiger Eye or killed her
outright when she went against the elders' wishes. Instead we
sided with her. So we're liable to be tossed too."

Tiger Eye wiped tears off her cheeks with scabby scarred
fingers. "The elders said the volcano would subside and it
did. There's no proof we saved the island. But they can prove
I disobeyed orders. Their word is law. To go home is to die."

The party was quiet for a while, then Eli cleared his throat.
"Maybe we should all stay away from these elders for a
while. They wanted us dead too. We'd just as soon run for the
coast and hop Mistroke Channel. We've had enough of this
cursed island. No offense, you all."

The boy warrior Aldar asked Zed, "Can't you jump us
straight home from here?"

Zed shook his head. "The Essence flows around the island
are raging. With all this magic that's been released, and the
volcanoes settling, they'll be a maelstrom for months. Or
years. And I'm spelled out. If I miscalculated by a hair, we'd
end up—Loremasters know where." He didn't add his private
thoughts, that he was in no hurry to separate from Tiger Eye.

"Well, while we're thinking on it," said Eli. "Let's get
walking south. Doing anything's better than doing nothing."

On that they agreed. The whole party would walk south.
Zed would try to jump the Fulcrumians across the narrow
channel: that might be safe enough. Otherwise, they'd fashion
rafts for the Fulcrumians. After that, Tiger Eye's warriors
could journey home to the great tree Calagrog. Without Tiger
Eye, they could argue she misled them and plead their lives.
They might be accepted back without punishment.

A decision reached, people relaxed and began to tie up their few belongings for traveling. Yet Tiger Eye walked away to the edge of the tier. In the middle distance loomed the giant trees of the Wyr Forest, like a green mountain range.

Zed joined her. "Where will you go, Tiger Eye?"

"It doesn't matter," replied the warrior woman. "I'm as good as dead."

Zed looked into her face, spotted brown and white like a horse's backside. "You don't have to go home. You could go away with me."

She whispered, "And never walk the trees again? That's the same as being dead."

Zed put his arm around her and didn't answer.

With Zed and Tiger Eye in the lead, the party descended the crumbling tiers of Tarek Nev and passed through the Red Gate named Teroglustrod. Their path was clear enough. Under Tiger Eye's guidance, they would circle the city to the north and strike onto the Fulcrumian army's cut road. That would take them directly to the southern channel in two or three days.

Once past the bridge, they spread out in marching order. Tiger Eye took the lead. She and her warriors carried wooden spears cut from apple trees, neither crooked nor forked. The Fulcrumians had picked up whatever swords, crude knives, or clubs they could find. The whole party was ragged, filthy, bruised, and hungry, but their spirits picked up as soon as they set foot outside the ancient city. Its time-slowed magic, stultifying air, and ancient history and horror were not for living beings. The marshland and forest seemed like old friends. The tropical heat felt cleansing, the earth felt springy and inviting (and didn't tremble), and the smell of flowers and birdsong was invigorating. It was with light hearts that they filed into the forest for the long walk home. Even Tiger Eye held her head high and smiled bravely at Zed behind.

Their happiness was snuffed out at the first widening of the trail. Tree folk stepped from the forest like ghosts. A triple phalanx of sharp crooked spears surrounded them.

"Stand or die!" barked their leader.

Prisoners, they were marched to a large glade and bound to cut sticks. Tiger Eye, her eyes downcast with shame, was lashed to a stick in the same humiliating fashion Zed had been. The leader of the Nureti warriors—this was most of them, some sixty—whistled shrill and fierce, and the gray-skinned, red-eyed flete swooped from the gray sky to snatch them up. Many of the Fulcrumians went up with a scream.

Zed watched the terrain sail below him idly. He wasn't bothered by the height. Either he'd grown used to it, or he was less afraid of dying. The wind whistled across his toes where they stuck out of his severed boot, chilling them. He worried about Tiger Eye. What would the elders do to her? Would they toss her? He tried not to picture her body lying maimed and twisted on the dim forest floor, food for ants and carrion. His heart sank as the flete dipped among the broad leaves and wide-reaching branches of the ancient forest.

Their landing space was a branch away from the community. At least, Zed could see no houses or children. Tiger Eye's warriors and the Fulcrumians were caught and rounded up one by one. Together, with arms bound to sticks still, they were marched over broad branches and hanging bridges. A double contingent of warriors accompanied them, twice as many warriors as prisoners. The Fulcrumians were hushed, awed, and they walked gingerly, as if one misstep might pitch them into open air.

The navigator could feel the electric charge in the air before he saw the great tree. They rounded a ledge and entered the broad plaza before the amphitheater entrance. They were surrounded again, and unbound. The men and women flexed their arms and wrists.

Two warriors accosted Tiger Eye and ordered her to fall in between them. She went, without giving Zed even a backward glance. Head down, she marched toward the entrance to the amphitheater and her audience with the elder council.

Zed rubbed his fingers back alive. He pressed through the crowd of prisoners and confronted the Nureti leader who'd captured them. This was a big man, broad in the chest and scarred across one shoulder, white hair spiky. Zed told him, "Good sir, I should accompany Tiger Eye. I can speak in her behalf before the elders."

The man sneered. He loomed over Zed's dirty face. "You can stand right here, earthworm. If the elders wish to speak to you, they'll send word. Though I doubt it."

Zed held on to his temper. A navigator's greatest skill was

in negotiating, after all. He tried again. "Surely you can allow me a small audience. I have knowledge that would benefit the elders and your tribe. A loyal warrior like yourself, a man used to command—"

The tree warrior would have none of it. He batted Zed in the chest with the butt of his spear. "Your knowledge, we hear, amounts to nothing! I, a loyal warrior—"

Zed lost all art of negotiating as his temper flared white-hot. His anger lent him the strength of a lion. He slapped the spear back into the man's chest. While the man was off-balance, Zed swung a fist and smashed him in the broad face. Zed felt a knuckle in his hand pop, but by then he had bulled the man aside and was running. Before the two guards by the door could even take a step, Zed had dashed between them and into the amphitheater.

Inside the vast room were only seven people. The three elders sat on the dais at the center of bench rings, with their attendants behind them. At their feet stood Tiger Eye, her hands by her sides, her head bowed. The elders were all visibly angry, and the pipe-smoking woman was berating her.

"—not the place of a warrior to *question*, it is the place of a warrior to *obey*. We have lived *five times* your life span, and we have seen *five generations*, and we have the *knowledge*—"

"Halt!"

Zed was as surprised as they that he had called out. But he marched down the paths between the benches. The elders gaped at him with tight-clamped mouths and burning hatred. Behind him he heard the slapping of feet as a dozen warriors pursued him. But Zed pressed ahead until he stood beside Tiger Eye, glaring back at the elders. Beside him, Tiger Eye's eyes were shining.

He called, "I am Zeddeth Toog Niarmon, Navigator of the Guides of Vurn-kye, and I *demand* an audience!"

Warriors streamed across the benches to capture him, but they froze as the male elder raised a hand. Zed took advantage of the space to bellow, "I *demand* an audience to speak on behalf of this woman! You know me! You have tortured me and condemned me to death!" He grasped his thin chemise in both hands and rent his shirt to the navel. "I sustained your torture of hot coals, and I survived being tossed from the highest branches! You cannot kill me, you elders of the

Nureti, rulers of the Ancient Tree Calagrog. so you will *listen* to me!"

The elders glanced at one another as the warriors, sprinkled throughout the benches, waited. Finally the elder male said quietly, "Speak, then."

Zed spoke. He told them everything, starting with the first contact between an assessor navigator and Aroth called Cutthroat, through the journey overland, through his capture and rescue by Tiger Eye, through their treaty with the Fulcrumian army, the sundering of the army, Cutthroat's disappearance, the entrance into the city, the journey to the temple and outworld, their Essence flow escape, their teamwork in evading the city monsters, the final betrayal of Belkor and his death with Orgiana, and Tiger Eye's saving the island by carrying the helm into the volcano. He glossed over nothing, left nothing out. It took a long time. By then the warriors had sat down, and more had trickled in, until when he was almost finished, he was surprised to find the entire Nureti community had gathered: four hundred men, women, and children.

Flushed, arms waving, the navigator wound up his argument. "So know this! It was my knowledge and her spirit that saved you and all yours! Do what you want, but you can't change the truth of that!"

He stopped, head held high, and gulped air.

Unexpectedly, the gathered Nureti sent up a cheer. They shouted and sang, whistled and hooted, waved their arms and spears. They called, "Ti-ger Eye! Ti-ger Eye!" and "Zed! Zed! Zed!" The noise and celebration went on and on, and Zed found himself blushing. Beside him, her head still down, Tiger Eye smiled at him.

The elders ignored the noise. They signaled to their attendants and their chairs were tugged together for a private conference. After a few whispers, they were cranked about again. The eldest woman took her pipe out of her mouth and stood up. The room fell into a hush.

She tottered forward on the dais and signaled Tiger Eye to her. The elder put her hand on the woman's white scruffy head. "If all this be true—and it has the ring of truth—you have done well by your tribe, our daughter. We thank you, and drop upon your shoulders the mantle of hero."

Cheering made the walls rings, but the hush fell again when she beckoned Zed forward. She laid a hand on his head.

"You, Zeddeth, have aided Tiger Eye in her quest and helped to save our home. For this act, we thank you, and drop upon your shoulders the mantle of—friend."

Zed blushed anew. He croaked, "Thank you, elders."

The cheering went on and on.

A celebration feast was hastily pulled together, and the drinking and singing and eating went on long into the night. Tiger Eye and Zed were never more than a foot apart.

The Nureti elders and Eli of the Fulcrumians were all of an age and so able to converse about the folly of youth. The Nureti acknowledged the secret of their existence was out, though they assured everyone it wouldn't change much in their tribe or way of life. Eli, speaking for the largest clan of Fulcrumia, agreed to recognize the Nureti's sovereignty, and the Nureti blandly returned the favor. Inevitably, as two neighbors will, they entered into negotiations. The Nureti admitted they could use more steel goods. The knives and swords and other utensils they had looted along the Fulcrumian trail did not go far. They would like to have blades, needles, nails, doctoring tools, saws, and more. Eli said he could provide them, if the Nureti could guarantee a supply of the marvelous quick-healing salve, a good quantity of which he and his men and Tiger Eye and Zed were wearing. The Nureti could provide it, as well as other medicines they could gather from the forest reaches. The bargain struck, the elders shook hands all around.

Zed bargained also. He asked for and received permission to install a locater focus on the plaza before the great tree Calagrog. Once the focus was in place, a team of navigator engineers could erect a black obelisk, from which anyone could summon a navigator and thence travel anywhere. The Nureti would be able to travel to the ends of Kulthea and step right back into their own treetops. The elders shook their heads. Why, they asked Zed again, would anyone want to travel from their home? But they eventually gave up, muttering about young, restless blood. Then they retired to their council room, to smoke their pipes and assess what it all meant to the Nureti, now once again a people of the world.

And that mission accomplished, Zed filled a wooden noggin full of pale ale and toasted his success. When he lowered the cup, Tiger Eye was standing before him.

She had combed the sticks and scabs out of her hair and trimmed it short, though she was still bald on one side. Her stretches of new pink skin had already begun to tan: she'd be a uniform toasted brown in a matter of days. Her skin was dusky in the firelight. She'd donned a leather tunic, one closely fitted to her curves. She handed Zed a bundle. It was his navigator's tunic, stitched neatly and scraped clean. Sheepishly, he pulled it on, and rebuckled his broad black belt with its compass pouch.

The woman took his hand and led him away, far down the tree branches until the noise and frivolity were left behind. They sat on a branch against a trunk, side by side and holding hands, their feet dangling, and listened to the breeze rustle the leaves.

"I can see why you love this place so much," Zed murmured. "It's beautiful."

Tiger Eye laughed gaily, the first time he'd ever heard her do so. "I thought you said it was a hellhole."

Zed smiled and shook his head. "No, that must have been some other man. I find this place paradise."

She took his hand in the dark. "Then must you leave? You could stay here—with me."

He squeezed her hand back. "Must you stay? You could leave—with me."

She sighed. "I've much to do. I have to fashion another spear and learn its balance. I have to regroup my squad of warriors and train them to work together. I must scout the forest floor and learn what's changed. It will all take time."

Zed told her. "I have duties too. But I'll come back, soon. I have to bring another locater focus. One of your forest floor monsters probably ate the first one."

She laughed again, lightly. "It's dangerous on the forest floor."

"Anyway, I'll bring one back through a portal. It will take me several days to get it anchored and adjusted. I'll be around then. And when the engineering team gets here, I'll have to protect them from the savages. They'll stay for a month or more."

She stirred against him, laid her head on his shoulder. He could feel her soft hair brush his cheek, and he kissed the top of her head. She whispered, "And then?"

"Then—more traveling. It is my work, after all. Though a man can't travel all the time, or forever . . ."

Tiger Eye nodded against him. "I understand. I've always wanted to travel."

Zed laughed. "I've always wanted to live in a tree."

Tiger Eye snuggled closer and sighed in contentment. Zed squeezed her close.

Together they dangled their feet from the tree branch and listened to the song in the leaves.